ACCIDENT . . . OR MURDER?

"It is my opinion that William Farley was murdered, even if the scene of this crime has been carefully staged to look like an accident," Amanda Hazard stated with conviction.

Officer Nick Thorn glared at the meddling female. One dead body lying around and *poof!* Ms. Hazard, the lady accountant who was too attractive and too self-confident for her own good, imagined herself to be a homicide detective. Wasn't that typical of women? They thought they knew everything there was to know.

"Look, lady. I'll do the job I'm paid to do and you do yours. Just stick to your clients' financial accounts and stop reading so many murder mysteries. Those of us on the police force would appreciate it if all you armchair detectives would leave crime-solving to the proper authorities."

Amanda knew right then and there that Officer Thorn was not going to take her suspicions seriously. It was up to her to provide the evidence and possible motive to assure this skeptical police officer that her assumptions were indeed correct.

AN AMANDA HAZARD MYSTERY

DEAD IN THE WATER
CONNIE FEDDERSEN

ZEBRA BOOKS
KENSINGTON PUBLISHING CORP.

ZEBRA BOOKS are published by

Kensington Publishing Corp.
475 Park Avenue South
New York, NY 10016

First Printing: October, 1993
Printed in the United States of America

*This book is dedicated to my husband Ed
and our children, Christie, Jill and Kurt.*

*Special thanks to Tammy Monroe.
Your efforts, dedication, and hard
work are greatly appreciated!*

One

Amanda Hazard breezed through the door to order a cup of coffee. Her arrival earned her several nods of greeting and the waggle of a few male eyebrows, for compared to the coffee shop's other patrons Amanda was over-dressed. The rural community was situated within easy driving distance of Oklahoma City, however the life-style in Vamoose did not move at a hectic pace, a source of pride to Vamoosians. "If you like it country-style, then Vamoose" was the motto posted at the city limits.

The main occupations of the town's residents, and of those in the surrounding area, were farming and ranching. And each time Amanda happened into the Last Chance Cafe, the hodgepodge of conversation testified to the primary concerns of the community. Today was no different.

In one corner of the restaurant, Glenn Chambliss and Preston Banks were swapping philosophies and grousing about the government's idiotic agricultural programs and farmland restrictions. In the opposite corner, Frank Hermann and three other overall-clad ranchers were debating whether there was more money to be made grazing cattle on wheat pasture or preserving the entire grain crop for summer harvest. In yet another corner of the crowded establishment, the local beautician, Velma Hertzog, was giving free advice to

7

the small silver-haired woman who sat at the table adjacent to her. Near the counter, two men were debating whether the hard freeze of two nights' past would diminish the number of insects that damaged the crops. Thus far, the arguments for and against were inconclusive.

Since Faye Bernard, the waitress, had sashayed over to Velma to eavesdrop, Amanda poured herself a cup of coffee and left the correct change on the counter. Pivoting toward the door, she then reflected on life in the country. What a change of pace this small town was from her previous life-style! The laid-back atmosphere was what had lured her into giving up the lease on her apartment in the city and renting a partially modernized farmhouse a few miles south of Vamoose.

Amanda had grown tired of the rat race, the singles bar scene and the executive types who flirted for the sport of it. Although she still made the drive to Oklahoma City three times a week to handle the accounts of her clients there, she had been in town long enough to develop a rapport with the citizens of Vamoose. Several of them had even become clients, and several more were contemplating making the switch for the convenience of close-to-home consultation.

Glancing at her watch, Amanda suddenly realized she'd be late for her eight A.M. appointment if she didn't leave immediately. Walking away from the counter, she found her way blocked by the imposing Officer Nick Thorn.

"Ms. Hazard."

"Officer Thorn."

Amanda and Nick Thorn had never been formally introduced, but in Vamoose's casually friendly atmosphere that hadn't been necessary. Displaying a cordial smile, Amanda sidestepped the local police officer, who continued on into the restaurant, as she made a hasty departure.

Despite her efforts to ignore the man she couldn't help but admit that Thorn was sexy, exceedingly handsome and well proportioned—all six-feet-two of him. His high cheekbones and bronzed complexion indicated Indian ancestry, as did his thick dark hair and sparkling black eyes.

Amanda doubted that many women in the area minded when Officer Thorn pulled them over to lecture them on the hazards of speeding. Even the prospect of being presented with a citation seemed almost pleasant.

Discarding her wandering thoughts, Amanda again checked her watch and quickened her step. If there was one thing she wanted to avoid it was being late for her appointment with William Farley. He had called the previous evening, demanding that she meet him at his ranch at eight and not a second later. William Farley, Sr., was not a patient man, and he had sounded distressed when he'd spoken with her.

William had a fetish about organizing the daily tasks he intended to accomplish in his cattle operation, right down to the minute. He expected the world to operate on his time schedule—no deviation allowed. William was also Amanda's most important client in Vamoose. He owned and rented more farmland than anyone in the county. Although he had been labeled the local scrooge, and was called the Scourge of the Western Plains behind his back, resentful neighbors and acquaintances still listened when William Farley spoke. He had a knack for making money.

After easing past the stop sign without actually making a complete stop, Amanda guiltily glanced over her shoulder, hoping Officer Thorn was not behind her. Heavy-footed, she then sped down the blacktop and veered off onto a gravel road, the only way to reach Farley Farm unless one chose to travel by horseback. Amanda did not own a horse, didn't know the first thing about them and couldn't saddle or ride one if her life depended on it. God forbid it ever came to that.

She muffled a curse when her Toyota hit a bump and swerved into the wide ruts that had frozen solid after a recent snowstorm. The Styrofoam cup that sat on the dashboard plummeted to the floor, catapulting coffee onto Amanda's skirt and hose-clad legs.

"Damn county commissioner. Doesn't he ever send out a crew to grade these damned roads!"

The country roads around Vamoose had been neglected for months. Frozen ruts left by cattle trailers, tractors and pickups formed a maze that could easily break the axle of Amanda's compact foreign car. She decided she'd better purchase a four-wheel-drive truck if she continued this practice of making house calls to generate business.

While coffee dripped through the defrost vent onto her navy blue pumps, Amanda jerked the steering wheel to the left before the Toyota dropped into a Grand Canyon-sized pothole. She finally decided the incline of the ditch was smoother than the road, and she gave it a try. By the time she reached the entrance to Farley Farm, she was five minutes late and completely out of sorts.

Amanda glanced around at the endless number of granaries, workshops and sheds that surrounded the two-story brick farm home. Farley Farm certainly appeared to be a busy place, though untidy. Stacks of scrap metal from William's welding repairs were strung along the fences, and old model trucks that had been robbed of parts cluttered one corner of the yard. From all indications, William Farley threw nothing away. He was a collector, and his farm was a junkyard paradise.

Two raps on the door produced no results, and Amanda began to wonder if William had lost patience and rambled off to tend to his chores, making her wait until he returned. It was then that she noticed his battered four-wheel-drive Ford pickup was not among the fleet of vehicles that lined the driveway.

Pulling her coat tightly around her to ward off the brisk January wind, Amanda walked along the porch to survey the area. Where the hell was the old coot? Was this his form of punishment for her tardiness?

In the distance, Amanda spotted the green pickup sitting in the pasture beside an outdated windmill. Since the path that skirted the wheat field looked no more hazardous than the country road, Amanda headed for her car. If she blessed William with her most charming smile, perhaps he would forgive her for keeping him waiting. She doubted it, but it was worth a try. It couldn't hurt to kill William with kindness.

There had been several matters Amanda wanted to discuss with William, even before he'd called and demanded this appointment. It was tax time again, and Uncle Sam raised an eyebrow when an accountant could not justify a client's expenditures. Amanda had been puzzled by several substantial withdrawals that William had made from various bank accounts over the past few months. This was the perfect time to request explanations.

She was sorry to say that William Farley's bookkeeping was in the same state of disarray as the supplies scattered around his farm. Although he organized his time schedule to ensure that his herd of cattle expanded and prospered, he let other facets of his farm operation go to hell. Each month, William dropped shoe boxes of canceled checks and bills on her doorstep, leaving her to sort through them.

Some of Amanda's clients were as organized and methodical as she was. Some were not, and William was the worst of that lot. The man had no idea how much money he made or spent during the course of a year — until he penned his name to the state and federal tax forms. His checkbook was a disaster. His receipts for

11

newly purchased machinery, mechanical repair and fuel looked as if they had been wadded up and tossed in the glove compartment of his truck to gather a few layers of dust before he dumped them in a box and put them in Amanda's hands.

The personal checks that William, his son and daughter-in-law wrote were deducted from various bank accounts, none of which were designated specifically for farm or personal use despite Amanda's insistence that this be done. It was left up to her to find some method to William's madness. It gave her migraines just thinking of the time and effort required to keep the Farleys in good standing with Uncle Sam. She definitely earned every cent of her fee as William's accountant and tax consultant.

All William really cared about were his vast herds of cattle that grazed all over the county. Developing superior beef cattle was his obsession. He had no hobby other than farming and groused constantly about the oil-field trucks that damaged his crops and pastures when they came and went, carrying oil and gas from his money-making wells. The man was stinking rich, but he didn't care. He just wanted cattle, cattle everywhere, wearing his brand like a British coat of arms.

In short, William Farley was a wealthy, grouchy old rancher who was accustomed to having his own way. He thumbed his nose at anyone who disagreed with him. But Amanda and William had found common ground. Neither of them approved of the county commissioner and his lack of attention to country roads. Consequently, Amanda and William had developed a working relationship, despite the fact that she was a woman. William had forgiven her for her accident of birth after she had performed her duties more efficiently than the male accountant he had just fired.

Amanda gritted her teeth when the Toyota sailed over the ridge of the terrace and bounced along the crude path that led to the water tank. Maybe if she began the conversation by complaining about the gravel roads in the area, William would forget about her tardiness.

Screeching to a halt behind the idling farm truck, she scurried forward, her greeting smile intact. However, she soon stopped short, immobilized by shock.

There was no need for her to attempt to charm William into good humor or to blame her late arrival on deplorable road conditions. William would not be the least bit receptive to anything she had to say. She could not kill William with kindness since he already looked as dead as a man could get.

William's body was jackknifed over the edge of the stock tank — head submerged, feet dangling. His faded OshKosh overalls were soaked from the waist up.

When Amanda peered more closely into the tank she saw the billfold William always carried in his chest pocket lying on the bottom. With his arms floating outward, Farley looked as if he were reaching out to retrieve his soggy wallet.

The electric heater that prevented the water from freezing bobbed lazily on the ripples caused by the wind. In the near distance, a cow bellowed. Every bovine eye was focused on Amanda. When she lifted her hand to touch the body in order to confirm her worst suspicions, the herd retreated in synchronized motion.

Sure enough, William Farley had vamoosed from Vamoose. The farmer-stockman had stacked his last hay bale and planted his last wheat crop. He was on his way to reap his reward at the Eternal Harvest . . .

Two

Amanda's heart felt as if it were about to pop out of her chest, and her knees knocked together. She gave herself a mental slap, refusing to let panic crumble her composure. She had watched enough detective shows on television — "Magnum, P.I." was her favorite — to know that eyewitnesses were expected to survey the scene of accidents so they could answer the numerous questions posed by investigators.

With deliberate concentration, Amanda took inventory of her surroundings. She was standing in a sprawling pasture, kept company by inquisitive cattle. The twelve-foot, circular water tank sat beside a broken-down windmill and the electric pole to which the floating de-icer was attached. To the right, a stone's throw away, stood a clump of willows that surrounded one of the many buffalo wallows that still existed in Oklahoma.

Farther down the hill was a meandering creek. To Amanda's left was the wheat field, the only patch of green in a winter world of dried grass and leafless trees. This was farming and ranching country, suited to crops and livestock. Nothing seemed out of the ordinary . . . except the lifeless body.

Swallowing the lump in her throat, Amanda tried to collect her wits and determine if it was advisable to drag William's bulky corpse from the stock tank — no small feat! — or to leave it untouched.

The herd of cattle had now formed a semicircle around the tank, but seemed no more eager to approach William than Amanda was. The creatures stood there, forgoing drinks of water, watching, waiting.

The only sound to penetrate Amanda's ears was the lowing of the same cows that had broken the silence earlier. On wobbly legs, Amanda circumnavigated the tank to view William from a different angle. Unfortunately, he looked just as dead no matter where she stood. But to her surprise, another body lay on the opposite side of the tank.

A frown knitted Amanda's brow as her gaze bounced back and forth between William and the small calf that looked to be no more than a few days old. Her attention shifted to the murky water, the ring of ice around the perimeter of the tank. Still baffled, she stared at the floating heater that drifted on the water. Although the de-icer looked as if it were functioning properly, Amanda was hesitant to stick her hand in the water. If the de-icer had shorted out, she could wind up as dead as William.

Again, Amanda glanced around the herd of cattle, wishing one of the creatures could explain what had happened to William. No help there. The herd continued to peer at her with huge brown eyes.

Still shaky, Amanda clambered back into her car and whizzed off. She prayed Nick Thorn was still at the Last Chance Cafe, taking his coffee break. Being the local representative of law and order, he was the man she should contact first. He would know the proper procedure for handling this sort of thing. He had probably encountered more dead bodies than she had. Accountants usually dealt with live ones, and Amanda preferred to keep it that way.

In her haste to contact Nick Thorn, she set a speed

record on the local roads. She knew her Toyota would never be the same after bouncing over bumps and ruts at seventy miles per hour. For one frantic moment, she'd thought she was going to wind up in the ditch, staring at the world upside down. Luckily, she regained control before the deep ruts jerked her sideways, launching her toward the steep incline and the steel fence posts beyond. With intense concentration, Amanda then negotiated her way back to town to find help.

Amanda heaved a sign of relief when she spotted the patrol car cruising down the blacktop, west of Vamoose. She blinked her headlights and honked the horn to gain Nick's attention. But before she reached him, a rear tire blew out, and her car, which had just been through the most rigorous road test imaginable, ground to a halt with a strange clanking sound. Amanda leaped out, waving her arms in a windmill fashion.

The police car zoomed toward her and, with a squeal of tires, screeched to a stop. Amanda yanked open the door and collapsed on the passenger seat.

"William Farley's farm, and step on it," she croaked, indicating the direction with a trembling finger. "He's dead."

Nick floored the accelerator, and the car gained speed like a launched rocket.

"I had an eight A.M. appointment with William, but he wasn't at the house when I got there. I spotted his truck in the pasture, so I followed the path to the stock tank." Amanda gasped for breath, realizing she was talking too rapidly.

"Did William collapse at the wheel?" Nick asked in a voice that was noticeably calmer than hers.

"No, he was draped half-in and half-out of the water tank," she reported.

"Heart attack," Nick diagnosed. "William collapsed five years ago and was hospitalized for two weeks. Dr. Simms told him to slow down, but he refused. His collapse didn't affect him more than one flea affects a dog. William was supposed to carry nitroglycerin pills to put under his tongue when he felt the pains coming on, but he never bothered."

The news didn't surprise Amanda. William was as likely to thumb his nose at a physician's advice as he was to scoff at anyone who disagreed with him.

"I'll have to contact Bill Farley," Nick mused aloud. "He flew to Denver for the Western Polled Hereford Sale. He's a sponsor and he'll be auctioneer."

Amanda knew Bill Farley spent a great deal of time on the road and in the air, leaving his father to manage the farm. Bill's expense accounts were tied into William's. Farley Farm was a conglomeration of financial disorganization. Like father, like son.

"Hold on, Ms. Hazard," Nick advised, taking the turn onto the gravel road with more speed than caution.

Amanda grabbed the seat belt and snapped it around her. The car bobbed over the washboarded road and bounced through ruts.

"Damned county commissioner. If he ever had to travel this route, he'd have a crew here smoothing out these mountains and valleys he calls a road."

"Ms. Hazard, do you have any idea how many miles of country roads Commissioner Brown is responsible for?" Nick quizzed, his dark eyes glued to the rough terrain.

She should have known one local official would defend another. "I suppose you and Brown are good buddies."

"Casual acquaintances," he clarified. "And if you handled the county government's accounts, you would know there aren't enough funds to upgrade and repair the dozers and graders, much less purchase a sufficient amount of gravel to cover hundreds of miles of roads."

Amanda flung Nick a sharp glance. "So we should all bite our tongues and make the best of it, is that it?"

Nick spared a moment to stare at his companion before refocusing on the road. "Something like that. Or you could move back to the City. I thought you were a little out of your element when you moved to Vamoose. I doubt the night life around here is what you're used to."

"I'm not the only one around here who disapproves of these roads, you know. William complained about them too. Surely you don't think *he* was out of his element!"

Damned cop. He and his holier-than-thou attitude! Who did he think he was, sitting there passing judgment on her? God's brother?

"William complained about everything." Nick swerved to miss a deep rut and took the corner on two wheels.

A dull groan tumbled from Amanda's lips as her head slammed into the side window. "I don't know why you're driving like a bat out of hell. William is as dead as he can get. Five minutes one way or the other won't affect him now."

Nick flung Amanda a hasty glance. "If that's so, why were you driving like a maniac to flag me down, and why did you tell me to 'step on it'?"

Amanda slouched down in her seat and exhaled the breath she felt she'd been holding since she'd arrived at the scene of the accident. "Touché, Mr. Policeman.

I guess I panicked. This is my first corpse."

Nick tried to calm down. Something about Amanda Hazard riled him, making him unnecessarily defensive. Some kind of personality conflict, he deduced.

"Sorry, Ms. Accountant. I should have considered that."

Nick did slow his swift pace as he turned into William Farley's driveway. Amanda, however, forgot to brace herself when the car bounced over the ridge of the terrace. Her head hit the ceiling, and she saw double as they sped over the dirt path that led to William's cattle tank.

"Sorry about your head, Ms. Hazard."

Amanda didn't think he sounded all that apologetic. Just what she needed, a country cop with an attitude. If the truth be known, Nick Thorn was probably as much a novice with corpses as she was. But since men tended to have stupendous egos, he'd likely shoot himself in the foot before confessing his lack of experience.

After Nick brought the patrol car to a grinding halt, he unfolded himself from the seat to investigate the scene. William Farley was still draped over the stock tank. The upper portion of his body dangled in the water, arms outstretched. His face was a distasteful shade of blue.

"He must have leaned over to test the electric heater and collapsed," Nick speculated. "Either that or he tried to grab hold of the tank when the pains overcame him. He could have stumbled forward, too weak to right himself."

Amanda circled the tank and stopped short. "It's gone!"

A curious frown creased Nick's black brows. "What's gone?"

19

"The calf." She indicated the vacant spot. "There was a dead calf lying here fifteen minutes ago."

A chuckle reverberated in Nick's chest as he ambled up beside Amanda. "The little critter obviously wasn't as dead as you thought he was. Being a city slicker, I don't imagine you're all that familiar with the habits and peculiarities of newborn calves. They sleep so soundly their mothers often have to nudge them awake."

Ignoring the subtle insult, Amanda studied her surroundings. Since the ground was frozen, there was no visible evidence that the calf had been dragged or carried away. But at the same time, there was no evidence that it *hadn't.* When she surveyed the herd, Nick gestured to three small calves that were staring in their direction.

"Could one of those newborns be your dead calf, Ms. Hazard?"

"How would I know? They all look the same to me. If you've seen one Salers calf, you have seen them all."

"That is pronounced Sah-lairs," Nick corrected her. "And these are not pure bred. They are Polled Hereford and Salers crosses."

Amanda did not appreciate the fact that her ignorance was showing, or that Nick Thorn was there to notice. "Well, whatever they are, none of those calves is the one I saw. It was dead."

"Right."

Nick didn't call her a liar, but his glance indicated he didn't think she knew what the hell she was talking about. Amanda, however, was not convinced she had made a mistake. And as she looked around, she noticed that the dish-faced cow that had been standing at the front of the herd earlier had since abandoned ranks. Amanda specifically remembered that particular cow because it looked as if someone had taken a

20

sledgehammer to its face. Then she saw it. It had wandered away from the herd and now stood bellowing beside the clump of willows.

While Amanda was mulling over the unexplained disappearance of the calf, Nick called for an ambulance and the medical examiner. After giving directions to the scene of the accident, he propped an arm on the hood of the car and thoughtfully surveyed the statuesque blonde who looked sorely out of place in business suit and pumps, surrounded by a herd of cattle.

Before him stood five feet, five inches and one hundred twenty-five pounds of sassy conceit. Hazard was a former homecoming queen, Nick guessed. Her stunning good looks had certainly gotten her plenty of attention, and she was accustomed to getting her way. Men probably came to heel when she crooked a finger in their direction. Most likely, she had been born rich and insisted on always going first class and in the latest style.

"Mind if I ask you something?" Nick queried.

"No," she absently replied.

"Just what *is* a woman like you doing in a town like Vamoose?"

Amanda quickly took offense. Her head snapped up, and crystal blue eyes drilled into the country-bumpkin cop. "What do you mean—a woman like me?"

"A woman completely out of her element," Nick specified with a goading smile.

Amanda did not consider herself a staunch women's libber, but after her divorce seven years past, she had lost a great deal of respect for all men. Reckless flirtations of white-collar executives and rude propositions of drunken patrons at singles bars had not helped their cause. Nick Thorn was exactly like the rest of his gender—thoroughly agitating. And further-more, what business was it of this country cop, whose lazy drawl was reminiscent of Andy Taylor's "Mayberry RFD," where she had her mail delivered?

"Where I choose to live is none of your concern, Officer Thorn." *In the side,* she silently tacked on. "I would expect you to be paying attention to the scene of this crime rather than passing judgment on where I belong."

"Scene of the crime?" Nick threw back his head and laughed out loud.

Poking fun did not endear Nick to Amanda. For years she had battled the infuriating stigma of "dumb blonde." Blue eyes, blond hair and a reasonably good figure did not signify anything whatsoever about her intelligence, but men rarely got past a woman's appearance.

True, times had changed somewhat. The women's rights movement had improved conditions in the working world. But some men—obviously Nick Thorn was one of them—still had strong genetic links to Neanderthals. One of Amanda's pet peeves was males' lack of confidence in the analytical and intuitive workings of the feminine mind. She was intelligent, and was a damned good accountant, even if she was blond and had been cursed with the figure of a Las Vegas showgirl.

"I am not thoroughly convinced that William Farley died of a heart attack," she burst out. "The sunken wallet and the dead calf provide reasons to doubt it."

"Ah yes, the invisible dead calf."

Twinkling brown eyes peered down at Amanda, silently mocking her conclusions. She was sorely tempted to kick Officer Thorn's shins because he refused to take her seriously. Despite what he thought she was certain there was something fishy about Wil-

22

liam's sudden death. Irregularities in William's checking accounts had caught her eye, and the phone call she'd received the previous night had indicated William was angry and upset. His voice had fairly boomed over the line. It was entirely possible that he had come upon information that had earned him an early grave. Amanda would not shrug off the incident as death by natural causes until the calf's disappearance and the dislodged wallet were explained to her satisfaction.

When she continued to glare at him, Nick sighed audibly. "Okay, Hazard, what makes you think a crime has been committed?"

"I already told you." Her voice rustled with frustration. "There was a dead calf lying beside the tank, and now there is not. Aren't you going to check the water for contamination or test the electric de-icer for a short circuit? Maybe William was electrocuted."

"That doesn't appear to be the case," Nick said reasonably. "If he had been shocked, there would be burns on his hands. I don't see any."

"Maybe someone tried to steal his wallet and battled for possession of it until William's heart gave out. Perhaps I showed up and frightened the thief away before he could retrieve the billfold. And who knows? There may be a bullet hole or a knife wound in William's chest. You haven't even bothered to fish him out and take a look."

"I am waiting for the coroner and the ambulance!"

Evidently he thought her deaf as well as stupid. His voice boomed like a jet breaking the sound barrier. The harder he glowered at her, the higher Amanda elevated her chin, until she was looking down her nose at him from the lofty heights of indignation.

Damned sassy witch, Nick thought irritably. One

dead body lying around and *poof!* Ms. Hazard, the lady accountant who was too attractive and too self-confident for her own good, imagined herself to be a homicide detective. Wasn't that typical of women. They thought they knew everything there was to know!

"Look, lady, I'll do the job I'm paid to do and you do yours. Just stick to your clients' financial accounts and stop reading so many murder mysteries. Those of us on the police force would appreciate it if armchair detectives would leave crime-solving to the proper authorities."

"I would be only too happy to yield to a competent authority, but I am not totally convinced you are one. It doesn't seem to me that you have been very thorough, Thorn." Watching his lips curl and his eyes narrow into thin black slits. Amanda reciprocated in like manner. She could look as mean and nasty as he when she tried. "And don't threaten to have me arrested for badgering an officer of the law. You started this, making your wisecracks about my being out of my element."

Women. They had a most infuriating knack of turning everything around, always making things a man's fault. They had queen-sized chips on their shoulders. The married ones nagged their husbands to death, and the single ones were so damned bossy and independent a man could barely stomach them.

Nick had become set in his ways over the years, and this sharp-tongued accountant reinforced his belief that bachelorhood and his lone-wolf profession were all the satisfaction he needed in life. Besides he'd known the first time he laid eyes on Amanda Hazard that there had to be something wrong with her. If she had been good wife material, some guy would have snatched her up years ago and kept close tabs on her.

Now he knew why she was unattached. Although she had the body and face of a goddess, she had the disposition of a rhinoceros. But Hazard wasn't his problem, thank the Lord. He just wished this accountant-turned-detective would shut her trap and leave him the hell alone.

Except for the cow that bellowed in the distance, nothing broke the brittle silence. Amanda and Nick stood there, mentally listing all the reasons they disliked each other, until the roar of an approaching ambulance and the squeak of shocks interrupted them.

Nick gestured toward the squad car. "Why don't you have a seat? I'll take your statement after the coroner makes his examination and the body is removed."

In other words, thought Amanda, butt out. She did, but with ill-concealed vexation. Nick Thorn, in her estimation, was handling this case as if it were open and shut. Amanda was not an authority on criminal investigation. Her only connection to detective work was her fascination for Tom Selleck as Magnum in reruns. But the sunken wallet and the disappearance of the calf had caused suspicion to cloud her mind.

Maybe William Farley had died of natural causes, but could it hurt to consider other explanations and pose a few questions around town? What else did this country cop have to do besides write citations and help little old ladies across streets? Vamoose was not exactly the crime capital of the world. There weren't all that many unsolved crimes for Thorn to investigate. Surely he could spare the time to ensure there had been no foul play here.

In Amanda's opinion—and she was rarely without one on any issue—Nick Thorn was a great deal like the do-nothing county commissioner he'd so quickly defended. They both sat around drinking coffee and flapping their jaws. Officer Thorn and Commissioner Brown could have picked up a few pointers about efficient time management from the recently departed Farley. William might not have been the best-loved citizen in Vamoose, but he deserved a little consideration. At least the man accomplished something during the course of the day, unlike Nick Thorn of Vamoose P.D.

In silence, Amanda watched the ambulance driver check the electrical de-icer for a short circuit. Finding none, the group of men pulled Farley's six-foot, two-hundred-pound body from the tank and loaded it on a stretcher. The coroner, a wiry little man with a mustache that completely concealed his upper lip, gave the body a quick going-over. He exchanged comments with Officer Thorn and then chuckled as he glanced in Amanda's direction.

Amanda suspected the country cop had made reference to her remark about checking for bullet holes and knife wounds. They were both having a laugh at her expense.

When the ambulance sped off, Nick strode back to the patrol car, noting Amanda had refused to climb inside as he had requested. Another indication of her independent streak. For the sake of avoiding an argument, he overlooked her defiance.

"If I could impose on you to drive Farley's pickup back to the house, we can be on our way. You do know how to drive a standard shift, don't you, Hazard?"

For that, and everything else that had happened in the past hour, she could have hit him. But she had already stooped to harassing a law officer. She hesitated to add assault and battery to her list of offenses.

With her nose in the air, Amanda stamped toward

Farley's pickup. Behind her, she heard the roar of the patrol car zooming across the pasture. In front of her, she saw the same dish-faced cow bellowing at the clump of willows. Determined to satisfy her curiosity, Amanda shifted into first gear and circled the herd. The cow still hadn't stirred a step. Its attention was focused on the trees.

Thorn could wait. Amanda went to investigate.

After a bit of a search, Amanda found what she was looking for—the missing calf. Sure enough, it was as dead as it had been when she'd seen it beside the stock tank. If she could have picked the creature up, she would have taken it with her to prove to the thick-skulled Thorn that she knew what she was talking about. But the calf was too heavy. Her only option was to bring the muleheaded cop to the calf.

A crackling of twigs somewhere nearby brought Amanda's head around. Had the mother cow come searching for her calf?

She swore she then heard the snapping of twigs coming from another direction. Unfortunately, she did not have time to investigate. The cow had spotted the calf and now charged at Amanda who was standing much too close to it. Though Amanda's coffee-stained pantyhose ripped, she managed to remove herself from the cow's path and return to the pickup more or less in one piece. She would see what Officer Thorn had to say about this intriguing development.

Three

"What the hell took you so long? Having trouble shifting gears?" Nick questioned when Amanda brought the farm truck to a stop in front of the house.

"I was investigating a mysterious disappearance." She indicated the passenger door. "Get in. I have something I want to show you."

"Find another dead body, did you?" Nick questioned as he swaggered toward the passenger side of the truck. "You have had a busy morning, Hazard."

Amanda stamped on the accelerator before Nick could settle himself comfortably on the seat. If the sarcastic cop suffered whiplash, he deserved it.

"Don't add reckless driving to your list of offenses."

"Then don't provoke me, Thorn. I am not having a good day."

"I'm beginning to think you woke up in a world of bad days."

"Don't start with me, Thorn. You may think I'm a pain in the ass—"

That was certainly an accurate assessment of how Nick felt about Amanda Hazard.

"—but I'm not all that fond of you either."

28

Amanda shifted gears and cleared the ridge of the terrace in a manner that would have done "The Dukes of Hazzard" proud. The pickup rocked on its suspension springs and whizzed down the dirt path toward the stock tank. "Doesn't it pique your curiosity in the least that a deceased calf got up and walked off?"

Nick braced himself for the upcoming hairpin curve at the gate that led to the pasture. "The only one who saw a dead calf was you. And I must admit I am skeptical about your credibility. Now would you mind telling me where we are going?" Nick requested impatiently. "I have a statement to take, reports to file and calls to make."

"There's something in the grove of trees you need to see."

"I've seen my share of willows, thank you very much. I grew up in Vamoose—"

"And lived here all your sheltered life. It figures."

"I was in the Marines and served on the Oklahoma City police force for several years," he said, offended. "I've been around, Hazard, a lot more than you have, I'll bet. I just happen to have gotten my fill of stabbings, rapes and drug dealings in the metropolis. I was tired of living in the fast lane so I moved back to Vamoose."

Amanda was not ready to apologize for thinking Officer Thorn had never been outside his own jurisdiction. She was still peeved at him for refusing to take her seriously. When he apologized for thinking she was a lunatic, then she would apologize for thinking he was a jerk.

"Follow me." She climbed down from the truck and hiked along the same path she had taken to locate the calf. To her utter disbelief, the little critter had disappeared—again! Lord, she was losing her mind. Now cow and calf were nowhere to be seen.

Nick came to stand directly behind her, staring over her head to survey the thick underbrush and tangled willow branches. "Now what was it you wanted me to see?"

Amanda wheeled around to stare up into chocolate brown eyes brimming with doubt. "I swear to you, I saw the dead calf right here, at this very spot."

"You swore an hour ago that the dead calf was beside the tank. Now which is it, Hazard?"

"It *was* beside the tank, but—"

"It got up and moved over here? Give me a break. I don't have time for your wild-goose chases and weird suspicions."

Nick grabbed Amanda's arm and uprooted her from the spot on which she had planted herself. He forcibly towed her through the willows and stuffed her into the passenger side of the truck. That done, he climbed behind the wheel, wishing he wasn't in the company of a wacky witness who obviously had a strain of insanity in her family.

Amanda sighed in frustration. "You don't believe me."

Nick stared incredulously at her. "Would you believe you, if you were me?"

Amanda massaged her aching temples. The stuffy air in heated vehicles was giving her a headache. Her sinuses were rioting, and exasperation was eating her alive. She knew she had not been hallucinating. She had seen what she'd said she saw.

"Do you want to know what I think, Hazard?"

"Not particularly," she muttered.

"I think the shock of finding Farley caused you to suffer a trauma. It happens. Shock is a natural reaction. Trauma can distort normal mental functions. I can't tell you how many times I've questioned eyewitnesses to the same accident, only to receive contradictory accounts."

"Perhaps the emotionally unstable have mental lapses, but"—Amanda bared her teeth when Nick sent her a look that indicated he thought she had described herself perfectly—"I am *not* psychologically imbalanced, Thorn. You are going to feel very foolish indeed when I get to the bottom of this murder."

"Murder?" Nick squawked like a crow. "There was no murder. Old man Farley had his second severe heart attack in five years. This one was fatal. He never took care of himself properly. He was known to drink to excess on occasion, and he always overexerted himself. How he managed to survive this long is the only mystery that baffles me. The medical examiner concluded that Farley's heart gave out. If the coronary didn't kill him right away, then dangling there with his head immersed in water caused him to drown."

"Someone could have held his head underwater," Amanda speculated.

Nick gave his dark head a contradictory shake. "There were no marks on his neck or shoulders."

"He could have struggled with his assailant over the possession of his wallet and collapsed."

Nick glanced skyward, as if seeking angels to deliver him from this madwoman. "I am taking you back to town for a cup of coffee to settle your nerves. After that, you can go home, take a couple of aspirins and go to bed."

31

"Aspirin upsets my stomach."

"Then take Tylenol or Alka-Seltzer, and avoid watching detective shows for at least one week," her self-appointed physician prescribed.

"I suppose you have a medical degree too, Dr. Thorn," she said snidely. "My, my, such a variety of knowledge stored in one man's thimble-sized brain. Amazing."

Nick ground his teeth until he very nearly wore off the enamel. "The point is, I have dealt with enough eyewitnesses to unexpected deaths to recognize the symptoms of emotional stress."

Before Amanda could protest his second reference to her "frazzled" mental condition, the pickup ground to a halt in Farley's driveway. They had yet to seat themselves in the squad car when a Cadillac sped toward them. Janene Farley appeared, dressed in a costly Western ensemble, right down to her shiny lizard boots.

"Is something wrong, Nick?"

Amanda detected Janene's apprehension the moment Nick approached her. And she knew the instant Nick conveyed the grim news. Janene's well-manicured hand flew to her mouth to muffle a wail of grief. Within seconds, the brunette had braced herself against the side of the Caddy to absorb the shock. While Nick continued speaking, Janene nodded at irregular intervals. Then, drawing herself up, she wobbled toward the house she and her husband had shared with William.

Having delivered the bleak news, Nick seated himself in the patrol car beside Amanda. "Janene is going to try to get in touch with Bill in Denver."

Amanda was silent during the ride to town. She had voiced her opinions, and Nick had said his piece. He didn't believe her tale of the mysteriously disappearing calf, and she could not rid herself of the notion that foul play had been involved. There was nothing left for her to do but conduct her own investigation in the spirit of Magnum, P.I. The logical explanation of William Farley's heart attack and subsequent drowning just didn't answer all of her questions. What about the soggy wallet and the missing calf?

What had become of the dish-faced cow that had exhibited protective maternal instincts? If the cow had previously lost its own calf it might be reliving the loss. Or did the calf actually belong to that particular cow? As Nick delighted in pointing out, Amanda was not familiar with the habits of livestock. She was operating only on speculation. The results might or might not apply to the bovine species.

There were no tracks on the frozen ground to substantiate Amanda's theory that someone might have attacked William or tampered with evidence. But that did not discredit her suspicions. In her estimation, the calf and/or the wallet were vital keys to the truth.

"If you'd buy a well-built American car, you wouldn't be left afoot right now," Nick said, dragging Amanda from her pensive musings.

She glanced up to see that he had pulled in front of her abandoned Toyota.

"Better yet, if you plan on paying house calls to your rural clients, get an American-made truck," he advised before climbing out of the patrol car.

Amanda refrained from launching into a spirited debate about purchasing foreign or American-made products. She was certain that she and Officer Thorn held opposing views on that subject, as on most subjects.

"Well?" Nick stared down at her from his towering height.

"Well what?" Amanda snapped irritably.

"Are you going to change your tire, or do you want me to do it for you?"

Amanda compressed her lips before she yielded to the impulse to bite Thorn's head off. He was waiting to hear her admit she didn't know anything about changing tires. Well, he wasn't going to gloat at her expense. She would change the damned tire—one way or another.

After fishing the keys from her purse, she stomped around to the trunk. Nick sauntered after her when he heard the clank of metal against metal. With arms crossed, he studied the curvy derriere that protruded from the trunk. Nice view. Nice legs. Nice a—

"What in hell is this thingamabob for?" Amanda wheeled around with pipe in hand, infuriated that she couldn't make head nor tail of the unassembled tools and jack. Catching Nick gawking at her while she was half-sprawled in the trunk, she thought of a use for the tire tool that had nothing to do with replacing a flat.

Before Amanda hammered him over the head, Nick grabbed the jack. "You'd better let me do this, Hazard. I suspect you're as knowledgeable about automotive repairs as you are about livestock."

When he squatted down to tend to the task, Amanda mentally kicked him in the seat of the pants. She knew he was gloating, assuring himself that she was totally incompetent as well as irrational.

Within a few minutes, the tire had been replaced and Nick had stashed the tools in the trunk.

"Thank you." Amanda nearly gagged on the words.

"You're welcome."

Burdened with the unsettling incidents of the morning, and her clash with the countrified law officer, Amanda stepped into her car. She waited for Nick to hook up the chain and tow her to the auto mechanic's located a hop, skip and jump away from the Last Chance Cafe.

With a curt and foul-tasting "thank you for the assistance" on her tongue, Amanda coolly dismissed Nick Thorn and turned her attention on Cecil Watts. The mechanic was covered with a layer of grease that made it impossible to determine the original color of his shirt. The stubble on his face indicated at least three days of five o'clock shadow. His straight brown hair hadn't been trimmed in months. His belly avalanched over his belt buckle, and there were enough holes from dripping battery acid on his jeans to cause frostbite on his lower extremities. If Cecil's appearance bespoke his mechanical aptitude, Amanda was in serious trouble.

He nonetheless informed her that he could not work on her car for at least two days because he had other customers scheduled ahead of her. Amanda wasn't surprised by the news. Considering the awful morning she'd had, she was now operating on the philosophy that if anything could go wrong, it would.

Amanda slung her purse over her shoulder and collected her briefcase. She didn't bother detouring into the cafe for a bolstering cup of coffee. She simply began her three-mile hike toward home. She hadn't walked a quarter of a mile before Nick pulled up beside her.

"Get in. I'll give you a lift." He handed her the promised cup of coffee. "You can give me your statement. Then our business will be concluded."

Amanda consented to climb in, but only because she was half-frozen and her feet were killing her. It had nothing whatsoever to do with the fact that Nick Thorn's dark hair and eyes and his physique appealed to the feminine eye. The man annoyed the hell out of her, and she refused to forgive him for believing her to be the local lunatic. He was only taking her statement because it was procedure. He had already passed judgment on the Farley incident and had put the case to rest. Despite his opinion, however, Amanda gave her account and voiced her suspicions — again.

When Nick pulled up to the stone farmhouse Amanda called home, he made only a half-hearted attempt to conceal his mocking smile. "Be sure to call me if you sight any UFOs tonight."

At that moment, Amanda came as close as she ever had to striking a police officer. The infuriating man had deliberately offended her every time he got the chance. Amanda decided, right there and then, that she wanted no more association with Officer Thorn-in-the-flesh.

Before she resorted to physical violence, Amanda slid out of the car. Flashing Nick a look

36

as cold as the Klondike, she slammed the door and stamped up the steps to her house.

Chuckling, Nick put the car in gear and made his appointed rounds to ensure the local teenagers didn't run each other down in their haste to rush from high school to the cafe for lunch. From what Nick had learned about Amanda Hazard during the course of the morning, he concluded the woman detested the possibility that anyone might think she was human. She refused to admit the incident had upset her, and she had a condescending air that fairly shouted, Keep your distance.

Nick wondered if an unpleasant love affair was responsible for her standoffish attitude and her seeming resentment of men. Not that he was concerned with changing her. Attractive as Amanda Hazard was, with her silky blond hair, bright blue eyes and sexy figure, she was definitely not Nick's type. What man in his right mind wanted to be treated as if he were inferior to a conceited accountant? As far as Nick was concerned, Amanda Hazard could take her vital statistics and her suspicions and stuff them . . . in her file cabinet.

After a much-welcomed shower and several cups of coffee, Amanda spread William Farley's financial file on the dining-room table and meticulously poured over the accounts. The amount of cash that flowed in and out of the Farley family's hands was staggering. William had spent scads of money on land investments and in the acquisition of cattle and farm machinery, while his son and daughter-in-law were prone to personal extravagance. Janene spent a fortune on clothing and withdrew a good deal of cash. Bill wrote dozens of checks posted as "miscellaneous" on his expense account. It was no wonder William Farley had worked from dawn until dusk. The rest of the family spent money as fast as they could scrawl their signatures on checks.

As cranky as William could be at times, Amanda still felt sorry for him. It seemed to her that his family did far more taking than giving. She wondered how he'd felt about his son and daughter-in-law and their extravagance. Knowing William, whose philosophy was that money should be invested to make more money, she was sure he did not approve of his family's habits. In fact, he had made several remarks during the past year that suggested friction. But Amanda was not well enough acquainted with the younger Farleys to know whether one of them had wished William would take a permanent vacation.

She set the file aside and stared at the wall. How did an amateur detective go about making subtle inquiries without drawing suspicion? She had no desire to invite the kind of ridicule she had earned from Nick Thorn. He thought she had leaped to all sorts of ill-found conclusions. The entire community would peg her as a loon if she voiced her doubts about William's untimely death without backing them up with substantial evidence or plausible motives.

Now, where could one glean bits of information without appearing obvious? The Last Chance Cafe.

When word of William's death spread, the coffee shop would be buzzing like a beehive. That was where farmers and ranchers did their gossiping, even though they swore up and down that spreading rumors was a characteristic exclusive to women.

And where did women exchange tidbits of information? At Velma's Beauty Boutique. In small-town America, one could find out everything one wanted to know at the cafe and beauty shop.

Amanda grabbed the phone to schedule an appointment with Velma Hertzog. A wry smile quirked her lips after she replaced the receiver. The following morning she would park herself in a booth at the Last Chance Cafe to eavesdrop on the latest gossip before she kept her appointment at Velma's. By late afternoon, she would know whether or not there was reason to suspect foul play in William Farley's death.

She still had one problem to resolve, though, her lack of transportation. As slow as Cecil Watts was at auto repair, she might be afoot for a week.

A possible solution popped to mind and Amanda dialed the mechanic's number. In a matter of minutes she had made arrangements to purchase the twenty-year-old Chevy pickup that sat outside Cecil's garage. She had noticed the For Sale painted on the truck's window with shoe polish. Although the sides of the old pickup looked as if it had been used for a fund-raising car bash, Cecil assured Amanda that its motor purred like a pussycat. And he promised to deliver registration, title and truck to its proud owner after he closed the shop at five-thirty. Slow as Cecil was, Amanda didn't expect him until six.

Cecil arrived at seven.

Amanda heard him coming from a quarter of a mile away. He'd neglected to mention that the

39

gas-guzzler needed a new muffler to pass motor safety inspection. Of course, he said he'd be glad to see to the matter when he caught up on his work.

Four

Amanda was seated and waiting when the early wave of farmers and ranchers arrived at the Last Chance Cafe to drink coffee and shoot the breeze. As she had anticipated, the previous day's incident was on every tongue, and her booth was soon filled with curious patrons who had heard through the grapevine that she had found William in his stock tank.

"Well, I can't say I'll spend too much time grieving," Glenn Chambliss remarked between sips of coffee. He stretched out his long legs beneath the table. "And I know it isn't Christian to speak ill of the dead, but Will was an orncry cuss and as tight with his money as bark on a tree."

"I take it that you and William had a few conflicts over the years," Amanda asked shrewdly.

This was just the opening she had hoped for. Now that William wasn't around, the locals were ready to reveal what they really thought of him. It made Amanda wonder what sort of comments would be expressed over her remains when she traveled to the hereafter.

"A *few* conflicts?" Preston Banks piped up. His barrel-shaped chest and abdomen swelled when he inhaled deeply. "Every farmer and rancher whose land adjoins Will's had conflicts with him. Will

41

and Glenn even came to blows back in their younger days. One year the Farley cattle broke through the pasture fence to help themselves to Glenn's wheat crop. Between the unseasonable rains and the hungry herd, Glenn's stand of wheat looked as if it had been trampled into the ground. And worse, Farley cattle had helped themselves to the hay bales stacked up beside the waterway."

"I expected Farley to offer to pay for the damages to my wheat and hay, but he insisted it was my fault because I was responsible for that stretch of fence between our property." Glenn's bushy brows, which looked like fuzzy caterpillars, flattened disapprovingly over his gray eyes. "The man never replaced a barbed-wire fence in his life. I swear some of his fences are the original posts and wire that his granddaddy put on the homestead."

"Damaging a neighbor's stand of wheat isn't the only complaint you'll hear about William Farley, either," Frank Hermann contributed. "I was on my way to town with a load of wheat at harvest two years ago when one of Farley's bulls wandered out of the ditch and onto the road. Since I was carrying a full load of grain, I couldn't slow the truck down fast enough to avoid a collision. I tried to swerve toward the ditch to miss the damned bull, but you know how these country roads are. My truck skidded in loose gravel and landed on its side, spilling grain all over the ditch."

"What happened to Farley's bull?" Amanda questioned.

"Expensive hamburger," Frank grunted. "Of course, Farley raised hell with me because he lost his prize bull, the first one he'd had shipped here from France to start his experiments with Salers and Hereford crossbreeds. When I put up a fuss, reminding him that it was a farmer's responsibility to keep his livestock inside the fences and off the roads, he said he'd pay for the six hundred bushels of lost wheat and the damage to my grain truck. But I never did get a cent out of that tight-fisted rascal. When I practically beat down his door and threatened to sue, he pulled a gun on me."

Amanda was beginning to see there was no love lost between William Farley and his neighbors. The man was stinking rich, but he refused to pay one red cent for damages. Generosity was not one of William's saving graces. Neither was a sense of fair play. He had virtually isolated himself in the community so that only hostile acquaintances were left to mark his passing.

"I don't know what'll become of the farming operation now that Bill's in charge of his father's land holdings," Preston Banks commented, settling his oversized body more comfortably in the booth. "Bill's on the road more than he's at home."

"Can you blame him?" Glenn interjected with a snort. "The two of them squabbled constantly. According to Will, Bill never did anything right in his entire life, especially when it came to marrying Janene. She can spend money as fast as the old man made it."

Amanda could attest to that. The first lady of Farley Farm could match the Queen of England's expenditures on clothing.

"I think Will took losing his younger son out on Bill," Frank remarked and then paused while Faye refilled his coffee cup. "Robert was the spitting image of his father, and he seemed eager to follow in his old man's footsteps. Will doted over Robert, teaching him all there was to know about farming and ranching. When Rob drowned in the pond on

43

the farm two years back, it crushed Will."

Drowned . . . Was it just a coincidence that William had also drowned? Amanda wondered if there might be a connection between the accidents. Of course, with Nick Thorn in charge of the investigation, there would be no suspicion of foul play. He opened and shut case files as if they were cabinet doors.

"What exactly happened to Robert?" Amanda inquired.

"William was too tight to run a water line and electricity to the pasture he owns east of town," Preston explained. "Since we were having a hard winter, the ponds were frozen and the cattle had no place to drink. Will sent Rob down to chop a hole in the ice, and Rob found one of the cows floundering on the frozen pond. When he tried to run the cow off, the ice cracked and they both went down. At least, that's how Nick thought it happened. Since there was no one around, it was only speculation."

Although Amanda would have been perfectly content to continue her subtle line of questioning, she had an appointment to keep. If Velma Hertzog was as informative as her male counterparts, she'd have come a long way toward understanding William's position in the community. She already knew no streets would be named after him. William Farley was not being given a fond farewell in Vamoose but a hasty good riddance.

Amanda had just stepped outside to face an icy blast of wind when Nick Thorn pulled into the parking lot. He watched with amused glee as she piled into the dented red pickup and rumbled off

44

with only a nod of greeting that matched the frigid temperature.

Well, he hadn't expected that sassy blond to forgive him for ribbing her unmercifully. If the truth be known, and he had no intention of letting that happen, his razzing was a defensive tactic. Nick was definitely attracted to Amanda Hazard. She was one of those women who stirred the man in him. But the best way to avoid getting involved in a dead-end relationship was to build walls. The less that blue-eyed terror liked Nick, the easier it would be for him to keep his distance.

Over coffee, Nick swore he disapproved of Amanda even more than he had the previous day. Everybody in the cafe was reciting grievances with William Farley. Old feuds that had been laid to rest were cropping up like unearthed ghosts, and recent conflicts were being heatedly discussed.

Nick held Amanda personally accountable for inciting this situation. She was obviously operating on the theory that Farley had been murdered, searching for motives and possible suspects. Damn it, she was taking an open-and-shut case and making it a crime. Her crazed notion of foul play was going to have Vamoosians in a tailspin. He and this amateur sleuth were going to have a long talk. Real soon!

Amanda inwardly cringed when Velma Hertzog clamped her stubby fingers around a clump of blond hair and stared at their reflections in the mirror. When Velma glanced down, it exposed her double chin and sagging jowls. The hefty beautician towered over Amanda like an Amazon, making her even more apprehensive about putting herself in the woman's hands.

45

"Whatcha want me to do with ya, hon?" Velma asked between chomps of chewing gum. "You want the tapered look or just a trim?"

What Amanda wanted was pertinent information. She would have preferred that Velma leave her hair alone. If the beautician's beehive hairstyle was an indication of her outdated tastes, giving her free rein might result in Amanda walking out of the Beauty Boutique looking like a younger version of the middle-aged Velma!

"I just want to experiment with a few new styles this week," Amanda explained. "Nothing drastic on the cut—maybe only a fraction of an inch."

Amanda knew beauticians were notorious for getting scissor-happy. She had learned that years back. If a customer asked for a short haircut, she could be looking at a scalping.

Velma led Amanda to the sink and pressed her into a seat. Gritting her teeth, Amanda waited for the shampooing to end. That done, she was herded back to her original seat to begin phase two of the scalping.

For a full minute, Velma twisted silky strands around her fingers, holding the tendrils one way and then another; elevating, extending and pulling hair away from Amanda's oval face.

"You've got a perfectly shaped face"—chomp, chomp, crack—"for wearing any style you want, hon. I'd kill for a face and hair like that."

An alarm went off in Amanda's brain. *Kill* was not a word Amanda took lightly these days. Her gaze automatically flew to the scissors Velma held in her poised hand. Metal was already grinding against metal.

"Why don't we try sweeping my hair up like Janene Farley wears hers," Amanda craftily suggested.

46

Velma sniffed distastefully and popped her gum. She began clipping hair as rapidly as she spoke. "Janene is too highfalutin' to grace my doorstep, much less allow me to lay a hand on her precious mop of hair. She dyes it, you know. I can tell at a glance. She came to Vamoose with her nose in the air, and she will leave the same way, I suspect." Snip, snip.

Amanda bit back a wail when a large clump of hair drifted to the floor. "Janene isn't from around here?" Her voice was one octave higher than normal.

"No way," Millicent Patch interjected from the corner. She set her magazine aside, tugged her polyester skirt over her knees and joined in the conversation. "Janene's family owns a fancy horse-breeding ranch south of the City. She's used to money, and it shows. She wouldn't be caught dead driving an economy car or buying clothes that don't come from the fanciest Western stores in the City or Fort Worth. She wears eight-hundred-dollar ostrich and lizard boots, flaunts diamonds and turquoise big enough to choke a horse and she has her hair styled at some la-de-dah place in the City. You never see her unless she looks her very best."

Amanda braced herself when another clump of blond hair dropped to the floor. Courageously, she concentrated on the information Millicent and Velma were supplying. All in the line of duty, she reassured herself. Losing her hair was the price she had to pay.

"Bill ran into Janene at one of those honky-tonk bars in the City after he had organized a brood-mare auction for her daddy," Velma reported. "He fell for her skin-tight jeans and her silicone-implanted chest." Snort, clip, chomp. "I never did hold with tampering with one's body to attract men. I say we've got what we got and we should make the best of it."

Amanda bit her tongue and refrained from accusing Velma of manufacturing her scant beauty from bottles and boxes. When one is under the gun—or under the scissors as in this case—one does not invite discord.

"Exactly right," Millicent inserted. "My Henry, God rest his soul, never complained that I didn't have Marilyn Monroe's figure."

"Marilyn bleached her hair too, you know." Snap, crackle, pop. Snip, snip.

"How long have Janene and Bill been married?" Amanda inquired, refusing to look in the mirror for fear the shock would kill her.

"Only about five years." Millicent leaned down to pick up her discarded magazine. "And she is at least twelve years younger than Bill. I never thought the marriage would last this long, what with Bill traveling all over the country, conducting livestock sales. But he and Janene get along better when they don't see each other. With Will Sr. gone, the fur will probably fly. Since Janene's brother came to work for Farley Farm as the resident veterinarian she spends more time with him than with Bill. I don't know who Bill is spending his time with or how he is spending it."

Amanda blinked, surprised. "I didn't know Janene and Luke Princeton were sister and brother."

"They are." Clip, chomp. "Luke got his degree at Oklahoma State, but Janene never went to college. She may be long on beauty but she's short on brains. When Will found out about Luke, he saw his chance to hire a private vet. But he kept Luke on call twenty-four hours a day. He treated him like a high-priced farmhand. If Will thought one of his prized cows might have trouble calving, he sent Luke to the barn to spend the night. And if Will brought a truckload of steers to graze on wheat pasture, he would have Luke down at the corral, inoculating the livestock, even if it was after midnight," Velma added disapprovingly.

"It seems William was notorious for taking advantage of people." Amanda cautiously shifted in her chair between snips.

"That's the understatement of the decade." Millicent sniffed in disgust. "I never did like the man myself. Will was a tightwad. He was forever borrowing equipment and tools from my Henry and never bothering to return them. If Will's tractor broke down near our farm, he just waltzed into the workshop and took what he needed for repairs. And when Henry went to retrieve his tools, William threw a fit, insisting they belonged to him.

"The time Henry and William tried to rent the same farmland from Mrs. Baxter, after her husband died, they nearly came to blows. And from what I've heard around town, William didn't always pay his rent for wheat pasture. No wonder he made money hand over fist. He grazed far too many cattle on his neighbor's wheat crops, taking the profit and neglecting to pay his expenses. I swear that man cared more about his cattle than his fellow man."

A teasing smile settled on Millicent's wrinkled face. "Of course, there was a time when Velma had eyes for William and defended his unscrupulous business dealings."

The comment caused Velma to snip even faster. Amanda grabbed the beautician's wrist before the

49

Amazon cut off all her blond hair. "I think that will be enough trimming, Velma. Could you blow my hair dry and style it. I have an appointment with a client later this afternoon."

With a nod of her dyed-red hair—she would swear the color was natural to her dying breath—Velma tossed the scissors aside and snatched up the dryer. "You would have to bring that subject up, wouldn't you, Millie? Okay, so I had a thing for Will for a year or so. All his money could turn a woman's head, and he could certainly be charming when he felt like it. He was lonely after his wife died. But Bill didn't approve of me any more than Will approved of Janene." She flung Millicent a firm glance. "And contrary to what you and the other busybodies probably thought, all Will ever got from me was free haircuts."

"Did I say anything?" Millicent put on an innocent look, but Amanda and Velma didn't buy it. Avoiding their unblinking stares, Millicent removed her glasses and cleaned the lenses on the hem of her blouse. "Well, what were the rest of us to think, Velma? You were both of legal age. And Will did pay house calls to Rose Chambliss and Violet Banks while their husbands were away. I saw Will's pickup at their doorsteps one too many times not to suspect there was hanky-panky going on. William Farley didn't live in celibacy after Margaret passed on, I can tell you that. And if you ask me, he was friendly with Rose and Violet up 'til the day he died. That's probably what killed him—too much exertion for a man his age!"

Amanda was beginning to wonder if that was what killed William, but not in the way Millicent suggested. The grudges that Glenn and Preston held against William Farley might have gone much deeper than conflicts over farming interests. Of course, considering the sensitivity of the male ego, neither rancher would admit another man was capable of taking his place. Cuckolded husbands had a tendency to let their resentment fester like boils. But then, so did wives cursed with cheating husbands.

Amanda had suffered from cynicism after her husband came home from the office one evening to inform her that he had found someone else. The shock, the feelings of rejection and betrayal had lingered for years. As a result, she would not permit herself to trust men farther than she could throw them. She suspected Glenn and Preston had developed strong resentments toward William, if what Millicent said was true.

"I heard William had been trying to buy Glenn's and Preston's quarter sections that join the Farley place on the north and west. Both men are in debt up to their eyeballs," Velma declared as she wound Amanda's hair around the brush and blasted her with the dryer's hot air. "I heard Glenn even stooped to asking Will for a loan because the banker wouldn't extend him more credit. Preston had to sell his John Deere 8960 tractor to pay part of his debts. There's no telling what sort of deals Glenn and Preston tried to make with Will to save their farms, even if they didn't like him."

Amanda found herself wondering if clandestine loans might explain the checks William had written—the ones Amanda had questioned but had never brought to his attention.

"With wheat prices so low and beef sales on the decline, profit is skimpy. All those oil wells on Farley ground have kept him going. Some of the farmers and ranchers weren't so lucky," Millicent added. "They already have their belts tightened as far as they will go."

Since Amanda did not handle the books of Glenn Chambliss and Preston Banks, she could not attest to their financial situation. But she knew times were tough. Wheat prices were as low as they had been thirty years earlier, but the cost of equipment, fertilizer and land had escalated at phenomenal rates. The Environmental Protection Agency had placed so many restrictions on pesticides that there were times when farmers had no choice but to watch while insects and weeds overtook their crops, wiping out what little profit could be gained.

Some farmers and ranchers employed the "plunge and recover" method of finance, hoping prosperity was just around the corner. Nowadays, banks owned more land and farm machinery than the farmers and ranchers themselves.

William Farley was one of the fortunate few who didn't have one leg sunk in debt. It made Amanda wonder just how far bitterness and jealousy might drive a man toward wanting to see his *un*favorite neighbor bite the dust.

Could William Farley have had an argument with one of his neighbors—a heated confrontation that brought on a second heart attack? William had definitely sounded upset the night he'd called Amanda. He had ranted about switching accounts and writing enormous checks for more cash without stating the whys and what-fors. Had he been blackmailed? Or had he been blackmailing someone else? Amanda wished she knew!

"So, Amanda, how do you like living in Vamoose?" Millicent questioned, tiring of the previous topic of conversation. "We have produced several

52

celebrities, you know. Billie Jane Baxter made it big in Nashville, singing country tunes. We all knew she was talented while she was growing up in Vamoose, entertaining at high school and church functions. Now her records are at the top of the charts."

"And there's Buddy Hampton, the nationally known horse breeder. He made a name for himself with the American Paint Horse Association. Buddy hired that good-looking trainer from Texas to get all those fancy horses ready to compete in the national shows and livestock sales held all over the Midwest." Chomp, chomp.

When Amanda frowned pensively, trying to associate names with faces, Velma started rattling off explanations in an effort to help her make the proper connections.

"You know Buddy Hampton. He's the bean-pole cowboy who always comes into the Last Chance Cafe with his jeans tucked in the top of his boots. He wears a black Stetson with a brim as wide as his shoulders. He married Mrs. Baxter's youngest daughter, Bobbie Sue. That's Billie Jane's little sister. And Randel Thompson"—Velma cracked her gum and sighed with feminine appreciation—"he's the one with those bedroom, blue eyes and the body like Hercules. I hear Randel is as good at handling women as he is with horses."

Before Velma veered off into somebody else's family tree, Amanda said, "Yes, I remember seeing both of them."

"And, of course, there is Bill Farley, who travels the country auctioning off cattle for the National Cattlemen's Association," Millicent added. "There is also that famous author who lives here in town and does freelance work for magazines, besides writing

53

those steamy novels that keep me reading all night. Vamoose does seems to breed all sorts of success."

Amanda had no opportunity to interject a comment because Velma attacked in a flurry of hairpins and a fog of hair spray. By the time she'd finished gluing every stray hair in place, Amanda looked as if she were wearing a ten-gallon hat. Her hair was piled so high on her head and sprayed to such an extreme that a cyclone couldn't budge her coiffure.

"There. All done." Velma backed away proudly to admire her creation.

Amanda called upon her acting ability to compliment a hair style she would not have considered wearing to a costume party. "You did a splendid job, Velma."

Velma's pudgy face beamed with delight. "I also have certification in cosmetology," she boasted. Smack, smack. "Would you like me to—"

Amanda leaped out of her chair as if she'd been sitting on red ants. "We'll experiment with makeup another day. Thursday perhaps?"

Velma thumbed through her appointment book and penned Amanda in for the afternoon. Amanda shuddered to think what she would look like when she turned Velma loose with mascara, blush and eye shadow. But if Thursday turned out to be as productive as today, she would have gained more information to help her understand William Farley and his relationships with his family and his neighbors.

Amanda wondered if William would have appreciated the sacrifices she was making in his behalf. If foul play was involved in his death, she was going to discover who had played him foul. And if she was leaping to wild conclusions, as Officer

54

Thorn insisted she was, then all she had wasted was time and a few dollars for extra coffees and beauty parlor appointments.

Five

Taking an impulsive turn in the opposite direction from her home south of town, Amanda steered her pickup toward William Farley's farm. The newborn calf that had twice disappeared still disturbed her. She could not help but think the calf's relocation held some clue to the circumstances of William's death. Someone obviously did not want that calf seen. Had it belonged to one of William's neighbors? Amanda hadn't thought to check for a brand or identifying mark on the poor animal. Was some old-fashioned rustling going on around Vamoose?

Amanda recalled what Millicent and Velma had said about Glenn and Preston being heavily in debt. Had William been hiding some of his neighbor's livestock among his own herds until after the bank decided whether or not to foreclose on outstanding debts? Or perhaps the cattlemen had devised some method of hiding, and later selling, livestock?

If Glenn or Preston had used their cattle as collateral for loans, they might have resorted to illegal means to acquire cash to keep them afloat. Had William offered to assist one, or both, of his neighbors and then threatened exposure if the favor wasn't returned to his satisfaction? Had William's form of blackmail resulted in his cleverly arranged death? And without the missing calf, how could

56

Amanda hope to prove he did *not* die from a natural cause?

Pulling the rattletrap of a pickup to a halt, Amanda studied the stretch of fence that separated William's pasture from the gravel road. At the expense of snagging her slacks on barbed wire, she eased through the fence and hiked up the hill toward the grove of willows.

No calf. No tracks. No nothing. *Damn!*

Refusing to be discouraged, she trekked toward the creek that cut a lazy path through the pasture. A thorough search of the area turned up nothing out of the ordinary. Amanda was beginning to think she was as crazy as Nick Thorn swore she was.

And then she saw it. Or at least she thought she did.

In a narrow neck of the creek, she spied a hoof protruding from a clump of half-submerged tumbleweeds. This time Amanda checked for a brand, but there was nothing to identify the unfortunate calf. Now maybe Nick Thorn would believe her!

Determined of purpose, Amanda jogged back to her pickup and sped off. Her feeling of smug satisfaction evaporated when she flagged down the patrol car, only to discover Nick's evening replacement was making the rounds.

Benny Sykes directed Amanda to Nick's house. According to Benny, Nick lived on his family's farm, ran a few head of cattle and sheep and grew enough wheat to pasture his herd. Until that moment, Amanda had assumed Nick Thorn had no other interests besides patrolling the streets of Vamoose and ridiculing her at every chance he got.

She expected to find a run-down farm house and unpainted outbuildings that begged for attention. However, that was not the case. A well-kept brick home, freshly painted fences and sturdy corrals greeted her. From all indications, Nick Thorn spared the time and energy to give his property the care a rural home and surrounding acreage required. She was sorry to say her rented place looked shabby in comparison to Thorn's. That came as a blow to her ego. She didn't want to feel inferior to Nick Thorn in any way.

After she rapped several times at the door, Nick answered, wearing a bathrobe that revealed a dark matting of hair on his muscled chest. Amanda found herself inspecting his legs, those very masculine columns that glistened with water droplets.

Tom Selleck had nothing on Nick Thorn, not as far as Amanda could tell. She wished she hadn't noticed. Unfortunately, her gaze kept straying where it didn't belong, even when she tried to focus on those dark eyes that were surrounded by long lashes—eyes Velma Hertzog probably would have killed for. So she wouldn't have to resort to wearing the false eyelashes she denied owning.

"Wanna take a snapshot, Hazard? Or do you have a photographic memory?"

The taunting remark provoked Amanda to bristle in self-defense and jerk herself to attention. "I wasn't expecting to be greeted by a man in a bathrobe."

"I wasn't expecting to have my shower interrupted by someone who sounded intent on beating my door down."

"I have something I want you to see." She changed the subject and shifted her gaze to a safe object—the brick facade of the house.

"Your new hairdo? I'm sure the bees will love their new hive."

Since Nick had not been courteous enough to ask

her in out of the cold, Amanda invited herself. "I found the missing calf," she announced. "Do you want to dress before I take you with me, or do you prefer to hike through Farley's pasture practically naked?"

Nick rolled his eyes and expelled an audible sigh. "Not again." Amanda's unblinking stare assured him that she was not leaving without him, no matter how many times he insulted her. "Oh, all right, Hazard. Give me a few minutes to dress." He gestured toward the kitchen before he pivoted toward the bedroom. "Make yourself at home. There's fresh coffee on the counter."

After tromping around in the cold, steaming coffee sounded heavenly. It took Amanda a while to find the powdered cream and sugar since Nick's kitchen wasn't alphabetically organized as hers was. The sugar should have been sitting between the salt and tea, not stashed beside the bread. The man had no sense of order.

Within a few minutes Nick returned wearing a faded red flannel shirt and trim-fitting jeans that accentuated his broad shoulders, lean hips and sturdy legs. He smelled as good as he looked. Amanda wished she hadn't noticed that, either. Her only interest in Nick Thorn was a confirmation that she had seen the dead calf that had been relocated twice for reasons unknown.

"I'm ready for another wild-goose chase," Nick declared, grabbing his down-filled jacket.

Amanda propelled herself toward the door. "You can apologize for being an ass after I tell you I told you so."

By the time Amanda drove back to Farley's pasture, darkness had descended. It was difficult to retrace her path with only the use of Nick's flashlight.

"Are you sure you know where you're going?" he questioned after several minutes of circling and doubling back.

Amanda flashed him a glare that even the darkness couldn't hide. "Do you think I was an Indian scout in a previous life? Have a little patience, Thorn. I'll find the calf eventually."

"I may freeze to death first," Nick muttered.

Amanda finally located the bend of the creek where the calf had been camouflaged in weeds. With immense satisfaction, Amanda called her doubtful companion's attention to the corpse. "Was I right?"

Nick studied the carcass for a long moment. "This is the same calf you allegedly saw lying beside the stock tank?"

"There is nothing alleged about it," Amanda huffed. "Someone moved the carcass and my inquiring mind wants to know who and why."

When Nick pivoted on his boot heels and ambled away, Amanda stared incredulously after him. "Well, don't you have something to say?"

"Yes," he said without a backward glance. "I'm cold and hungry. I'll buy you supper."

"I want you to open an investigation!"

Nick halted, grumbled under his breath and wheeled around to fling Amanda a you're-wasting-my-time glare. "If I investigated every dead calf in the vicinity of Vamoose, I would get nothing else done."

"You get nothing else done anyway," she declared with certainty.

His teeth clenched. For a satisfying moment he envisioned himself curling his fingers around her throat and shaking the stuffing out of her. With commendable self-control, he refrained from doing her bodily harm.

"It's a fact that newborn calves die occasionally. It could have been premature or—"

"Or it could have been killed the same way William Farley was."

"The medical examiner's report indicated no presence of poison, no injury that might have resulted in death. Farley's heart gave out. Now give it up, Hazard!"

Headlights speared through the darkness. A pickup veered around Amanda's parked vehicle and sped away. She thought she recognized Glenn Chambliss's truck with its white tool box bolted to the bed. But in the darkness she could not make a positive identification.

"Hurry it up before somebody comes along and collides with your truck," Nick demanded.

Amanda followed in Nick's wake, suspicious of everything that moved, especially the unidentified truck that sailed over the hill and disappeared from sight. Had the driver of the truck returned to remove the calf from Farley's property under the cover of darkness? Amanda made a mental note to check the spot in the light of day to see if the calf had vanished again.

Deciding to join Nick for the evening meal, she drove home. But she volunteered to fix sandwiches so she could speak with him privately. However, when she unlocked the door and switched on the light, she was met with darkness.

"The bulb must have burned out." Nick handed her the flashlight. "Bring me a replacement."

Amanda moved swiftly across the front room to the closet. Her hand stalled in midair, and she

61

frowned, dumbfounded. She could have sworn she had placed a package of bulbs on the second shelf. Pivoting around, she sped into the kitchen to rob a bulb from the fixture over the sink. The flick of the switch produced no results. What the hell was going on?

Not one to be easily discouraged, Amanda zipped down the hall to retrieve the bulb from her bedroom lamp. Dragging a chair back with her, she held the flashlight while Nick climbed up to replace the overhead bulb in the front room. Light swallowed the shadows.

While Amanda went in search of another bulb to replace the one over the kitchen sink so she could prepare sandwiches, Nick wandered around the room. It was evident that Amanda was one of those individuals who believed everything had its place and that things should be immediately returned to their places after use. Magazines were stacked in alphabetical order. Old newspapers had been discarded. No glass sat about on a coaster. Undoubtedly it would have been carried to the kitchen and promptly washed.

Nick paused to study the family portraits, curious. He had imagined Amanda to be the homecoming-queen type, but her high-school photo projected the image of a chubby teenager with cheeks like a chipmunk's.

"Not what you expected, Thorn?" Amanda questioned from behind him. "I was a late bloomer and noticeably overweight until I entered college and escaped Mother's cooking. She tried to keep me on four-hour feeding schedules. I didn't lose my baby fat until I was twenty. Despite what you probably thought, I was not very popular. In fact, I was a pudgy bookworm overlooked by the boys. During college, I suddenly found myself receiving a great deal of masculine attention."

Amanda set the tray of food and drink on the coffee table and eased onto the sofa. "I, of course, was the same person I had always been. I had shed a few layers of flab and *poof!* I had more offers for dates than there were nights in the weekend. It occurred to me that men were far more attracted by looks than brains and they didn't care all that much about the real me. I never quite forgave you all for being so shallow."

"And I have not forgiven you since I walked into the cafe this morning to discover you had stirred up old hostilities against William," Nick countered, jumping to another topic of conversation.

Amanda munched on her ham sandwich and chased it with Coke. "Can I help it if the customers brought up the subject? I was the one who found William, after all. Everyone wanted to hear the gory details."

"And you were digging for information to support your absurd theory. Admit it, Hazard."

"Fine. I admit it. But several people in Vamoose may have had good reasons to want William dead."

"Hearsay and speculation are not admissible in a court of law, thank God. If they were, you would have everyone who ever had an argument with William in handcuffs. I've had a few confrontations with him myself. Do you plan to make a citizen's arrest after supper?"

"I'm considering it. You seem very eager to look the other way when I suggest things are not as simple as they appear. Are you protecting yourself or are you avoiding the extra effort involved in investigation?"

Nick scowled at his plate. "I wish to hell you

would stick to your profession and leave me to mine!"

Amanda decided she was using the wrong approach to gain this mulish man's cooperation. But then, she seldom employed the right approach with men. She had always been too persistent and straightforward, refusing to pamper the fragile male ego. Men had difficulty coping with pushy women. They seemed to resent determination in their female counterparts, though they admired the quality in themselves.

"I suppose if I asked you to go to bed with me, you would be willing to at least consider my theories about William Farley." That, in Amanda's estimation, was something the male mind could understand—swapping favors for favors.

Nick stared at her as if bees were buzzing from her beehive hairdo. Okay, so he had considered the possibility once or twice in his weaker moments. Single men did such things on occasion. Speculation wasn't against the law. However, the last thing he'd expected from her was a remark like that. He had come to expect insults, but that comment offended him.

Nick gathered his feet beneath him and stood up. "I think I'd better leave."

Amanda decided he had better do that. It had been a tacky thing for her to say, and she had accomplished nothing by it. But nothing infuriated her more than a man's refusing to take her seriously.

"I'll get my keys," she said without a glance in Nick's direction.

The phone rang just as she hurried by it. She snatched it up and burst out with a sharp "Hello."

"Hi, doll. It's Mother. I just called to tell you that

your brother and his family are coming over for Sunday dinner. I thought you might want to come too."

Amanda's mother cleared her throat. "Your brother needs advice on budgeting. I swear that boy has forgotten everything Daddy and I taught him."

No, he hasn't, thought Amanda. Her brother just happened to enjoy doing things his own way after escaping the nest. "I'm sure Brad is managing quite well. He has a good job and—"

"And two children who go through his money as if it were water!" her mother groused. "I don't know how he makes ends meet." She sighed melodramatically. "Well, enough about your brother and his problems. Are you coming to dinner? We'll expect you at one o'clock."

"I don't think—"

"Did you send your niece a card yet? Her birthday is a week from tomorrow. Your aunt—Grace—has a birthday next month. Don't forget to mark it on your calendar."

"Yes, Mother," Amanda gritted out in the most pleasant tone she could manage.

"Well then, I'll see you on Sunday. Don't forget to mail those cards . . . and don't forget to buckle your seat belt."

"Yes, Mother." Amanda's voice was reminiscent of a hiss, though she tried admirably to disguise that.

She slammed down the receiver after she heard the click on the other end of the line. A conversation with Mother was all she needed after a frustrating discussion with Nick Thorn-in-the-side. Both of them could turn her mood black as pitch in nothing flat.

* * *

Neither Nick nor Amanda uttered a word the first two miles of the return trip to Nick's farm. The silence was awkward, but Amanda reminded herself there was nothing wrong with letting silence be a part of communication.

After a while, she felt the reluctant need to apologize for the ludicrous question she had flung at Nick in a moment of irritation. "I'm sorry. I shouldn't have said that."

More silence.

Not until the truck rolled to a halt did Nick comment. He climbed out and poked his head back inside the lighted cab. "Don't proposition me again, Hazard."

She stared straight ahead. "I said I was sorry."

"Now that that's settled and out of the way, do you want to go to bed with me? For a quick tumble, I'll listen to your weird theories."

Her head snapped around and she glared daggers at him.

"Insulting, isn't it?" An ornery smile quirked his lips. "The hell of it was, I was tempted when you made your sarcastic suggestion. I'm curious to find out whether you look as good in a sheet as you do in a business suit. That's the man in me talking. Not the police officer." Nick could have cut out his tongue for admitting he wanted something he knew damned good and well he shouldn't have. He and Hazard were at opposite ends of the personality spectrum. To save face, he added, "However, I intend to see that logic prevails over lust. We are going to keep this relationship respectable."

Amanda couldn't say why she felt flattered by this backhanded compliment, but she was. Of course, she would not have admitted to it, even under penalty of death. She had made a pact with herself years ago to never let a man come close enough to hurt her again. Unfortunately, she had difficulty squelching the tingles of arousal elicited by this sexy country cop.

"You looked pretty damned good in a bathrobe, Thorn. But take time to dress if I ever pay you another visit. I don't like being a little bit tempted either. If offends my strong sense of integrity."

Amanda shifted into reverse, stripping the opened door from Nick's hands and leaving him to stare bewilderedly after her. Now she had done it. She had let Thorn know the physical attraction was mutual. It was begrudging and reluctant for both of them, but mutual nonetheless.

By the time Amanda reached the bridge over the river and turned south, she had herself in hand again. She was going home to wash off the gallon of hair spray and go to bed—alone. She was not going to get involved with Tom Selleck's clone, the one without the mustache. She'd had her fill of marriage and relationships that were more trouble than gratification. Nick wanted no complications, and all Amanda wanted was his professional expertise in solving this mystery. She wasn't likely to get it, but *that* was all she desired.

Six

The next few days passed in a flurry of activity. Amanda went twice to Oklahoma City to confer with metropolitan clients at the firm of Nelson, Blake and Cosmos, where she dodged the flirtations of two roving-eyed executives. She also attended William Farley's funeral and accepted an appointment to counsel Bill Farley on his father's estate.

And she had made it a point to stop by the Last Chance Cafe to keep abreast of gossip. She had detained Officer Thorn long enough to inform him that she had returned to check on the vanishing calf, which had been moved again to a location unknown to her. And what did that suggest? she had asked him with a smug smile before making a theatrical exit from the cafe.

She had received her weekly call from Mother who reminded her it was time for her annual dental checkup and cleaning. This reminder, unbeknownst to her mother, was one that the dental receptionist could handle. After all these years, Amanda's mother still treated her as if she were a child. And her mother's habit of clearing her throat before initiating a new topic of conversation, as if demanding absolute attention, still annoyed the hell out of Amanda. She prided herself on being an independent, responsible modern woman. Her mother couldn't accept that. Mothers rarely did.

Cecil Watts had left a message on Amanda's answering machine, informing her that her Toyota would be out of commission longer than he'd anticipated. It might be a week before he completed the repairs. Knowing the snail's pace Cecil set, Amanda thought he was being too optimistic.

An ice storm pounded central Oklahoma the morning Amanda drove out to confer with the Farleys. Although bad road conditions caused her to be a few minutes late, Bill did not call attention to the fact as his father would have done.

Bill Farley was a tall, good-looking man with a knack for making a person feel welcome — also uncharacteristic of his sire. No doubt, the need for good personal relations in Bill's line of business contributed to his conscious effort at projecting a personable air.

Janene, on the other hand, was polite but distant. Amanda remembered what Millicent and Velma had said, and she attributed Janene's demeanor to an unwarranted air of superiority. As usual, Janene was immaculate, not a hair out of place. Her Western wear looked so crisp and colorful that Amanda wondered if the woman ever wore the same ensemble twice. Even her ostrich boots looked brand spanking new.

"I was hoping I could count on you to handle all the financial statements for me, the same way you did for Dad," Bill said, handing Amanda a cup of coffee.

"Of course." Amanda opened her briefcase. "There are a few canceled checks here that I would like to question you about . . ." Amanda frowned, bemused. She had paper-clipped the three checks to the inside of the file earlier in the week. Now they were gone. How odd. "Um . . . I must have set the checks aside to ask your father about them and then neglected to replace them in the file."

Although the missing checks disturbed her, she retrieved the detailed accounts of William's holdings and presented her client with a copy to be relayed to the family lawyer.

"I'll see that Lloyd Bascom gets the papers as soon as possible," Bill promised. "I have an Angus cattle show to organize this weekend, but I'll stop by Bascom's office before I fly out."

The comment drew a peevish frown from his wife. "Another trip? What if disaster strikes again while you're gone? You weren't even where you were supposed to be when I tried to contact you about your father."

Janene's accusing stare suggested there was more she would have said, were it not for their guest. Husband and wife exchanged hostile glances, and the tension in the room increased, making the silence awkward and uncomfortable.

To Amanda's horror, she found herself clearing her throat as her mother had always done when she'd switched topics. "I should be on my way. I know you have dozens of obligations to fulfill. If I can be of any further assistance in finalizing the estate, let me know."

Leaving her black coffee untouched, Amanda took up her briefcase and left. What was Janene suggesting? Amanda wondered. Had Bill mixed business with pleasure during his trip to Denver?

She quickly recalled what Millicent Patch had said at the beauty shop. *And I don't know who Bill is spending* his *time with*. The comment suggested Bill might be fooling around while Janene cried on her brother's shoulder.

Growing suspicion prompted Amanda to make a mental note to check the arrival and departure times of Bill's flight. She then detoured to Nick Thorn's farm to gather further information.

Nick appeared at his front door clad in faded blue jeans. Amanda was disappointed. Her traitorous eyes and sordid mind had hoped for the shower-fresh bathrobe look, even when her sense of propriety objected to it.

"I wondered if I might borrow a copy of the *Farm Journal*," Amanda requested politely.

Nick scrutinized her for several seconds before stepping aside to let her enter. "Thinking of taking up farming, are you, Hazard?"

"Maybe. You seem to enjoy ranching on a part-time basis. I thought I might endear myself to my rural clients if I bought a few cows." She could be as much of a smart ass as Nick when she was so inclined.

"Cut the crap, Hazard. What are you up to now?"

"Nothing." She graced him with an angelic smile. "If you can't part with your most recent copy of the *Farm Journal* for a few days, I'll borrow one from somebody else."

Scowling, Nick wheeled around to rummage through the stack of magazines on the end table.

"If you compiled your reading material in alphabetical order, you could put your hand on anything within seconds," Amanda suggested, just to get his goat. Sure enough, Nick did have a goat to get.

71

"I don't happen to want my life categorized alphabetically, thank you very much!" Nick finally located the publication and pivoted to slap it into Amanda's outstretched hand. "What crazed lead are you following now, Detective Hazard?"

Amanda thumbed through the magazine in search of the article about the stock show and auction held in Colorado. "According to Janene Farley, Bill wasn't where he was supposed to be when she tried to contact him about his father's death." She called Nick's attention to the ad. "According to this itinerary, the auction and convention adjourned two days prior to Bill's return to Oklahoma."

"So?"

"So we all know Bill and William were in conflict. William did not approve of his son's marriage or Bill's lack of attention to the farming and ranching operations. Bill did not approve of William's friendship with Velma Hertzog after Margaret Farley's death. There has been bad blood between father and son for years, and that's been aggravated by the torment William underwent when he lost his favorite son in another so-called accident. One that you investigated. I wonder where Bill was at the time of *that* accident?"

Amanda paused only long enough to allow Nick to insert two muffled oaths. "It is entirely possible that Bill could have returned early to arrange his father's murder, left town again without anyone knowing he had come and gone, and then made his appearance after Janene got hold of him."

"Hazard, you are nuts! Do you stay up nights dreaming up these crazy ideas of yours?"

Nick grabbed his coat with one hand and latched on to Amanda's arm with the other. "You are coming with me while I check my cattle and feed the

72

sheep. And on the way, I am going to tell you just how crazy you are."

Despite Amanda's objection, Nick propelled her toward his pickup and planted her on the seat. After he took a few swipes to clear the icy glaze from the windshield, he sped toward the barn.

Gesturing for Amanda to accompany him, Nick tramped inside to retrieve a square bale of alfalfa hay. Employing a whistle that blasted Amanda's eardrums, he called to the flock of sheep. Creatures that resembled oversized cotton balls bounded around the corner of the barn. They collided with each other in their haste to reach the blocks of hay Nick had scattered in the straw.

"I think you are overfeeding your sheep," Amanda declared as she watched the flock mill around her. "You should consider cutting their rations in half. These sheep don't walk; they waddle."

Nick grinned at Amanda's ignorance. "You would waddle too if you were expecting twins within the month."

Amanda felt foolish and she sorely resented the fact that Nick Thorn constantly delighted in calling attention to her lack of knowledge about livestock.

"Sheep usually have twin lambs, and occasionally triplets," he informed her. "These ewes, with their thick wool winter coats and slender legs always appear fatter than they are. Only when they have been sheared in the spring can you tell at a glance how much weight they are carrying. These Suffolk ewes don't need to be put on a diet, Hazard."

"Oh," Amanda said sheepishly.

Her attention shifted to the Great Pyrenees sheepdog that trotted in with the flock. The huge white dog sniffed Amanda up and down.

"That is Napoleon, defender of the flock," Nick

73

announced before he ambled off to get dog food. "He keeps the flock from wandering off and protects them from coyotes. Napoleon lives with the sheep and only makes occasional appearances at my doorstep."

Amanda bent over to pat the dog's broad head. "Nice to meet you, Napoleon."

"Watch out for the—"

Nick's abrupt warning came a second too late. Amanda stood facing him, unaware that the ram had darted around the corner and spotted a vulnerable target. The ram's forward momentum sent Amanda stumbling into Nick's waiting arms. Cursing the ornery animal, Nick swung Amanda out of the way to swat the buck between the eyes. The ram charged again, and Nick retaliated with another discouraging blow.

Amanda massaged her stinging backside and glared at the offending buck. Now she knew why rams were said to have the hardest heads in the animal kingdom. The blows Nick rendered to the ram didn't seem to faze him. Only after the ram had made the point that he was king of this flock did he raise his arrogant head and trot off to munch his alfalfa.

"I forgot to warn you that Atilla has a nasty disposition," Nick said. He walked over to scoop up pellets and sling them in the feeder, providing the flock with the second course of their meal. "You never turn your back on bucks. They have appropriately earned the name of *rams*."

Amanda committed that valuable piece of advice to memory. She never took her eyes off Atilla while she and Nick exited from the barn to climb into the truck.

She had just settled herself on her aching backside when Nick shifted the pickup into reverse. A pained groan erupted from her lips when he smashed into the round hay bale that sat behind them. He had lowered the hydraulic cylinder-operated hay fork that had been bolted in the bed of his pickup. It stabbed the thousand-pound bale. After Nick levered the bale off the ground and drove off, he flashed Amanda a stern glance.

"Bill Farley did not plot to murder his father because there was no crime committed. There is no ongoing investigation. Only you harbor the ridiculous suspicions that satisfy your incredibly active imagination.

"Robert Farley fell through the ice in his attempt to rescue one of his father's highly prized cows two years ago. I don't believe Bill resented his little brother or his father's favoritism. You are trying to glue unrelated incidents together to support your absurd notions of murder and I want your meddling stopped!"

"Don't you think it rather odd that Bill did not return to Vamoose until two days after the convention and auction adjourned?" Amanda opened the magazine and thrust her forefinger at the dates listed on the ad. "Forty-eight hours, Thorn. Forty-eight unaccounted-for hours. Where was Bill Farley? What was he doing and with whom?"

"You are driving me berserk, Hazard!" Nick stomped on the accelerator and zoomed through the open corral toward the pasture where twenty purebred Salers cows anxiously awaited their breakfast.

"Your cattle look like some of the ones in William's pasture," Amanda noted.

"Yeah, I suppose you want to make something of that too. Bill bought these Salers heifers for me at auction. They are an up-and-coming breed because the cows drop small calves without many complications during labor and delivery. However, there are always a few complications to be expected with first-time heifers, no matter what the breed. I anticipate a few problems this first year," he added.

"Experiments with Salers indicate promising weight gains as beef cattle. This breed can withstand harsh weather conditions like the ones we face in Oklahoma." His eyes narrowed on Amanda as he continued. "And before you accuse me of rustling, the brand on the hip belongs to the breeder in Wyoming. I won't brand my herd until I gather them in the corral to vaccinate the new calves in late spring."

Amanda remained silent while Nick lowered the hay bale and hopped out to cut the nylon strings that held the straw together. "Is there any particular reason why you don't let the cattle eat around the string?" she questioned curiously.

"Two reasons," Nick explained without glancing in her direction. "I don't want the cows and calves to entangle themselves and risk injury. Neither do I want the knotted strings clogging up the workings of my swather when I mow the pasture for prairie hay this summer."

That sounded sensible. But why hadn't William Farley followed that practice? Amanda had noticed wads of nylon cord strung around the stock tank in William's pasture. Obviously he hadn't been as particular in that department as Nick was. William had been one of those farmers who took from the land without much thought of giving back. He did not see the beauty of the country, only its worth to him as a stockman. William overgrazed his pastures and wheat fields, as well as those of his neighbors. He patched fences rather than replacing them. He left piles of old machinery and trucks sitting around to spoil a grand view of wide open spaces.

But Nick Thorn was an environmentalist and conservationist who tried to live in harmony with the land. He believed in preserving the beauty of nature while he reaped its benefits. Amanda favored Nick's approach. She wasn't about to tell him so, but she did.

With practiced ease, Nick drove away from the hay bale, elevating the spike as he went. The hay fork attached to his black pickup reminded Amanda of a bumblebee with its protruding stinger. Although the device looked a little peculiar jutting out from the end of the truck, the mechanism apparently saved farmers a great deal of time and extra work in feeding large numbers of cattle.

William Farley also had a fork attached to his green truck, enabling him to feed cattle without the exertion of manhandling bales. Gone were the days in which square bales were used exclusively. No longer did a labor crew have to gather small bales from the field in trucks, unload and restack them in barns, and then reload them in pickups to deliver to livestock. What time and energy-saving devices would they think of next?

"Have dinner with me tonight," Nick said out of the blue.

Amanda stared at him as if he were insane. "What's the matter? Haven't you poked enough fun at me for one day?"

Nick stopped the truck and gestured for her to join him at the rear of the truck bed. He handed her a block of salt and then slung a sack of mineral supplement over his shoulder. Amanda hadn't realized ranchers had the extra expense of providing salt and minerals for their livestock. She naively presumed ranchers simply enclosed their cattle in pasture or wheat fields and let them graze to their hearts' content. Obviously she had a lot to learn about the new breed of farmers and stockmen.

Although William had doted over his cattle, he hadn't bothered to look into updated procedures or modern technology to improve his livestock's health. He had raised cattle the old-fashioned way, letting the animals take their chances against Mother Nature as they had done in the past. Amanda was beginning to think William Farley was not the model rancher he'd proclaimed himself to be. Nick Thorn was far more conscientious. But be that as it may, she still felt an obligation to investigate the circumstances surrounding William's death.

Absently, she followed Nick to the rubber feeder and dropped the heavy salt block, missing his booted foot by mere inches. Nick stared at her as if she had done that on purpose. Maybe she had and maybe she hadn't. Her carefully blank expression assured Nick that he would never know for sure. Wisely, he continued with the previous topic of conversation and ignored the near miss she'd scored with the heavy block of salt.

"You fed me supper a few nights ago," he belatedly responded to Amanda's question. "I am merely reciprocating. But if you don't want to drive to the City with me for seafood, that's fine. I just thought I'd be polite and ask."

"I thought cattlemen promoted their industry by eating nothing but beef," Amanda replied.

Nick shook out the contents of the sack, ensuring that every last granule of mineral found its way to the feeder. "I do enthusiastically support the beef industry. I just happen to have a soft spot for crabs' legs and lobster."

78

He was tempting her. The mere mention of seafood caused Amanda to salivate. "I love legs and tails."

The smallest evidence of a smile curved Nick's lips. His dark eyes measured the lower half of Amanda's torso, but he made no reference to her remark. He didn't have to. Amanda knew what he was thinking. The worst part of it was, she had unconsciously invited his speculative glance by the wording of her remark. Or had her subconscious deliberately baited Nick? Amanda Hazard inviting a man's sexual speculations, absurd!

"I'll pick you up at six o'clock."

"I suppose I won't be permitted to mention the Farley case." Amanda turned toward the truck.

"Mention it if you wish," he generously offered. "Just don't expect me to participate in any conversation that deals with the possibility of murder."

"You're going to feel immensely foolish when I dig up evidence to support my theory."

"I won't hold my breath waiting for that to happen, Hazard."

"I wish you would," Amanda grumbled spitefully.

When Nick stopped to check the water level of the stock tank, Amanda stared at the floating de-icer that looked exactly like the one she had seen in Farley's tank. Even though the water temperature was below freezing, the tank was devoid of ice. But it was not so much the familiarity of the de-icer that drew Amanda's pensive gaze as flashbacks to unpleasant memories.

"These contraptions have saved farmers a great deal of time," Nick stated, misreading the attention Amanda was paying to the heater. "When I was a kid, one of my after-school chores was to chop ice at the pond so the cattle wouldn't walk out for a drink and fall through. I haven't lost a single head of cattle since I started using a tank de-icer. Preston Banks lost eight head last winter when he neglected to chop the ice on his pond before his cattle got so thirsty they walked out on the frozen pond."

Amanda frowned, recalling her conversation with Preston, Glenn and Frank. One of the men — she couldn't remember which one — had ridiculed William for being too stingy with money to water his cattle from a tank. The oversight had cost Robert Farley his life. But Preston had not bothered to mention that he had lost part of his own herd in the pond. Why?

"A rancher can't insure against this kind of loss," Nick was saying when Amanda began to listen again. "Neither can he afford to lose eight steers that would have brought over six hundred dollars apiece at the stockyard. Nobody wants to buy frozen beef on the hoof these days."

"My, you are a wealth of information, Thorn. If I do decide to invest in livestock, I will be sure to consult you before I purchase a herd and lease pasture."

For the life of him, Nick could not picture this classy female garbed in faded flannel and denim, caring for livestock. It was ridiculous. She might break one of her polished fingernails.

"You'd better stick to accounting, Hazard," he advised.

"And maybe you should consider full-time farming and ranching, Thorn," she suggested flippantly. "I'm not sure you're qualified for police work — at least not the investigative end of it."

"Give me a break," Nick grumbled. "This is my day off."

"Crime never takes a holiday, even when you turn

your back and pretend it hasn't happened." When Nick's fingers curled like a choke necklace that was two sizes smaller than her throat, Amanda smiled impishly. "Still want to take me to supper?"

"Certainly," he said through clenched teeth. "I want to get my hell over with on earth so I can book a straight flight to the pearly gates when my time comes." He paused for effect. "You're my hell, Hazard."

"You aren't exactly my idea of heaven, Thorn," she flung back at him.

Amanda stole one last glance at the stock tank before she climbed into the truck. Try as she would, she could not erase the image of William Farley doubled over his stock tank, arms outstretched, staring sightlessly at his sunken wallet. Had William truly been struck down by heart failure? Amanda still didn't think so, but she was having one devil of a time proving it . . . and an even harder time convincing Nick Thorn to open an investigation.

Seven

A startled yelp erupted from Amanda's lips while she was rummaging through the dresser drawer in search of pantyhose. Out of the corner of her eye, she saw a gray shadow dart across the floor and disappear under her bed. Mouse! No, she corrected, *Mice!*

Mother always contended that if you saw one mouse there was an entire nest of them casing the place. The repulsive thought caused a shudder to snake down Amanda's spine. She would insist that Nick stop by the supermarket on their way home from dinner to purchase traps. She certainly was *not* sharing her residence with those filthy, beady-eyed little devils.

Dressing hurriedly, Amanda escaped the infested room and headed for her file cabinet to make one last search for the checks that had vanished from the Farley financial account. Along with the vanishing calf and the dislodged wallet, the three missing checks increased her suspicion.

Amanda had called the travel agency to check the dates of Bill Farley's departure and arrival. Just as she suspected, there was a discrepancy between his return to the ranch and his scheduled flight from Denver. Lo and behold, Bill had arrived at the

Oklahoma City airport two days before he'd showed his face in Vamoose. That was ample time for him to drive home, dispose of his father and hide out in the City. Of course, Bill may have had to stand in line to murder his father, Amanda reminded herself. William was not popular in Vamoose.

Using her professional position to secure answers, Amanda had posed questions at the local bank. Both Glenn Chambliss and Preston Banks were heavily in debt. Their loans had been called in. The assessor was scheduled to make his rounds the following week. William could have threatened to blow the whistle on either of his neighbors, and Chambliss or Banks could have retaliated. They might even have been in a conspiracy against William.

Desperation and fear of legal prosecution were possible motives. Men were known to employ drastic measures when backed into a corner, at least those who simply could not cope with the prospect of having their names and reputations besmirched. Fear of ridicule and humiliation drove some folks to extremes.

And yet, while Amanda was pointing an accusing finger, she could not rule out Janene Farley. She and William had reportedly got along as well as a cobra and mongoose. Janene could have disposed of her father-in-law while Bill was out of town. And come to think of it, who was to say that William had actually collapsed at the stock tank? For all Amanda knew, his body could have been planted at that location. Janene and her brother the veterinarian could have bumped William off. Luke had access to medication, and he would know how to administer drugs that might slip past an unsuspecting medical examiner who scoffed at foul play, especially after Amanda's talk of bullet holes and knife wounds. She might have unintentionally led one more person to discredit her suspicions rather than substantiate them.

A number of people might have wanted to kill William. Amanda would have to make out a list of suspects and methodically narrow it down. She would also have to determine how the deed was done.

And while Amanda was jotting down suspects, she could not overlook Velma Hertzog. The large woman could probably hold her own against any man. Velma had been involved with William, and was the only one who knew to what extent. Millicent seemed to think more had been going on than Velma wanted to admit. Jilted lovers have committed their share of crimes.

Don't be ridiculous, Amanda scolded herself. Velma could not have been responsible . . . could she? And yet . . .

The rap at the door jolted Amanda from her pensive contemplations. She reached into the closet for her coat, recoiled and screamed her head off. There, scrunched in the corner, was a rat. Not a tiny little mouse but a huge, hairy, revolting rat!

Nick came through the front door like a speeding bullet. "What the hell's wrong?"

Amanda stabbed a shaky finger toward the closet and the offending creature inside it. Nick peered into the dark cubicle to see the same set of beady eyes. He wheeled toward the kitchen to locate a broom, and like a warrior charging into battle, he attacked, emerging victorious from the closet.

Shuddering in revulsion, Amanda watched Nick carry his enemy out the door on the broom. When he returned, she didn't ask where or how he had disposed of the rodent. She didn't care, as long as it was gone.

"I don't recall being overrun with pests last year," Amanda reflected.

"That's because you didn't move in here until spring," Nick explained. "When the dead of winter strikes, rodents seek the warmth of houses. They must have gotten under the flooring and gnawed their way inside. In the past Preston Banks lined wheat-hay bales along the pasture fence north of your house. He had to use so many bales because of the bad winter, his stack is nearly depleted. The rats make their nests in it, and feed on the wheat seeds. With their shelter and food source gone, they probably migrated to your house."

"Thank you, Preston Banks," Amanda muttered.

She could imagine hundreds of rats abandoning their location in the hay bales to infiltrate her home. The incident had ruined her appetite. She hoped she'd regain it by the time they reached the restaurant.

"I thought you liked seafood." Nick sat across the table in the exclusive restaurant, watching Amanda push grilled shrimp from one side of her plate to the other. She hadn't even touched the crabs' legs and he could attest to the fact that they were delicious. "I didn't think you were all that squeamish, Hazard. You disappoint me."

To save face, Amanda nibbled on her shrimp. "I hate mice and rats. They're filthy creatures. I feel the urge to return home and clean my house from top to bottom to remove all traces of them."

"You could move in with me for a while," Nick suggested with a wry smile.

That snapped Amanda out of her sulky mood in

a hurry. She attacked the crabs' legs with a vengeance. "I don't think that would be a good idea, Thorn."

"Don't you trust yourself alone with me?" He waggled his eyebrows.

Amanda noted that Nick had not questioned whether or not she trusted *him,* but rather *herself.* The comment implied he thought she found him irresistible. She did find him too appealing for her own good, but she would have sewed her mouth shut before she'd confess that. The only investigation Amanda planned to conduct was the one concerning William Farley's death, not one of Nick Thorn's magnificent body.

"Eat your lobster and clam up." Amanda sent him a disgruntled glance. "You probably consider yourself God's gift to womankind, but I do possess a tremendous amount of self-restraint. If I did accept your offer, though I most certainly would not, I could keep our relationship on a purely intellectual plane. Continued close proximity would make no difference," she said with absolute confidence.

Nick shrugged a broad shoulder, neither challenging her declaration nor accepting it as gospel. "I have a few kittens in the barn that are past weaning age. You are welcome to them. They would made good mousers."

"How are they with gigantic rats?" Amanda wanted to know.

"If they tag-team wrestle the rodents to the floor, they might be able to bring down pests the size of the ones that have taken up residence with you."

"I think I'll stick with traps and poison," Amanda mumbled, desperate to change the subject. This particular one promoted indigestion. "I spoke with Janene and Bill today."

"So you told me." Interruption didn't slow Amanda down for a second. Nick hadn't thought it would. She had a mind like a steel trap.

"When I opened my briefcase, the three checks William had written out to cash were nowhere to be found. I'd set them apart because they'd aroused my curiosity."

Nick rolled his eyes and slouched back in his chair. "I was hoping we could enjoy dinner without dwelling on your obsession with murder. Another dashed hope." He sighed theatrically.

Amanda knew she might as well talk to a wall. It would be as receptive as Nick Thorn when he was in one of his stubborn moods. "All right then, we'll talk about something else. Tell me about yourself, Thorn."

"I am not an interesting topic," he said modestly. "I police the streets of Vamoose and farm and ranch in my spare time, as you already know. I grew up with a fond appreciation for the rural way of life, and I have never been married."

"Why?"

A mischievous smile pursed his lips. "Why do I appreciate rural life?"

Amanda shot him a withering glance. "No, why haven't you ever married?"

"The time never was right. Working as a detective with the OKC P.D. consumed too many hours a day, leaving little time for recreation. By the time I switched jobs and took over my father's farming operation, all the prospective brides had been snatched up. Now I am too set in my ways to change my habits. What about you, Hazard? Have you been married?"

"Long enough to know what a mistake it was." Amanda took a sip of wine to lubricate her vocal chords and continued. "I also discovered that I was not a good judge of men. My ex-husband was none of the things I'd thought he was. I suppose I was guilty of seeing only what I wanted to see in him. Opposites seem to attract for a time, but Jason eventually found someone more like him. I was the last one to know he had been out looking. I guess I was too methodical and practical for his tastes. He preferred a reckless and impulsive woman to a sensible and dependable one."

Amanda smiled with wicked glee. "Jason filed for bankruptcy a few months ago. He never was good with budgets. Money burned holes in his pockets. Though it's a small consolation and spiteful for me to say so, he had it coming."

"So you swore off men after you got hurt. Better to have backed off than thrown yourself into an endless string of meaningless affairs just to have some sort of twisted revenge on him."

"How do you know I didn't?" One perfectly arched brow lifted to challenge Nick's belief that he had her all figured out.

Nick grinned. "Because, as you said, you are too sensible—"

"Except when it comes to preoccupation with a murder you swear up and down has not been committed," she shrewdly tacked on.

"Drop it, Hazard." Shifting in his seat, Nick flagged down the waiter and requested the check. When Amanda fished into her purse for her billfold, Nick stared at her disbelievingly. "I offered to take you out to dinner—"

"Which you did. I accepted. I did not, however, agree to let you pay for my meal," she clarified. "The sandwich and drink I served to you only cost a few dollars to prepare. This meal cost a good deal more."

"I still intend to pay." Nick snatched up her fifty-dollar bill and shoved it back into her purse. "Call me old fashioned if you want, but I still believe a man should pick up the tab when he invites a woman out."

"But *I* am not old fashioned, and *I* do not believe a woman should feel a man is due any sort of compensation when he insists on paying the bill in full," Amanda declared.

He didn't assist her out of her chair; he hoisted her up beside him, and none too gently. "Did I ask for compensation, Hazard?" Dark eyes drilled into crystal blue.

"Are you planning to, later?"

"I was the one who initially turned you down, remember?"

"That was a rhetorical question and you know it, Thorn. I did not say I was going to ask you to go to bed with me, only that such a suggestion would probably be the only way to ensure a meager amount of cooperation."

Nick paid the check and escorted Amanda toward his pickup before he rounded on her, still wondering how this female had acquired the knack of getting under his skin when he had vowed not to let her.

"Let's get one thing straight, Hazard. Yes, I find you physically desirable. And yes, I have had one or two fantasies about the two of us in the sack together. But I do not consider buying your dinner foreplay. If there comes a time when I decide I want to kiss you, and I am not saying the time will *ever* come, then I will give you the option of accepting or rejecting. Who knows, neither of us might find the experience pleasant. But at least we will finally know one way or the other, won't we?"

"If it is a question you think will eventually have to be answered, why don't we just get it over with instead of dragging it out," Amanda suggested as she settled herself in her seat.

Nick slid beneath the wheel and laid his arm over the back of the seat. "Fine, Hazard. I'm game. Since you're a liberated woman, will you be offended if I initiate this experimental kiss?"

Amanda found herself in one of her contrary moods. She, of course, blamed Nick for it. "The parking lot of a restaurant doesn't seem the right place. I'm not a lovesick teenager, after all. The thought of gathering mouse traps to alleviate my pest problem seems more important than satisfying my curiosity about a kiss that will probably turn out to be disappointing anyway."

There, let him cope with that insult. That should put a dent in his stupendous ego and bring him down a notch.

Serenaded by country music on the radio, Nick aimed the pickup toward the nearest supermarket to let Amanda buy her mouse traps and rat poison.

This was the strangest date he had ever had. Talk of mice and murder was not his idea of a good time. But at least Amanda Hazard was unpretentious. She was what she was. She would always be consistent in her beliefs and behavior. She was firm in her conviction regarding equality of the sexes, and she did not hesitate to speak her mind. There were times when Nick did not consider Amanda's predominant qualities assets.

He reminded himself that he possessed many of the same characteristics, so who was he to complain? Even so, he was frustrated. Not because this gorgeous blond could irritate the hell out of him, but because he was attracted to her when he didn't

90

want to be. Even when she annoyed him. Now *that* really rankled.

Accompanying her into the store, Nick found his irritation changing to amusement while he stood back to observe Amanda gather up her arsenal of weapons against the rodent invasion. She compared prices against the quality and quantity of her purchases. The accountant in her had already tallied the total expense before she'd reached the register. She, of course, handed over the correct change.

That thought caused Nick to frown as he followed her out into the icy wind. If Amanda was so efficient, how could she have misplaced William Farley's canceled checks? What if she actually was onto something and someone *was* removing evidence?

No, he reassured himself. He had simply allowed Amanda's suspicions to cast shadows of doubt where none should have been. If he didn't get a grip on himself, he would be treating mere coincidence as evidence, as Amanda was.

For his own good, Nick decided he should dump Amanda on her doorstep and go home. If he spent too much more time with her he might begin to think like her. He made up his mind, right on the spot, that this would be his first and last date with Amanda Hazard. There would be no goodnight kiss, no nightcap of coffee that contained enough cream and sugar to pass as hot chocolate. Nothing.

"Thank you for dinner." Amanda reached for the door latch once the truck rolled to a stop in her driveway.

She realized she was clutching her grocery sack to her bosom like a shield and took time to ask herself

91

why. *Come on, Hazard, admit it. You're afraid you've gotten attached to this guy. He's right. You aren't sure you
trust yourself with him.*

Nick's dark brows elevated, as he watched emotions cloud Amanda's exquisite features. "Something
wrong, Hazard?"

"No." The reply was too hasty, too insistent.
Amanda backed down. "Yes."

"Well, which is it?"

Amanda set her grocery sack aside and leaned
over to plant a kiss on Nick's lips. The appealing
scent of his cologne closed around her like a mouse-
trap. She had to force herself back into her own
space. She also had to force herself to stay in it
while she stifled the warm tingles of pleasure that
radiated through her.

"Now we know, don't we, Thorn? The ice has
been broken. One of life's great mysteries has been
solved."

She sounded in perfect control, didn't she? She
was in control. It had been a chaste kiss, the mere
meeting of two sets of lips. The earth hadn't moved.
Fireworks hadn't exploded in the heavens. No big
deal. Right?

Sure, Hazard, whatever you say, her conscience
snickered. I still think you're lying.

"I must be slower in coming to conclusions than
you are." Nick's arm glided around her shoulders,
pulling her against his chest, though he had vowed
to do no such thing. "I need a little more time to
decide what I like and what I don't. Mind if we try
that again?"

His mouth slanted over hers in an amazingly tender kiss. Amanda had not been prepared for the
world to shift a little bit sideways the moment their
lips met a second time. Neither had she expected to

92

see firecrackers exploding like the Fourth of July in her mind's eye.

This, of course, was a pure case of body chemistry, of reacting to an outside stimulant. Elemental compounds were simply changing forms, causing internal combustion which emitted heat. The tingles she experienced were nothing more than a natural response to biological changes. They didn't mean a thing.

Oh sure, Hazard. Now you think you're not only a private detective but also a clinical biologist. The next thing we know, you'll have yourself convinced that you're a nuclear physicist and you'll be delivering a dissertation on atomic reactors, fission and fusion.

Amanda knew she should have untangled herself from Nick's arms immediately, because her answering kiss displayed anything but the indifference she had tried to project moments earlier. A mental tug of war raged within her. She liked kissing Nick Thorn a helluva lot more than she was prepared to admit. She enjoyed feeling his masculine body pressed to hers. It had nothing to do with biological and chemical experimentation. There was cause and effect all right, but this was definitely sexual.

Snuggling up to Nick was like nestling beside a cozy hearth, aware that the leaping flames could scorch her inside and out if she came too close. It would have been easy to succumb to the passionate undercurrents that channeled through her. It had been a long time since she had been with a man, more years than she cared to count.

Walking alone into a house that had been overrun with rodents held no appeal whatsoever. Here she was warm and satisfied. But inside the cab of a pickup with an all-too attractive man like Nick, she

93

was also in clear and present danger. And she was making a fool of herself.

Nick could sense her womanly responses, and he could also detect a hint of hesitancy in the way she held herself in his arms. He knew that feeling well. Casual affairs weren't his forte, either. But on cold winter nights there was something very appealing about cuddling up with a warm shapely body. And there was no doubt about it, their bodies had been communicating in a language all their own for the past several minutes. Nick was positive his body would have a lot more to say if he let it. He was not going to.

Calling upon conscious restraint, he withdrew to stare at the porch which was illuminated by the headlights. "Do you want me to walk you to the door?"

Amanda drew in a deep cleansing breath, dismayed that the heady scent was still clogging her senses. Walk her to the door? Would that be as far as he got? She hadn't planned on kissing the man. Now look what had happened to that resolution. It had been shot to hell. But then, Amanda didn't relish balancing a grocery sack in one arm and negotiating the glaze of ice on the steps to the door. Why shouldn't she take advantage of his chivalry?

"I would appreciate that, Thorn." She scooped up her sack and retrieved her keys.

Cautiously, she navigated the path to the steps. Pantyhose and heels were inappropriate attire for tramping along icy ground. Now that she had relocated to this rural area, she really should consider changing her clothing style. Nick didn't seem to have that much difficulty enduring the bad weather in his western slacks and boots. For a woman who prided herself on being practical, she had forgotten to practice what she preached. First chance she got, she was going shopping for sensible country wear.

"Let me have the sack."

Amanda dumped the traps in his arms and stabbed the key into the lock. The door gave way without a twist of her wrist. "I swear I locked this before we left."

"In this damp weather, the door might have stuck before the bolt slid home," Nick speculated.

If Amanda had been alone, she might have been more suspicious. But she felt well protected. There were certain advantages to associating with a cop, not the least of which was his training in self-defense. Even if Nick wasn't packing his pistol, he had dealt with danger often enough to cope with unexpected adversity.

The instant Amanda switched on the light a gray shadow zipped across the carpet toward the sofa. Ripping plastic bags apart on her way to the kitchen, she quickly baited the traps. She knew she wouldn't get a minute of sleep. Mouse traps would be banging all night.

Nick, Amanda noted, was being a good sport about their unconventional date. He positioned traps around the baseboards of the living room and kitchen before carrying an armload down the hall.

"Would you like a cup of coffee? We might as well have refreshments while we wait for the evening's entertainment."

"Bloodthirsty little thing, aren't you?" Nick razzed. "I think you derive wicked pleasure from killing pests. If they all turn out to be males, that would really make your night."

Amanda plugged in the coffeemaker and reached for two cups, checking closely to ensure the mice hadn't left tracks on the shelves. Disgusting thought!

"I believe in living and letting live," she philosophized. "Until repulsive rodents invade my territory. Then it's all-out war."

While the coffee perked, Nick and Amanda waited expectantly for the traps to snap. Sure enough, the two in her bedroom sprung. That was the last place she had expected to find the filthy varmints.

"Are you sure you don't want to spend the night at my place?" Nick heard himself ask a second time. Then he wondered why the thought disturbed him. He hadn't planned on kissing Amanda or on following her into the house. Several of his good intentions had already gone awry. What difference would one more make?

The offer was all too tempting, but Amanda was determined to set a precedent. She had to prove to Nick, just as she had proved to every other man, that she could function alone, even if she had to battle a horde of rodents.

"No, I'll stay here and man the artillery."

"Have it your way. I'm sure you usually do, Hazard." Nick pushed away from the counter and ambled toward the living room to fetch his coat. "I'll take a rain check on the coffee. I'd better go home to see if varmints have invaded *my* house. You might not be the only one with uninvited guests."

"Nick?"

He pivoted as he stabbed his arm into his coat sleeve. "Yeah?"

"I had a good time. Thanks."

"Yeah, right."

His tone of voice suggested he wasn't convinced of her sincerity.

"I really did."

Sure, that's why she'd refused his offer to abandon her mice-infested house for a peaceful night's sleep. Well, it was for the best, Nick thought as he braced himself for a blast of wintery air. If she had come home with him, they might have wound up in bed together. Not that he really objected to the idea. He was all for it, but it killed him to have to admit it.

For damned sure, the coffee wasn't the only thing percolating while he'd been standing beside Amanda in the kitchen. Be that as it may, it was too soon for anything remotely intimate between them. Her divorce had made her extremely leery, and she was probably even more suspicious of a man who had never been married. Hell, with that inquisitive mind of hers, she'd probably leaped to the conclusion that there was something wrong with him if no woman had wanted him.

Go home and get to bed before you analyze everything to death, Thorn. You are beginning to sound just like Hazard.

Nick took his own advice and did exactly that.

Eight

Amanda awakened bleary-eyed, having gotten only a few hours of sleep. Just as she had predicted, mouse traps snapped like corn popping all through the night. She had spent the midnight hours searching every nook and cranny, hoping to discover where the varmints had infiltrated her home, but had turned up nothing for her efforts. There were no holes gnawed in the Sheetrock at the backs of closets or under the cabinets. Obviously she had looked everywhere except the right spot. It could take her days to find the rodents' entrance. In the meantime, she would drive herself crazy searching for evidence of her uninvited guests.

Irritable from lack of sleep, Amanda stomped outside to keep her appointment at Velma's Beauty Boutique. This was the day she had designated to turn her face, as well as her hair, over to Velma for a makeover . . . all to investigate the murder Nick Thorn swore hadn't happened.

Tired though she was, Amanda congratulated herself for keeping the appointment. The moment she stepped into the shop, she knew it was worth the effort. The salon was buzzing like a hornet's nest. Two women were under the dryers. Looking pale and withdrawn, Rose Chambliss sat in one corner, quietly thumbing through a magazine. Amanda wondered if she was missing William Farley who was rumored to have paid her a number of intimate calls over the years.

Two high-school girls stood by the door, whispering and giggling, while Bobby Sherman was having his shaggy mane clipped. Velma also claimed to specialize in men's cuts and styling. She could make anybody's head look like a beehive, even the star of Vamoose's basketball team.

"So, how is the team doing, Bobby?" Amanda questioned, taking a seat.

"Ten and two." Bobby sat like a marble statue for fear Velma would snip off an ear. "We're playing our biggest rivals tomorrow night."

Another opportunity to pick up tidbits of gossip in the small community, Amanda speculated. If she wasn't doing anything, like fighting the cat-sized rats that had invaded her home, she might take in the game and mingle with the crowd.

"I'll do your makeup while Ginny and Marge are drying," Velma said between smacks of her gum. She gave Bobby's fluffy hairstyle one last critical glance and snipped off an errant strand of hair, barely missing his ear. "We'll do your hair later, Amanda."

After the six-foot-six-inch Bobby took himself, his size fourteen shoes and his two starry-eyed girlfriends out the door, Amanda planted herself in the chair, prepared for the worst.

"Have you heard the latest?" Velma popped her gum and extended a long arm to drag bottles, tubes and plastic cases of makeup beside her on the counter. "Word is Janene Farley is filing for divorce, soon as William's estate is settled. That woman will take Bill to the cleaners, mark my words."

No wonder Amanda had sensed hostility between

the married couple during their consultation. She had been standing on a private battlefield.

Velma leaned close so she wouldn't be overheard by Rose who was still in the corner, waiting her turn. Rose's face was concealed behind a magazine, and she appeared to be paying little attention to the world around her.

"First National is foreclosing on Glenn and Rose Chambliss." Smack, crack. "Just got word this morning. The bank plans to gather all his collateral and sell him out as soon as this stretch of bad weather clears up."

Amanda stared pensively at Rose. Was it the loss of her lover or the incipient bankruptcy that drained the color from her attractive face? Perhaps it was a combination of both. And then again, it might be much more than that . . .

"I heard Janene Farley packed up and moved in with her brother this morning," Ginny reported, poking her head out from under the dryer. "Millicent saw her hauling suitcases from the house to Luke's apartment behind the vet clinic."

"I met Bill on the highway—headed to the City—when I came home from work last night," Marge added her two cent's worth. "His daddy should rest easier now. William never did cotton to Janene and her extravagant tastes."

Rose Chambliss simply sat behind her magazine, keeping her mouth shut.

"I wonder if Bill plans to keep Luke Princeton on the payroll. If it had been William, he would probably have sent Luke packing, just so Janene wouldn't have a place to stay. William was a spiteful old rascal." Ginny tested the dryness of her hair and resituated herself under the dryer. "But Bill probably needs Luke's expertise on the ranch. Somebody has

100

to take care of all those herds of cattle that are scattered all over creation."

Amanda noticed Velma hadn't defended William or sided with Ginny and Marge. She'd merely loomed over Amanda, applying a layer of moisturizing base as if it were a thick coat of paint. One layer of base became a foundation for another. The makeup was so thick Amanda swore it would crack if she changed expression.

Velma's silence, with the exception of the steady snapping and popping of gum, drew Amanda's curiosity. It was out of character for the woman to leash her tongue.

Rose Chambliss set her magazine aside and moved mechanically toward the door. "I have a few errands to run, Velma. Since you're so busy, I'll stop by later for a shampoo and set."

Amanda had the feeling gossip would fly the minute Rose made her exit. She was right, of course.

"I heard Preston Banks is really sweating it out now that First National called in Glenn's loan," Ginny declared.

"Rose will have to give up everything, even her home. Glenn borrowed in order to buy everything he ever bought. I bet Rose is feeling as if her whole world is crumbling around her." Marge peeled rollers from her salt-and-pepper hair and continued. "Preston's head will be the next one on the chopping block. It seems the whole community is falling apart since William died. Coincidence, I guess."

Amanda wasn't so sure coincidence had anything to do with it. More than likely, it was the domino effect. No one claimed to have had much affection for William Farley, but he and his money were the glue that held Vamoose together. Amanda could attest to the fact that she had experienced nothing but bad luck since William had passed on. It was as if plagues were descending on Vamoose — bad weather, foreclosures, pests, to name only a few.

"Now close your eyes so I can apply the eyeliner and mascara," Velma requested, jostling Amanda from her silent reverie.

Within minutes, Velma had Amanda's eyes so thickly caked her lashes stuck together when she blinked. Amanda thought she looked as though she were about to prance onstage under glaring spotlights for a theatrical performance. Of course, the other patrons raved about how glamorous Amanda looked. She thought the women were being polite. Mirrors didn't lie. This was a face only Frankenstein could love.

While the other two customers had their hair combed and plastered in place with hair spray, Amanda sat in the corner, awaiting the final phase of her "beautification."

She had a compelling urge to visit Luke Princeton's clinic to determine how well Janene was bracing up to her pending divorce. The woman may have discovered something sinister about her husband, like maybe why Bill hadn't shown up until two days after the cattle convention adjourned in Denver. Maybe Janene feared for her life and had sought the protection of her brother. Bill was last seen heading for the City. He could be planning to double back to dispose of his wife, just as he might have disposed of his father.

After the last two patrons exited from the shop, Velma crooked a pudgy finger, summoning Amanda back to the chair. "Let's try something flamboyant and elegant to match your face." Snap, crackle, pop.

Amanda cringed at the thought of Velma's version of elegance. In a flurry of curling irons, blow dryers, brushes and hair spray, Velma set about creating her masterpiece. Suddenly, she was back to her customary chatter, broken only by the chomp and crack of her gum.

"I didn't want to say much while Ginny was here. She is the worst gossip north of the Texas border."

Amanda decided Velma would know a notorious gossip when she saw one, the beautician being an accomplished pruner and nurturer of the grapevine.

"Ginny can take the truth, twist it and distort it until no one can recognize it. If I'd defended William, she would have made something of it, you can bank on it." Crack, pop. "And I doubt Preston Banks is sweating blood just yet. When he's short of cash, he always manages to come up with funds to save his farms. The original homestead has been passed down through generations, just like William's has been. Preston would never sell off more than just a few acres of his property. No matter what he had to do, he'd find a way to save it. His family's name and its traditions are everything to him."

No matter what . . . ? H'mmm . . . It made one wonder to what extremes a man might go to protect a family name that had been around since the virgin prairies of Oklahoma had been opened by land runs in the 1890s.

"I guess you know Preston is your landlady's son-in-law," Velma continued. "He's been renting farm ground from his mother-in-law for years without paying her."

So that was why Preston had hay stacked along the fences around her house, Amanda reasoned. The land belonged to his wife's side of the family.

"How can Emma Carter survive if Preston isn't paying his due?" she questioned.

"Emma has always lived by modest means. She has her social security and rents out other farmland." Pop, crack, smack. "And of course, she has the rent you pay her."

Velma stepped back and held up her thumb like an artist measuring the symmetry of the mountain she was about to commit to canvas. "I went to school with Preston. He can be a sneaky rascal when he wants to be. I don't expect First National will be able to close him down. He's as slippery as an eel."

Twenty minutes later, Amanda emerged from the shop with a new face and another towering hairstyle that a raging gale couldn't touch. Wisps of blond hair angled at forty-five degrees from her face, falling into spiral curls that would have done Shirley Temple proud. Before Amanda could conceal the hairstyle under a scarf, the patrol car veered toward her and came to an abrupt halt.

Nick rolled down the window, looked Amanda up and down and shook his head. "You certainly spend a lot of time at the boutique, Hazard. Looking for the new you? Or is this your disguise for undercover investigation?"

The taunting remarks earned Nick a sharp glance and a cold shoulder as frigid as the wind.

"Maybe you should step inside Velma's salon," Amanda suggested, her nose in the air. "You ought to have her trim your tongue."

Having flung him that particularly frosty rejoinder, Amanda flounced toward her run-down truck and drove off with a cloud from the exhaust pipe billowing behind her. Nick Thorn-in-the-side seemed to get his kicks from harassing her.

Wasn't it enough that Amanda had thought about the annoying man more than she had planned to over the past few days? Must he badger her constantly? He was probably being spiteful because she hadn't fallen at his feet. Well, Amanda had learned to tell herself no.

A *disguise for undercover investigation* . . . Amanda huffed irritably at remembering Nick's snide remark. Well, maybe she did resemble Frankenstein's bride, but Nick didn't have to razz her about it.

The truck's bald tires skidded around the corner on the icy street, and it was all she could do to prevent sideswiping the parked car in her path. She didn't have time to give Nick another thought.

Inhaling a steadying breath, Amanda negotiated the slick patches on the pavement and aimed herself toward Luke Princeton's clinic. She wanted to see for herself what condition Janene was in. She would find some logical excuse for the visit by the time she arrived. Now that she had begun her private investigation, she had gotten good at dreaming up excuses.

Amanda found Luke Princeton dressed in tight-fitting jeans and a Western shirt that accentuated the broad expanse of his back. He was built like a rodeo steer wrestler, with shoulders like a bull and distinctly muscled thighs. His cream-colored Stetson sat low on his forehead, shadowing his face. With profound concentration, Luke was studying the electrical circuit box on the back wall of the clinic.

When he pivoted toward her, Amanda produced a cordial smile. "I'm Amanda Hazard." She marched forward and extended her hand. "We have never been formally introduced but I'm the Farley family's accountant."

Luke graced her with a winsome smile that cut dimples in his cheeks. Without hesitation, he accepted her proffered hand. "Luke Princeton. What can I do for you, Amanda?"

Tell me everything I want to know about the relationship between your sister, her husband and his father. Your sister has probably cried often enough on your shoulder for you to know the ins and out of the crumbling marriage.

She said aloud, "I was wondering if I could speak to Janene for a few minutes about the family's finances."

Luke smiled apologetically. "I'm sorry. Sis isn't here right now. She had a meeting and an appointment in the City this afternoon. I don't know when she'll be back. Can I give her a message for you?"

A wasted trip. "No, I'll be in touch with Janene later." Amanda glanced around the spotless facilities. She and Luke had a great deal in common. He was methodical and organized, just as she was. Shiny steel cabinets lined the walls of the clinic, and all the supplies were neatly tucked in their places. The tiled floor had recently been waxed. The animal clinic was as clean and as sterile as a hospital.

Amanda cast Luke a discreet glance, appraising him in a less professional and more feminine way. He was about thirty and extremely attractive, with sandy blond hair and pale blue eyes. Lean and powerful, he would have no trouble turning women's heads. Having his sister underfoot in his apartment had undoubtedly cramped his style, though. Bringing home a date for the evening would hold no appeal for him these days, Amanda imagined. His apartment was probably full of Janene's paraphernalia. The vanity in his bathroom would be over-flowing with cosmetics, and no doubt, Luke would have difficulty entertaining a lady friend with his sister as a chaperone.

"I heard you were the one who found William in the pasture," Luke commented, laying his tools aside. "I'm sorry. I imagine that was a most unset-tling experience."

"Extremely unsettling," Amanda said, staring curi-ously at the tools.

Luke chuckled when he followed her gaze. "Janene overloaded the electrical circuit while she was getting ready to leave for her meeting. She had too many appliances plugged in at the same time. William cut one too many corners when he had the clinic wired for electricity. The circuit box can't handle the kind of power surges my sister is famous for."

"Your knowledge of electricity must be as impres-sive as your training in animal husbandry."

Luke chuckled again. It was a pleasant purring sound that appealed to the feminine ear.

"You are giving me way too much credit, Amanda. I am barely adequate when it comes to electrical repair, but I do know enough to switch off the power before I start tampering with wires. I only hope I can keep from burning the place down, all in the name of repair."

Before Amanda could think of a tactful way to pose the questions that danced on the tip of her tongue, one of the local matrons waddled inside, carrying a poodle wearing a pink sweater. Amanda had wanted to interrogate Luke about Janene and Bill's falling out, but she was not to get the chance.

"Excuse me." Luke politely tipped his hat and

eased past her, only to have the frizzy-haired canine dumped in his arms.

"I'm worried sick about Fifi. She hasn't been acting like herself since this cold spell. She refuses to eat and . . ."

While the concerned owner recited the dog's symptoms to Luke, Amanda buttoned her coat and left the clinic.

It was apparent that, while Luke was employed as Farley Farm's resident veterinarian, he had been sought out by the locals to doctor the ailments of every animal and pet in the area. Of course, Luke always gave the Farley cattle first consideration, but he spared time for all creatures great and small. That was enough to endear him to little old ladies like the one who was just paying him a call.

Having accomplished nothing, Amanda returned home to wage the war on the pestilent mice. Once those fallen in battle had been carted off, she reset the traps and glanced over the journals of the client she was to meet the following morning at the offices of Nelson, Blake and Cosmos. After preparing her evening meal, she took to the shower to scrape off layers of makeup and to shampoo the hair spray away.

Although she had made another appointment with Velma, she wondered if the information she gleaned at the beauty shop was worth the expense. She recited a few consoling platitudes, reassuring herself that William would appreciate her efforts to learn the truth. Someone had to do it. The local police had discarded the case; Thorn was going to feel like an ass when she discovered evidence that pointed to foul play. Amanda only hoped she could solve the mystery before another body turned up. She anticipated a convenient accident or another death that would be chalked up to natural causes.

If her suspicions were correct, Janene might well be next in line. Or Luke might be caught in the crossfire and find himself managing that Great Dog Pound in the Sky. Amanda sincerely hoped her speculations were incorrect, but she knew instinctively that she was not wrong about William's demise. Either he'd known something he shouldn't have or he'd been using information to pressure the wrong person. William hadn't lived to tell who, how or why.

This, it seemed, was the fate of those who knew too much . . .

Nine

When Amanda entered the Last Chance Cafe the next morning for a cup of coffee, she heard the news that Janene Farley had been banged up in an auto mishap. According to the report, Janene's car had slid off the icy road and crashed into a fence. Luke had used William's four-wheel-drive pickup to tow the car back to the clinic.

Taking the Caddy to Cecil's for repair would have done no good. The man was as slow as a snail. Amanda could attest to that.

Still, news of the "accident" sent demons of doubts tapping at her mind. Amanda wondered if improperly functioning brakes might have caused it. The incident could have been a warning to Janene to keep her mouth shut. Janene's estranged husband might be the one who insisted on her silence.

Amanda's next scheduled stop was Cecil's Auto Repair. She inquired about her Toyota, only to learn her car still wasn't roadworthy. She wasn't surprised. Cecil had as many excuses for his inefficiency as a peach tree had peaches. He now informed Amanda, between chomps of his chewing tobacco, and in choppy sentences, that her Toyota might be ready the middle of the following week.

The mechanic got down on his hands and knees and pointed a greasy finger beneath the car. "See that thingamajig?"

Amanda doubled over, practically standing on her head to survey the object Cecil indicated. "Yes."

"Car won't run without it. Don't have one in stock."

Cecil levered his bulky body upright, grabbed the rag from his back pocket and cleaned off his hands. Why he bothered, Amanda didn't know. The rag was black with grease and his hands looked not one speck better after he'd completed the task.

Careful not to expose more bare leg than was decent, Amanda squatted down by the rear wheel. "How difficult would it be to unhook this brake line?" she questioned.

Cecil's smudged face puckered in a frown. "Why would you wanna do that?"

"I don't," Amanda assured him, studying the underside of the car. "I only wondered if it was much trouble."

"Not much," Cecil replied. Then he poked his head around the open door to spit an arc of tobacco. "If you know what you're doing, takes no time at all."

"Tell me, Cecil, are most of the farmers and ranchers in the area experienced enough to do some of their own automotive and tractor repair?"

"Small jobs," Cecil replied. "Have to. Never get their field work done if they couldn't. Machinery breaks down constantly. Gotta be a jack-of-all-trades to farm and ranch."

Amanda surged to her feet to smooth the wrin-

111

kles from her skirt. "Let me know how you progress with my car," she said before she left, still mulling over Cecil's response to her question about do-it-yourself auto mechanics.

If Cecil considered the task of dismantling the brakes to be quick and simple, then anyone with a little knowledge could sabotage a car—Janene Farley's Caddy, for instance. And, of course, if the car went crashing through the ditch, scraping its underside before smashing into a fence post, it might not look suspicious to have hoses and lines jerked loose. Hazardous road conditions would be blamed for the mishap.

Amanda piled into her pickup and headed for the City to keep her appointment with her client. She had lunch with the senior partner at Nelson, Blake and Cosmos and made copies of all existing files in the Farley account that she had stored at the office. Afterward, she went to the nearest Western clothing store to expand her wardrobe. Then she headed home, to the unpleasant task of disposing of more mice.

A wary frown knitted Amanda's brow when she took time to glance around her living room. Organized as she was, it didn't take her long to realize that several objects were out of place, as if someone had entered the house and rearranged her belongings.

Magazines which were usually stacked on the right side of the end table lay fanned across the coffee table . . . out of alphabetical order. The glass Amanda remembered setting in the sink that morning was on a coaster beside the reading lamp.

Wheeling about, she checked the house, searching for signs of a forced entry. Nothing. When she switched on the radio, it was set on a different station; rock music blared at her.

And that was when Amanda asked herself if these strange happenings were the work of a mysterious visitor who realized *she* knew more than she should have about William Farley's death. It gave her the willies to imagine someone wandering around her home, invading her privacy. But what other explanation could there be? The canceled checks she had intended to show to Bill Farley had turned up missing, and *someone* knew *she* knew it. Doors she'd sworn were locked swung open. Rodents infiltrated her house in droves. And now this . . . a subtle implication that whoever had been tormenting her could get to her anytime he pleased.

The unnerving thought caused Amanda's pulse rate to double. The next thing she knew she would feel compelled to examine open containers for fear her food had been laced with arsenic or some other poisonous substance easily accessible to farmers and ranchers. And she would check her vehicle daily to try to prevent brake failure and God knew what else.

Amanda picked up the phone to call the police. There was so much static on the line she could barely hear the dispatcher. Another sabotage of her personal property!

How could one tell if one's phone had been tapped? Amanda wished she knew so she could check it out immediately. Whoever was doing this wanted to make certain she knew her life was being carefully monitored.

* * *

Nervously wringing her hands, Amanda watched the squad car turn into her driveway. In one fluid motion, Nick Thorn unfolded his muscular frame from the car and ambled up the steps.

"Someone has been in my house," she said, not bothering with a greeting.

"Probably Goldilocks," Nick said with a straight face. "She has a criminal record of unlawful entering and breaking furniture to bits."

The last word sailed off his tongue in a rush because Amanda grabbed hold of his sleeve and jerked him inside. "Damn it, Thorn, what do I have to do to get you to take me seriously?" Her hand shot toward the coffee table, demanding Nick's attention. "That is not where I left my magazines. I keep them stacked over there"—she gestured toward the end table—"in alphabetical order."

"Now why doesn't that surprise me," Nick mused aloud.

"And listen to this!" She shoved the phone receiver at his ear, letting him listen to the crackling dial tone.

Nick's twitching smile evaporated, and he stared down at her with solemn obsidian eyes. "Hazard, you are going off the deep end."

She'd known he would say something like that, but it irritated her no less to hear it.

"Do you remember the night we came back from dinner and the door wasn't locked?"

"A result of cold, damp weather, old settling houses and sticking doors," he said, explaining everything to his satisfaction but certainly not to hers.

"And the missing canceled checks that I have

114

yet to find, the ones I specifically remember clipping to William's file?" Her glare challenged him to explain *that* if he could.

"You obviously misplaced them while you were distressed over finding William's body."

"I happen to be methodical and observant," she protested hotly.

Nick's thick brows elevated to a mocking angle. "If that's so, how do you explain the fact that you were the last one to know your ex-husband was having an affair." He stumped Ms. Know-it-all with that one.

Damn the man. He would have to use that argument against her. "I was trusting and gullible at the time," she muttered. "But no longer."

"True." His lips pursed, assessing the sultry blond. "Now you are suspicious and cynical to the extreme."

Amanda blew up. She had wanted sympathy and assistance, not ridicule. "Damn it, Thorn, someone has been in my house during my absence. These magazines are not where I left them and neither is that glass." She stabbed a forefinger toward the copy of the *Farm Journal* she had borrowed from him. "I left that magazine beside my recliner, not—I repeat *not*—on the coffee table!"

Nick crossed his arms over his chest and stared at Amanda for a long pensive moment. "What are you suggesting, Hazard?"

"I think someone knows I'm skeptical about William Farley's death—"

Nick groaned. "Dear God, here we go again."

"—and is badgering me, to warn me off. I think those mice and rats were deliberately planted—"

He emitted a bark of incredulous laughter. "One third of the residents in Vamoose have pest problems at this time of the year. Do you believe your murderer has been planting rodents all over town?"

Her chin went up, and she stared him down. "I cannot find one hole to indicate they gnawed their way inside my house."

"Maybe they unlocked the door, let themselves in and thumbed through your magazines. Of course, the mice, not being as organized as you, forgot to replace them in alphabetical order."

"Damn it to hell, Thorn! I expect you to take my speculations seriously," Amanda all but shouted at him.

"And damn it to hell, Hazard, I have better things to do than brush a crazy woman's house for fingerprints and mouse tracks," he replied in the same booming tone.

"Like what? Straightening stop signs that get bent sideways? All you do is cruise town, wagging your finger at teenagers who exceed the speed limit by a mere three miles an hour. Yesterday, I saw you pull Bobby Sherman and his harem of girlfriends over for easing past a pole that no longer has a stop sign attached to it. You didn't bother to track down the prankster who removed the sign; you simply sent a warning to the driver who did not observe the invisible sign."

Nick thrust his face into hers, displaying a full set of teeth. Mother would be pleased, thought Amanda. Here was a man who had taken the time to brush and floss several times a day.

"A man was killed in Vamoose," Amanda went on to say, despite the curling of his full lips and the flash of his stormy black eyes. "I am beginning to think those three canceled checks might

116

have been forgeries. And any time someone copies a signature to gain money, it's not only forgery but also fraud. And since you refuse to accept the truth because it might take some effort on your part to conduct an investiga—"

Nick yanked her to him so quickly that the last syllable came out in a whoosh. "Hazard, I have had just about enough of you."

Or maybe the problem was that he hadn't had enough. Amanda Hazard was classy, intelligent and independent and she challenged a man to exert control over her, if only to see if he could. And she also had the most kissable mouth ever to be carved on a feminine face . . . those lush pink lips drew his attention and held it like a magnet. He didn't want to stand here arguing with her; he wanted to kiss those luscious lips.

Nick expelled a what-the-hell sigh, pulled her rigid body against his hard contours and gave way to impulse. He didn't stop kissing Amanda until she got over being furious with him and yielded, in part, to the tantalizing pleasure he offered and hungered for in return.

Amanda was shocked by his unexpected embrace and even more stunned by her reaction to it. Instead of rearing back to slap him silly, as she should have done, she kissed him back—hard and hungrily. Her hands clamped onto his waist, as if to steady herself as a lightning bolt sizzled through her, and her fingers itched to bulldoze their way beneath his shirt to explore his muscular frame. He looked good. He felt even better. He kissed with a wild sensuality that demolished each and every one of her sensible resolutions—in alphabetical order.

And why shouldn't she want this powerful, sen-

117

sual male strictly for sex? Amanda asked herself. Men never gave a thought to anything but smoldering passion and physical satisfaction. So why shouldn't she? After all, she believed in sexual equality . . .

Careful, Hazard. You're letting dormant desire dictate when your mind should be in control. Do you want to be just another smile on a man's lips, a challenge conquered? Certainly not!

With more speed than grace, Amanda wrenched herself out of Nick's arms and took a fortifying breath. "What was that all about, Thorn?" she croaked in a voice that wasn't nearly as steady as she had hoped.

"You tell me, Hazard. You were as involved in that kiss as I was. Don't bother denying it because I refuse to believe it."

Amanda willfully ordered her heart to return to its normal pace. She focused on the strewn magazines and counted to fifteen. Counting to *ten* had never been ample for her to get herself in hand when dealing with this infuriating cop.

"I called upon you to investigate, as a professional, my complaints of illegal entry. I demand nothing less than your assistance and consideration, and I expect nothing more." Blue eyes sizzled over Nick like cold flames. "Is it customary procedure for you to kiss victims of forceful entry into silence?"

The jingling phone prevented Nick from responding to her caustic question.

Amanda jerked up the receiver and offered a clipped hello. She was met with static and heavy breathing. "I know what you are trying to do, but it won't work. And furthermore—"

Nick yanked the phone from her hand and

slammed it into its cradle. "Do you want the whole community to think you're as nutty as I do, Hazard?"

Her arm shot toward the door, as if he didn't know where it was. "Get out and don't come back. The next time I have trouble, I'm calling the county sheriff. That's what I should have done in the first place. If you refuse to take my complaints and suspicions seriously, I'll find someone who will!"

Nick pivoted on his heels and stalked out. The house vibrated when he slammed the door behind him. That woman was making him crazy. She was paranoid, cynical and so damned sassy that he wanted to shake her until her teeth fell out.

Muttering curses, Amanda stacked her magazines in proper order and returned the glass to the kitchen. That mulish man! Couldn't Nick get it through that chunk of rock he called a skull that someone was purposely setting her up to look the fool? But she had cried wolf so often that Nick would no longer listen, which was exactly what her mysterious prowler wanted, to discredit her in every way. The tactic was working superbly, much to Amanda's dismay.

But she knew what she was about and she vowed to find a way to prove to the bullheaded Nick Thorn that she was purposely being targeted by the same person who had murdered William Farley. Somehow or another, Amanda was going to smoke William's killer out, even if she had to become a target to do it. If she wound up dead, it would finally dawn on Nick Thorn that her demise was related to William's death. Then perhaps there would be an official investigation.

Better too late than never, Amanda thought grimly. She would show that infuriating Officer Thorn. She would come back from beyond the grave to say I told you so.

Ten

After Amanda changed into the jeans and the Western blouse and boots she had purchased, she grabbed the keys to her truck. She had opted to dine at the Last Chance Cafe, rather than risk being poisoned by the open food in her kitchen cabinets. It was small consolation that she saw Nick Thorn pull in behind her on the highway and follow her to town. If he thought keeping protective surveillance on her would return him to her good graces, he was sorely mistaken. And if he hoped she would invite him to her booth at the cafe to join her for dinner, he had also miscalculated.

Her first impression of Nick Thorn had been right on the mark. He was a laid-back country-bumpkin cop who didn't look for trouble and therefore didn't find any. To hell with her and her suspicions, huh? Well, to hell with him!

One greasy hamburger and basket of French fries later, Amanda climbed into her truck and skidded off to the high-school basketball game. The poor acoustics in the outdated gymnasium gave her an instant headache. The pep club shouted cheers, and the opponent's cheerleaders chanted back. Bobby Sherman and his fluffy new haircut were the highlight of the game.

By halftime, Vamoose had a twenty-point lead,

and Amanda adjourned to the hallway to drop deliberate hints about her suspicions concerning William Farley's death. She could almost see word spreading through the crowd like wildfire. She received several owl-eyed glances before neighbor leaned toward neighbor to convey the story. Of course, Amanda had no way of knowing how her comments had been distorted by the time they reached the opposite side of the lobby. But it didn't matter how twisted the tale bécame. Her primary objective was to plant suspicion and wait until the story was related back to her at Velma's beauty salon or the cafe. If nothing else, it would flush the murderer out of the shadows and into the spotlight. Hopefully, Amanda would live to see the results of her efforts.

She knew the very second Velma Hertzog got wind of the gossip on the far side of the lobby. Anybody with normal hearing couldn't miss the cracking and popping of her chewing gum. The story spread even faster after Velma got hold of it. She zigzagged through the crowd, relaying the information like a messenger passing the word through military troops.

Satisfied that the seed of suspicion had been planted and well watered, Amanda made her exit from the gymnasium. She predicted that by noon on Saturday everyone in town would be questioning what they had previously presumed to be death by natural causes.

Smiling in impish anticipation of Nick Thorn's reaction, Amanda climbed into her pickup and headed it toward the Farley Farm. Eventually, Nick would thank her for bringing this festering boil to a head. But he would be mad as hell for a while. Not that Amanda cared.

* * *

Amanda bumped along the pitted gravel road, scowling at the county commissioner and his invisible road crews. The radio station had updated the weather forecast. Another winter storm was rapidly approaching, bringing with it several inches of snow. Considering the frozen bumps and ruts that had not seen a road grader in months, the country byways would become even more treacherous.

She made a note to restock supplies of food in case the storm reached blizzard proportions. She still wasn't eating anything at home except previously unopened purchases. Otherwise, she might become deathly ill and never live to see how the Farley investigation turned out.

Panic shot through Amanda when she applied the brakes and skidded sideways into the driveway of the Farley Vet Clinic. She did manage to come to a halt before she sideswiped Janene's wrecked car. She doubted its owner would have noticed an extra dent anyway.

Amanda rapped on the apartment door and was met with silence. She stood by it shivering for several minutes before Janene responded. A curious frown hovered on Amanda's brow as she critically appraised the other woman. Janene's hair, which was usually styled to perfection, looked like a rat's nest. Her makeup was smeared, revealing a bruise on her left cheek and a scrape on her chin. And she was wearing a robe with very little beneath it. She seemed ill at ease at seeing Amanda, but that wasn't particularly surprising. Women like Janene prided themselves on looking their best. Any deviation from perfection witnessed by a neighbor, friend or acquaintance was likely to disturb her.

"I was sorry to hear about your accident." Amanda flashed the self-conscious woman a sympathetic smile. "I hope you're feeling all right."

"I'm fine." The reply was abrupt. "I only need to rest and recuperate."

In other words, go away and leave me alone. Amanda didn't take the hint. She manufactured another smile. "I'm also sorry to hear that you and Bill have split up. Is there anything I can do—"

Janene cut in. "My brother is all the assistance I need."

The wind swirled around Janene's robe while she blocked the partially opened door, refusing Amanda entrance. The slinky negligee beneath Janene's wrap drew Amanda's attention. Her gaze darted back to reevaluate Janene's appearance.

"I have a few questions to ask Luke about the clinic and his obligations concerning William's cattle operation. I wonder if I could impose on him for a few minutes."

"Luke isn't here."

No, but somebody was . . . or had been very recently. Amanda had the sneaking suspicion that Janene's ruffled appearance was the result of a tumble in the sack. The seductive lingerie gave her away. She had left her husband, but who was responsible for mussing her hair and smearing her makeup?

Amanda glanced back at the driveway. There were no extra vehicles to indicate another person was around. But that did not mean that someone had not been here and left before Amanda arrived.

124

Amanda would bet that Janene had not been resting and recuperating alone. She had been fooling around with a man. Amanda's last experience hadn't been so long ago that she didn't remember the look.

This unexpected incident threw a wrench in her theory. Was Janene on the rebound? Was she striking out to hurt her husband for something he had done, or something she thought he had done? Now Amanda wasn't sure whether Janene was a victim or a suspect.

Refusing to be discouraged, she bid Janene good night and returned to her truck. If the woman had been entertaining an unidentified guest and it wasn't her estranged husband, then who was it? And what was Bill Farley up to? He should have returned from his business trip days ago.

Amanda decided to pay another visit while she was in the neighborhood. She headed for the two-story brick house down the road and found Bill at home. He was nursing a drink—one of many, Amanda deduced. His eyes were streaked, and his greeting was slurred.

Now was the time to bait a trap or two, Amanda decided. If Bill was involved and he suspected she knew the truth—she just wished she did—he might become careless and give himself away. Then again, Amanda might be barking up the wrong tree. There were still Glenn Chambliss and Preston Banks to consider. They had clashed with William many times in the past. Outside pressure might have caused one of them to snap. Glenn faced the humiliation of foreclosure. Preston, a man full of pride and tradition, was next in line to feel the axe. They could have been scrambling to save themselves, and William could have been blackmailing them. That was not a good thing to do to men already walking on pins and needles in order to hold their businesses and their lives together. Such a threat could cause the strongest individual to snap.

"Bill, I know it's late, but could I beg a few minutes of your time?"

The door swung open and Bill Farley stumbled back a pace. He took another sip of his drink and wandered over to a chair, expecting Amanda to follow. She did.

"I have reason to believe three canceled checks which conveniently disappeared from my file were forged," Amanda said, cutting straight to the purpose of her visit. "I also have the uneasy feeling that foul play was involved in your father's death."

Bill blinked groggily. "What?"

"I think you should be the one to call for an investigation."

Silence. And more silence.

Amanda was prepared to judge Bill innocent or guilty, depending on his response to her declaration and suggestion. If he chose to do nothing, he was probably involved. If he agreed with her, he was likely to be innocent . . .

Bill just sat there for the longest time, contemplating the contents of his glass. Amanda began to wonder if he was trying to second-guess her while she was trying to second-guess him. If that was what was running through his mind, she should leave, having accomplished not one blessed thing except to put her life in jeopardy.

As the seconds ticked by, Amanda feared she had outsmarted no one but herself. This visit was a mistake. She should have stayed home with the mice.

"Bill?" she prompted impatiently.

He looked at her through glazed eyes. "What?"

Lord, the man barely knew where he was. He had not been able to follow her train of thought due to the effects of too much whiskey. Or was this only an act?

Amanda rose to leave, hoping to provoke some type of response. It was a wasted effort. Bill made no attempt to call her back.

Exasperated, she slammed the door of her truck and drove toward town, noting she was being followed. She detoured to purchase supplies in case the predicted blizzard descended, blanketing Vamoose with more snow. Still, headlights dogged her. Only when she pulled off the highway toward her house did her pursuer advance. Amanda held her breath, afraid to step outside and expose herself as an easy target.

She sighed in relief when she recognized Nick Thorn's patrol car pulling in beside her. She was still peeved at this country cop, but at least she did not now have to fear being struck down in her driveway by an assassin.

"Was I speeding, Officer Thorn? Or did I fail to use my turn signals?"

Nick resisted the urge to shake her when she climbed from her truck. "No, Hazard. You wanted protection from the mysterious evil force you insist is stalking you. I am here to ensure you return home safely." He pivoted and strode up the steps. "Let me check the door. I'm sure you locked it when you left, efficient as you are."

The door didn't budge when Nick twisted the knob. "No evidence of tampering."

Amanda elbowed past him, gouging him in the ribs before she stabbed the key in the lock. "I thought you would be off duty by now. Such dedication. I should be impressed. Too bad I'm not."

Nick stared at her shapely derriere, imagining how it would look wearing his footprint. "I'm working overtime so I can take tomorrow off. I have hungry cows to feed. If any of them drop calves during the storm that's coming, the subzero wind chill could cause difficulties. But I'm sure my problems are of no concern to you, now that you're moonlighting as a private detective and have so much to occupy you. How *do* you keep up with all of it, Hazard?"

The snide question was forgotten when the smell of smoke greeted them. Instinctively, Amanda bolted forward, but Nick yanked her back to surge past her. Within a few seconds he had determined there had been some sort of fire, but it had burned itself out. There was no uncontained blaze, no suffocating black fog.

Amanda darted toward the kitchen, one step behind Nick. To her frustration, she found the metal trash can, which usually occupied a corner in the utility room, positioned in the center of the room. Charred remains of trash and paper filled the bottom.

Amanda rounded on Nick before he lambasted her with sarcastic comments. "Don't you dare accuse me of burning my trash in the kitchen, damn you!"

"I am beginning to think you have been sabotaged." Nick scrutinized her carefully. "Either that or you've gone to extremes to convince me to believe your suspicions."

Amanda could have slapped him for that. "If you believe that, you are nuttier than you think I am!" She took a breath, prepared to continue her tirade, but strange scratching noises caught her attention.

"Christ. What now?" Nick muttered.

With the silence of a cat, Amanda inched down the hall, pausing at regular intervals to listen for the sound. She halted beside the wall of the spare bedroom that had become her office. The clawing noise continued. In the quiet house, it sounded as if a bear had been trapped inside the wall. Amanda shot Nick a belligerent glance, daring him to accuse her of planting another pest in her own house.

"Pack a suitcase, Hazard. You are coming with me." Nick spun around and paced down the hall.

"You are finally admitting that you believe me? The saints be praised!"

"I am willing to accept the fact that strange things are happening around here."

"Generous of you, Thorn," she said with an unladylike snort. "Obviously you are still reserving judgment on whether or not I am the culprit."

When Amanda refused to budge, Nick reversed direction and headed toward her bedroom. He flicked on the light and stomped toward the dresser. With swift efficiency, he gathered articles of clothing, Amanda loudly objecting.

"Give me those, you pervert." She snatched her bras and panties from his hands and glared at him.

Dark eyes twinkled devilishly as Amanda clutched lacy undergarments to her bosom, but Nick said not one word to set her off again. She was already irritated enough. In silence, he watched her cram her clothes into a duffle bag. Also in silence, he followed her down the hall, past the scratching in the wall.

"Weather permitting, I will investigate that noise tomorrow," he promised.

"Investigate?" Amanda scoffed at him. "I could have sworn that word was not in your limited vocabulary, Thorn."

"Come on, Hazard. It's been a long day."

"Where are we going?"

"To my place."

Amanda pulled up short. Up went the chin. A mule could not have looked more stubborn. "No."

"You want to stay here?"

"Not particularly."

"There are no motels in Vamoose, if you recall, and it's too cold to sleep in the cab of your truck. You can sleep on my sofa."

Amanda decided she'd be damned if she stayed home and damned if she left with Nick. There was danger in both places. At least she could see the devil who tormented her at Nick's house. Here, she didn't know her enemy.

"Leave your truck and come with me," Nick ordered.

For once, Amanda did not argue with him. She simply gathered her recently purchased food supplies and loaded them in the squad car. She wasn't thrilled at the prospect of having anyone see her vehicle sitting in Thorn's driveway overnight. Leaving her truck at home would squelch gossip.

One mile later Amanda groaned aloud. "I forgot my toothbrush and pajamas."

"You can borrow mine," Nick offered, never taking his eyes off the road.

"I refuse to share anyone's toothbrush."

"I have an extra one."

"I have serious reservations about this arrangement, Thorn."

130

"You aren't the only one, Hazard. I'm only of-fering you sleeping accommodations until the smoke clears out and I dislodge your latest pest from the wall."

"Your generosity and concern are touching."

"So is your gratitude."

Having exchanged insults, Amanda and Nick set-tled into their respective corners like boxers be-tween rounds, both lost to private thoughts.

Eleven

By the time Nick drove onto his farm, exhaustion had closed in on Amanda. It had been a long hectic day. One of many, in fact.

When they entered the house, the phone was ringing. Amanda dropped her duffle bag beside the sofa while Nick strode off to answer the call. She suspected, judging by the glares he flung at her while speaking, that the seeds of gossip she had planted earlier in the evening had sprouted—and in this cold weather.

"You really don't know when to quit, do you, Hazard?" Nick growled as he returned to the room and towered over her. "That annoying caller suggested I check into Farley's *murder*. I was informed that William drowned in his stock tank, rather than suffering a heart attack before collapsing into it. The story circulating around Vamoose is that William was overpowered and held down."

"Now, there is an interesting explanation."

"That is a bunch of crap and you know it," Nick snapped.

The phone blared again. Nick stormed off to answer it. He returned a few minutes later, still steaming.

"That version of the story had William suffocated

132

in his bed while he slept and later hauled to the stock tank," he reported, breathing down her neck in the process.

"At least the good citizens of Vamoose exhibit some imagination, which is more than I can say for you, Thorn."

"I am not into imagination; I deal in cold, hard facts. William Farley died of a heart attack." He made a stabbing gesture toward the Early American couch. "Go the hell to bed. You have caused more than enough trouble for one day."

"I haven't brushed my teeth, and you haven't offered me your jammies." Amanda cast a sunny smile at his thunderous frown. "You aren't a very gracious host. You were the one who invited me to sleep over. No wonder you aren't married. You aren't a very pleasant man."

"I was the epitome of cheerfulness until I got mixed up with you."

Nick tossed his coat toward the chair, not caring that he missed his target by a mile. Automatically, Amanda picked the garment up and hung it in the closet where it belonged. Typical of a man, tossing his coat on the floor. If Nick had done that at her house, the mice would have made a nest in it.

Moments later, Nick returned to toss a toothbrush and the top of his pajamas at her.

"You actually wear those things" Amanda asked, examining the garment with a look of dissatisfaction.

"I sleep buck naked, but I bought pajamas for my female guests," he snapped. "I do this sort of thing all the time, you know."

"As if I care."

"Did I say you did?"

Amanda clutched the toothbrush and pajama top

133

and marched off to locate the bathroom. She nearly scrubbed the fillings out of her teeth out of frustration. She did not wish to be here. And furthermore, she was outraged by the latest attack on her personal property. Had someone acquired a key to her house and then entered it to harass her? Who had access to her home, and how had he or she played these spiteful pranks? Only Amanda's landlady, Emma Carter, had an extra key. The elderly woman had moved into town several years earlier, leasing her farmland out to her son-in-law . . . Preston Banks.

The thought prompted a progression of thoughts — disturbing ones. If Amanda had her genealogy correct, Glenn Chambliss's wife was also a Carter. The flower sisters, Amanda reminded herself. Rose and Violet were Emma Carter's daughters. Rose had married Glenn and Violet had married Preston. They were both rumored to have been fooling around with William.

Everybody in Vamoose was related, somehow or another. Sisters, cousins, in-laws, nieces and nephews were everywhere. You couldn't swing a dead cat in Vamoose without hitting somebody's relative.

Amanda frowned ponderously. If Rose Chambliss was also a Carter, why had Emma rented family land to Preston rather than dividing the property in half and allowing both of her sons-in-law to farm and pasture it? Amanda didn't know the answer to that question. She could only speculate that Emma Carter had shown favoritism for one son-in-law, just as William Farley had favored one son over the other.

By the time Amanda had prepared for bed, the day's frustration had given way to pensive deliberation. Maybe her suspicions about Bill Farley were

134

off base. Maybe she should have been focusing on Preston and/or Glenn. Either one of them could have used their mother-in-law's key to enter her house. They had both been at odds with William through the years. And both men were in dire financial straits. They might even have conspired together.

Nick's breath lodged in his throat when Amanda wandered out of the bathroom, wearing his pajama top. It reached to mid-thigh. He should have offered her his robe to cover those long shapely legs.

Big mistake, Thorn.

Amanda's silky blond hair tumbled around her in disarray. Even with her face devoid of makeup, she was still gorgeous and sultry. Looking at her made Nick go hot all over. Inviting her to spend the night had definitely not been one of his brighter ideas.

Giving himself a mental slap, he propelled himself toward the linen closet to retrieve sheets and blankets for the sleeper sofa. "There's an extra pillow in my bedroom. Last door on the right," he said without looking at her. He couldn't.

Amanda padded barefoot down the hall, glancing in each room as she passed. Nick had converted one spare bedroom into a library and office. Bookshelves lined the north wall and a cluttered desk occupied the west side of it. The second spare bedroom had become a den filled with comfortable furniture and an entertainment center that boasted a collection of videotapes and stereo equipment.

When Amanda reached Nick's bedroom at the end of the hall, she switched on the light and sighed audibly. A fluffy patchwork quilt covered the antique brass bed. She felt like Goldilocks searching for just the right place to rest her weary bones. The room, decorated with an antique walnut dresser and matching commode, looked all too cozy and inviting. The temptation of curling up with Nick on a night like this in a bed such as the one before her was almost overwhelming.

Shrugging off her wayward thoughts, Amanda scooped up a pillow and reversed direction. She had to get her mind off sensual visions of cuddling up with a life-sized Teddy bear to ward off the winter chill. She was mature and sensible nowadays, and she could cope with sharing space with a country cop who kissed like nobody in living memory.

She could handle this challenge. No sweat.

The sleeping accommodations Nick had arranged for Amanda were nowhere near as inviting as the ones in his room, but tired as she was, she would hardly notice.

Nick tossed the television remote control to her—a great concession on his part, no doubt. Amanda knew how the male of the species treasured remotes. They were symbols of power and control to them. She had seen her own father get bent out of shape when someone dared to touch *his* remote control. And Amanda's ex had also suffered from the remote control syndrome. She decided it was a characteristic flaw that plagued those of the male gender.

"Since I am unaware of your customary sleeping habits, I don't know if you are into late-night television," Nick said, his voice showing evidence of strain. "I have a TV in my bedroom."

So she had noticed.

"I hope it won't bother you if I leave mine on while I doze off. It's a habit of mine."

"I'm sure I can find a detective show to watch before I drift off to sleep," Amanda said brightly. Then she switched on the set and zipped through all the channels, just for spite.

The look Nick tossed at her did not invite translation. Amanda ignored it.

"I'll leave a dim light on in the kitchen and bathroom in case you're prone to wander around during the night," he offered.

Was that a subtle invitation to come to his bedroom or was it an insulting suggestion that she was so mentally imbalanced she walked in her sleep? The first interpretation was foremost in Amanda's mind. She hated herself for pursuing the forbidden fantasy. Aware that Nick was fighting the attraction, just as she was, she admired his restraint. Yet, deep down, she resented it.

It was not particularly flattering that Nick hadn't even come within ten feet of her since he'd unfolded the hideaway bed. When he'd reappeared, wearing the trousers of his pajamas, he had avoided any physical contact with her. He had even tossed the remote control to her.

They now stood staring at each other, the bed between them like a river they dared not cross.

Amanda cleared her throat and then cursed the unconscious habit she had inherited from her mother. "Do you mind if I put my groceries in the fridge?" she asked. "I don't want the food to spoil."

"Make yourself at home, Hazard." Nick dropped an extra quilt at the foot of her bed and took a wide berth around her. "I'll take my turn in the bathroom while you're in the kitchen. I'll switch off the lights behind you."

Amanda neatly stacked her canned and boxed food on the counter. She had just bent over to line up her refrigerated goods on one shelf when she heard the sharp intake of breath behind her. Without looking up, she knew she had unintentionally given Nick an eyeful of barely concealed backside.

She smiled mischievously to herself and continued to arrange the food in alphabetical order.

"Are you about finished, Hazard?" Nick sounded like a bullfrog with a June bug stuck in its throat.

Amanda found the croak in his voice immensely gratifying . . . until she pirouetted around to view an appealing amount of bare chest, finely tuned muscles and fire-engine red pajama bottoms that rode low on his hips. Hot silk pajamas didn't lie. Nick Thorn was interested.

She had the most ridiculous urge to run her fingers through the mat of dark hair that covered his chest and descended into the waistband of his pajamas. And that was only the prelude. The rest of her fantasy was R-rated—to be viewed by mature audiences only. Amanda wasn't sure *she* was old enough for the erotic thoughts she was having.

Snap out of it, Hazard!

"I'm on my way to bed, Thorn."

Her voice sounded as if it had rusted. The acid of desire that was spreading through her had obviously corroded her vocal apparatus. Her pH balance was out of whack. Amanda grabbed a glass of water and the box of soda crackers to alleviate the problem.

But she found herself clearing her throat again. She cursed her mother for handing down that infuriating quirk, and, with firm resolve, circumnavigated the tantalizing hunk of masculinity who stood barefoot in the kitchen. Nick Thorn looked good enough to eat. Amanda stuffed a cracker in her mouth and headed for her bed.

"Good night, Thorn."

Nick flicked off the kitchen light, followed her through the dining room and switched off the living-room lamp. "Good night, Hazard."

Amanda propped herself against the pillow and swore inventively. She had picked up Nick's scent on the pillowcase. She had not grabbed the *spare* pillow, but *his* pillow.

Munching crackers, Amanda switched television stations and caught herself watching a romantic embrace in an old movie. Hurriedly, she changed channels. She concentrated on a commercial that advertised dog food. Safe. Maybe she should get herself a dog for a companion. The woman at Luke's veterinary clinic certainly had found contentment with a canine.

Once Amanda's bubbling emotions cooled down and she had satisfied her gnawing ache to some degree with soda crackers, she switched off the television and snuggled beneath the quilts. She could hear the drone of Nick's television in the distance. The flashing lights cast shadows on the wall in the hall, reminding Amanda that he wasn't too far away.

Was he lying there and thinking what she was thinking?

Go to sleep, Hazard. Your hormones could use a rest.

On that sound piece of advice, Amanda clamped her eyes shut, counted a zillion sheep and tried to relax.

Twelve

During the night, near-arctic winds howled, causing the guttering on the eaves to vibrate. Amanda opened her eyes to total darkness. The descending storm had obviously knocked down power lines. Great. No electricity. No heat.

Amanda lay still, unable to measure the passage of time, her teeth chattering. Nick had supplied her with an extra blanket and she had wrapped herself in the quilts as if in a cocoon. But she still could not generate enough heat to keep warm. In wide, open country, with nothing to block the icy blasts of wind, a farmhouse got cold in a hurry.

Amanda flung back the quilts and navigated around furniture. A groan exploded from her when her shin smacked an end table. She hadn't progressed five feet before she banged her head into the wall. She was not familiar enough with Nick's home to prowl around in the dark, searching for extra blankets, but she was cold and desperate.

"You okay, Hazard?" Nick's voice boomed from the inky blackness.

"Except for freezing to death and cracking my head and shin, I'm in splendid shape. Do you have a few more quilts?"

Amanda felt her way around the corner and into the hall. Stretching out her arms, she braced both hands on the walls and continued forward until she ran head-on into a warm, fleshy obstacle. Amanda yelped in surprised when she smashed her face into Nick's hairy chest. Reflexively, she retreated, stumbling over her feet and his. A muscled arm snaked around her waist, holding her upright. Amanda decided Mother Nature was out to test her willpower. She was alone in a dark house with no heat except the radiation of desire that streamed between her body and the physically appealing man meshed against her.

Snowflakes and raging winds swirled around the isolated house, and not another living soul was around to know Amanda was stumbling along the crumbling edge of temptation. When Nick's free arm slid around her hips, encircling her, traitorous tremors chipped away at Amanda's self-control. She was trembling, but it was no longer from the cold air.

She inhaled deeply, but took in the scent of the man who held her tightly against him.

"There is one sure way to conserve heat during a power outage, Hazard."

His rich baritone voice echoed in Amanda's ears, the tantalizing sounds vibrating down her backbone.

"You wanna risk it or not?" he asked.

Bless the man for offering her a choice and curse her for not having the sense to make the appropriate decision. "Do you snore and pull covers, Thorn?"

When a low rumble of laughter reverberated in that all-male chest, Amanda felt the tingles all the way down to her curled toes.

"I snore only when I'm exceedingly tired. Which side of the bed do you sleep on?" he asked in a husky voice.

141

The *wrong* side tonight, she said to herself. "Lately, I've developed the habit of taking my half in the middle — a hazard of sleeping alone too long."

Amanda cursed herself for letting her tongue outdistance her brain. *Way to go, Hazard. Let him know you've had your passions packed in ice for too many years.* Where was that biting sarcasm she usually employed to put men off? Now was not the time for honesty and sincerity. It would get her into trouble.

"I'm a middle-of-the-bed man myself," Nick admitted, guiding her down the hall. "We'll both have to adjust to an extra body."

All sorts of thoughts danced in Amanda's head while she was being propelled toward the bedroom. Did she dare? And if she dared, how would she react the morning after? If she and Nick stoked these banked fires, would it be a slow and tender flame or a heated blaze of long-denied lust? And how would Nick react later to what might happen while they were conserving heat to counteract the power outage? Would he graciously accept their night together, or would he kiss, gloat and tell? If she became the latest news in the Last Chance Cafe, she would kill him.

Nick was certainly suffering no power outage. His generator was humming along without missing a beat! He had lain awake for what seemed hours, Amanda's image floating above his bed like a haunting specter.

Was she really as cool and distant as she wanted the rest of the world, and all men, to believe? And if Nick did yield to his basic instincts, the ones that were burning inside him, where would he and Amanda go from here? They didn't agree on much of anything, except that they were unwillingly attracted to each other. Neither wanted to make the first move because neither wanted to face rejection. Nothing ventured and nothing lost, or something to that effect.

On the other hand, Amanda was a consenting adult and she knew how to keep score. If she wanted to say no, then she would. Hazard had never had difficulty declaring what she wanted before. Did she have a problem now? A man would never know what a woman's answer would be if he didn't ask.

Nick was beginning to wonder if he was the first man Amanda had spent the night with, platonic or otherwise, since her divorce. He would not have been surprised to discover that was the case. Amanda had shut herself off from the world of men, burying herself in her career, denying her natural affinity for companionship and affection . . .

When Nick reached the bed, he wavered in indecision for several seconds. Should he come right out and tell her what he was thinking, what he wanted? Or should he simply make his move and await her reaction? He was not about to do anything that would prompt her to accuse him of taking advantage of the situation, to claim he had overpowered her when she was not physically strong enough to put a stop to it. She would hold that over him for the rest of his life and give him hell for it. There would be equal participation, or there would be no participation at all, Nick promised himself, even when the prospect of *not having* was causing his blood to pound.

"You take the left side." Nick released his grasp on Amanda and circled around the brass foot rail.

The antique bed creaked when Amanda and Nick simultaneously sank onto it. She had developed a severe case of the jitters. Her heart was thumping against her ribs, and her senses were on full alert. When two hundred pounds of bone and muscle rolled toward her, Amanda's pulse leaped like a jackrabbit.

She was ashamed to admit it, but she was scared. In short, she was out of practice. And for crying out loud, she felt like a nervous virgin.

"Thorn?" Her wobbly voice indicated the turmoil inside her.

"What is it, Hazard?" Nick lay on his back. He and his erection were staring at the ceiling.

"I . . ." Amanda swallowed and inhaled an audible breath. "I . . . don't want anything to happen." She expelled air like a spouting whale. There. She had said it. Safe again. No humiliation. No embarrassment.

There was a noticeable pause. Only the raging wind broke the sound barrier between them.

"Could you be more specific about what you don't want to happen?" he requested.

"You know perfectly well what I'm talking about," she muttered.

"How do you know what I know? Are you lying there and reading my mind?"

"I'm reading your mood. Damn it, Thorn, don't make this more difficult than it already is."

"I wanted to keep it simple," he protested. "You are the one who is making it difficult."

"Oh, all right, since you are baiting me to say it, then I'll say it." Amanda's breath came out in an exasperated rush. "It isn't that I am not interested. The fact is, I am unsure of myself, and I'm not ready to . . . That is to say, I don't want *you* to be"—another gushing breath—"disappointed."

Seconds ticked past until a full minute had elapsed.

"If you aren't ready for anything to happen between us, then it won't."

Of course, Nick would burn into a frustrated pile of ashes, just like the residue in the trash can in Amanda's kitchen. She would awake to see his charred remains on the sheet. Either that, or the pressure of internal combustion would cause him to blow apart at the seams, leaving his remains scattered on the walls. Nick had gone to bed with far more pleasant thoughts than those of his own self-destruction.

Tentatively, Amanda reached over to pat his arm. It was not his arm she patted. Firm and hard? Yes. But definitely not his arm. She heard him groan. Amanda snatched her hand away with a jerk and a strangled gasp.

"Sorry, Thorn. I only meant to express my gratitude for your patience and consideration."

"Then do it verbally and keep your damned hands to yourself, Hazard," Nick unintentionally growled at her. "I may be understanding, but I sure as hell don't have a will of steel."

"No, not a *will* of steel . . ." Amanda burst into snickers and buried her head in her pillow, or rather his pillow, or rather their pillow. There was only one between them because she had left hers on the sofa.

Tension-releasing laughter shook her body, making the bed creak, reminding her of other reasons why beds creaked. Suddenly, Amanda was having a hysterical seizure. Tears dampened the pillow, and she fought desperately for composure. But each time she inhaled a cleansing breath, she remembered what she had said and another round of high-pitched giggles wafted around the room.

"Get a grip, Hazard. If you keep cackling, you'll

145

lay an egg," Nick snapped, grabbing her by the shoulder to give her a hard shake.

"I'm" — giggle, gasp — "sorry."

"So you said. Just go to sleep."

Amanda made a valiant effort to get herself in hand. But each time she settled down another giggle burst loose. Releasing tension in the form of laughter had been her remedy since she was a child. Nick didn't know that, of course. He thought she was a fruitcake, with nutty suspicions and all sorts of sexual hang-ups. Well, maybe that was what she was, a neurotic fruitcake. That sobering thought brought Amanda back to earth and into the creaking bed.

"I can understand why you aren't into casual affairs, Hazard. Going to bed with you is like attending a three-ring circus."

She countered with childlike vindictiveness. "Going to bed with you is like swimming around in a fish tank, the way you're thrashing about."

"You'll get finned if you don't hush up," Nick flashed back.

"Better finned than f—"

"Don't say it!" Nick interrupted in such a loud voice that he momentarily drowned out the wailing wind. "Just ask the Lord to keep you from being strangled before morning."

"Maybe it would be a blessing if I was," Amanda said, elevating her head from the pillow to stare at Nick's shadowed face.

"No, then I would become the prime murder suspect. And thanks to your gossip, the killing would somehow be linked to Farley's death. I would find myself in jail just because I resorted to choking the life out of you when all I really wanted was the satisfaction of sex. A crime of passion, Hazard. Now shut the hell up and don't provoke me again. I can be very mean and nasty when I am being deprived of s—leep."

Amanda lay there like a slug, relishing the warmth of the body beside her, but unable to achieve peaceful slumber. The wind howled like a pack of coyotes. The whole house rattled. Snowflakes beat against the windows like rioting butterflies. It would have been all too easy to succumb to the demands of her traitorous body. But she forcefully contained the pulsating sensations that channeled through her. *She* was the one who had a will of steel.

Nick lay on his side, his back turned to temptation. He stared unblinkingly into the darkness. Having that flaky blond so close and yet so tormentingly far away was hell on earth. Nick consoled himself by mentally listing all the other difficult and tormenting moments of his life. He had endured worse. He would get through this night. But one thing was certain. He was *not* going to find himself in this predicament ever again. He would rather freeze to death than burn alive.

Thirteen

"Drag your butt out of bed, Hazard. We have places to go and things to do."

Amanda awakened to shades of dreary gray and a booming voice that ordered her out of the cozy warmth that encompassed her. Obviously, Nick Thorn was not a morning person. He was grouchy and impatient, and she could not rise fast enough to suit him. Before Amanda could lever up on an elbow and claw the hair out of her eyes, Nick jerked back the quilts. Cold air swept over her.

"Without electricity, the heater at the stock tank isn't working. The water has iced over. The cattle have stampeded down to the frozen pond, looking for a drink. I've already driven them away once. And worse, one of my cows has decided today is the day to calve. She's having trouble and won't let me catch her." Nick tossed Amanda her jeans, shirt and a pair of insulated coveralls. "You have volunteered to help."

"What about breakfast? I'm starved." Drowsily, Amanda reached for her clothes.

"We'll eat when the cattle are fed and watered and the calf has been delivered. This will be good experience since you are planning to invest in a

148

cow-calf operation. Rule number one: the livestock come first in blizzards. If you lose your investment, you have no profit left to buy food."

Amanda pulled on her jeans and buttoned her shirt over the borrowed pajama top. When she stuffed her legs into the coveralls, she couldn't find her feet. The garment swallowed her.

"Hurry it up, Hazard."

"I'm trying, Thorn."

Seeing her problem, Nick knelt to roll up the bottoms and then pushed Amanda down on the edge of the bed to shove a pair of oversized galoshes into place. "The calf is coming backward. It will suffocate if we don't get to it soon. Damned cows. They pick the worst days for delivery."

Nick's sense of urgency rubbed the sleep from Amanda's eyes. Quickly, she thrust her arms into the coveralls and rolled up the sleeves. After Nick stuffed a stocking cap on her head, he shepherded her down the hall and out the door.

The wind scorched Amanda's cheeks like dry ice. The air was so cold it burned her lungs when she tried to inhale. The subzero wind chill was hell on man and beast.

Amanda developed a new sense of appreciation for the farmer-stockman while she blazed a path through thigh-high snowdrifts to reach the idling four-wheel-drive pickup. Ranching was the last frontier, a link with the Old West. It pitted man against nature. He battled for supremacy over land and animal. He fought flood, famine, drought and blizzard to survive.

Ranchers faced unexpected emergencies and challenges daily. The only consistency to ranch life was the inconsistency of it. Machinery broke down in the fields. Animals became contrary. Tempers flared

149

out of frustration. But the ever-present challenge to fight and conquer prevailed.

It's a little early in the morning to be so philosophical, isn't it? Amanda smiled to herself and blew her warm breath onto her icy fingers.

"Here, put these on." Nick handed her a pair of gloves without taking his eyes off the snow-packed path that led to the pasture. He stopped between drifts. "Open the gate and close it behind us. I don't want cattle scattered from here to hell and back."

"Oh sure, make me get the gate while you sit here, all warm and toasty in the pickup."

"If I let you do the driving, you'd find yourself stuck in a snowdrift. Now get your ass out. We don't have all day."

"What did you say, Thorn?" Amanda demanded in a sugary tone.

"I said *now!*"

Please obviously was not now in his vocabulary. Courtesy and politeness fell by the wayside when Nick was concerned about his livestock. He had done more cursing in ten minutes than he had in the ten days she'd been associated with him.

Inhaling deeply as if in preparation for an underwater swim, Amanda bounded from the truck and leaped over the drifts to reach the gate. It took a few minutes to clear a path through the shifting snow so the gate would open, giving Nick room to bulldoze through to the pasture.

Revving the engine, he plowed forward, sending up a mist of snow that soared off in the wind. Amanda blinked snowflakes from her eyes and shoved the gate shut. Employing the tire tracks Nick had left behind, she jogged to the pickup and climbed inside. She barely had time to close the door before Nick took off in a blast of speed. The pickup cut through the drifts, sliding sideways and bouncing over concealed bumps. Amanda gripped the door handle to prevent being flung helter-skelter.

Conditions were so bad that it was difficult to distinguish snow-covered cattle from drifts until the pickup was upon them. When Nick slammed on the brakes and spun the wheel to avoid a young calf that stood frozen to the spot, Amanda's head clanked against the dashboard.

"Where the hell did she go?"

She, Amanda presumed, was the aforementioned cow that was trying to deliver her calf on the worst day of winter. Of course, Amanda was no help in spotting the mother-to-be. Her vision was blurred by the blow to her head, compliments of Nick's wild driving.

After zigging and zagging all over the pasture, Nick finally located the cow. She had tucked herself against the south side of a hill to avoid the whining wind and blowing snow. The cow bellowed at the sight of them, but before the animal could turn tail and run, Nick bounded from the cab, grabbing his lariat on the way out. With experienced ease he flung the loop and caught the cow. She, however, had an aversion to ropes, as most cows do. Cattle do not take kindly to being restrained in any manner. And the greater the pain they're suffering, the greater their instinct to fight.

Amanda scaled the hood of the truck when the bellowing cow charged at her, jerking Nick off balance and dragging him behind her as if he were a skier behind a motor boat. The urge to rescue Nick from impending disaster dominated Amanda's thoughts, overshadowing her need for self-preservation. She jumped off the truck to grab the trailing rope. Digging in her heels, she slowed the cow down before Nick slammed into the fender of the truck. The extra pressure exerted on the cow's throat caused the creature to pause momentarily, giving Amanda time to prepare herself for what would inevitably become a sleigh ride minus a sleigh.

Nick, having plenty of expertise in roping contrary cattle on the wide-open range, scrabbled to his feet. Hurriedly, he dallied the rope around the hay fork that was bolted to the truck. The cow lunged forward, hit the end of her rope and bellowed for all she was worth. Nick snatched up a second lariat and waited for the cow to make her next escape attempt. He lassoed her hind legs the instant she moved and secured her hooves to the hay fork. The cow sank to her knees and rolled onto her side, eyes wide and nostrils flared.

"There is a short silver chain in the glove compartment," Nick informed Amanda. "Bring it to me."

"*Now?*"

"*Please.*" He managed a hint of a smile at the reference to his previous demand for immediate obedience.

Amanda hurtled a snowdrift to retrieve the chain. While the cow bawled and strained, Nick knelt behind her. "Give me a little cooperation," he cooed. "I'm as anxious to get this over with as you are."

As if the cow understood, which of course she didn't, she yielded to the demands of birthing. As soon as both small hooves were visible, Nick looped the chain around them.

"Grab hold, Hazard. It will take two of us to pull this calf out backward."

Amanda clamped her hands beside Nick's and

tugged steadily. "Are you sure two of us will be enough?"

"Do you see anyone else around here to help?" Nick gritted his teeth and reared back, using his legs for leverage. "Another rule of farming is that you do whatever it takes, no matter how hard or how long, to get the job done."

Amanda strained with all her might against the chain. "Any other rules, Thorn?"

"That rule pretty much covers all the other rules," he replied as he braced his legs and arched backward to employ every ounce of strength he possessed.

Slowly but surely, they made progress. Amanda strained and pulled until she swore her arms would give out. The instant the calf eased onto the ground, its body steaming in the icy air, Amanda half collapsed in relief. Nick, however, wasted no time in bolting to his feet. He grabbed hold of the lifeless calf, slinging it roughly around before bouncing its chest against the ground.

"Damnation, Thorn, give the poor creature a break," Amanda snapped, appalled by his insensitivity.

"The calf isn't breathing." Nick gave the limp newborn another hard shake and swung it in a circular motion before dropping it to the ground. "Swinging a new calf around is like swatting a newborn baby's bottom to cleanse his lungs and remove the mucous so he can catch his breath. Sometimes, Hazard, what appears to be cruel is the world's greatest kindness."

To lend credence to the remark, the bull calf inhaled his first shuddering breath. A feeble sound tumbled from his mouth. Amanda had never considered herself overly sentimental, but witnessing the

153

miracle of new life put a lump in her throat. The calf had come into this world backward to face a blizzard and had just taken its first breath. Big brown eyes blinked up at Amanda. Another weak bawl gurgled in the calf's throat. Amanda felt a tug on her heartstrings.

"Cute little thing, isn't he?" Her voice crackled.

"Much cuter than he would have been if I hadn't beat life *into* him," Nick replied, smiling down at the floundering calf.

While Amanda stood there dazed by sentimentality, Nick removed the ropes from the cow so she could tend to the cleaning up of her calf. "It will be a few hours before he can stand up and nurse." Nick coiled the ropes and placed them in the back of the truck. "We'll come by and check on him later."

Amanda stared at Nick as if he were a maniac. "You are going to leave him out here to freeze to death after all we did to bring him to life? He'll never get dried off in this weather."

"Well, I sure as hell can't haul him and his mama to the house, now can I? The electric heat pump isn't working, remember?"

"You could take him back to the barn," she suggested.

A devilish smile pursed Nick's lips. This city slicker didn't have a clue as to what hauling a newborn calf to the barn entailed. Maybe she should find out. "Okay, Hazard, we'll take him back with us after we chop the ice on the pond. You'll be responsible for the calf."

Amanda didn't know what that implied, but she nodded agreeably all the same. When Nick gestured for her to climb into the truck, Amanda hopped inside, giving thanks for the invention of automotive

154

heaters.

In a burst of flying snow, Nick zoomed across the pasture toward the pond. The cattle were testing the ice, and Amanda was given the task of shooing them away while Nick chopped holes where it was safe for them to drink. Amanda remembered what had happened to Robert Farley two years past when he had trotted onto the ice to save a prized cow and had lost his own life. She remained on the perimeters of the pond, just to be on the safe side.

"Grab the other hatchet, Hazard," Nick called over his shoulder.

Amanda lugged the hatchet to the edge of the pond and whacked away. By the time Nick called to her to halt she was completely out of breath and her arms felt like noodles. She sucked in cold air in great gulps while the cattle inched forward to drink. She hoped they were grateful. As for herself, she was exhausted.

"Let's go pick up the calf."

Amanda fell into step behind Nick's long, energy-efficient strides. In less than a minute, they were standing beside the sprawled calf. Nick scooped the wobbly creature up in his arms and deposited him on the bed of the pickup. The mother cow voiced her objections to being separated from her calf. Head lowered, she charged.

Nick scooped Amanda up and set her in the pickup bed before darting out of the cow's way. "You'll have to ride in the back and hold the calf down," Nick instructed. "Make sure his mama can see him at all times. This is going to confuse her. If she can't keep his scent, she will keep circling back to this spot to find him. This could take hours if you don't keep the cow and calf within sniffing distance of each other."

Now Amanda knew the reason for the scampish smile that had quirked Nick's lips earlier. He would be driving through the drifts while she froze her butt in the back of the truck, clinging to the struggling calf and blinking away an avalanche of snow.

While the cow sniffed her calf and bellowed in protest, Amanda hooked one arm around the hay fork and the other around the newborn. Nick had to stop twice and circle back for the cow. But the third time worked like a charm. The calf made a bleating sound that caught his mother's attention, and she followed the truck to the barn, sniffing continuously at Amanda and her calf.

By the time they reached the corral, Amanda was chilled to the bone. She hustled the calf farther into the bed of the truck and hopped down to open the gate. The cow was still in a state of alarm, trotting in circles and bawling at her calf. It took another few minutes to get the cow into the second corral and make sure the gate was shut behind her. While Amanda was leaping snowdrifts, Nick scooped up the calf and carried him into the barn, depositing him in a pile of straw.

Cow and calf were soon reunited.

"Satisfied now, Hazard?" Nick grinned when Amanda came inside, puffing and huffing, covered with a layer of snow.

"Yes. Can we have breakfast yet?" she asked hopefully.

"Not until the cattle have their hay and cubes." Nick grabbed her arm to shepherd her off in the direction she had come. "My flock of sheep also need a few blocks of alfalfa and a few gallons of feed to get them through the day."

"Ah yes, how could I have forgotten. Feed the critters and starve the slave."

156

Falling into step, Amanda trailed Nick to the east side of the barn to cut the wires on the square bales of alfalfa and scoop up feed for the ewes that were huddled against the south wall of the barn, avoiding the brisk wind. The flock was surrounded by a snowdrift that resembled an igloo. When the sheep spotted Nick and Amanda, they bounded toward their feed, nearly knocking Amanda flat in the process. When she saw the ram trotting toward her, she darted behind Nick, using him as her shield. Nick and Atilla then had their customary battle to determine who was the Prince of the Barnyard before the ram turned his attention to the feed. Napoleon, the sheepdog, paid his respects to Nick and Amanda before moseying over to eat his fill.

Wishing she had a fuzzy wool coat to fend off the icy bite of the wind, Amanda climbed into the truck to warm herself in front of the heater. Nick backed toward a round hay bale and speared it with the protruding prong while Amanda thawed her frozen fingers.

An opened and shut gate later, Amanda was back in the pickup, clinging to her door handle while Nick plowed down the path to unload hay and string out sacks of cubes for the hungry livestock.

In contented silence, Amanda watched him send a spray of snow swirling around them as they headed for the house. With the last gate shut, Amanda had visions of scrambled eggs, toast and coffee dancing in her head . . . until she remembered there was no electricity. Chilled crackers were not her idea of morning brunch.

"Wait here."

Nick slid off the seat and bounded up the steps to disappear into the house. He returned several minutes later with a grocery sack of supplies. Without offering an explanation, he drove to the workshop and motioned for Amanda to follow him. He had built a fire in the wood-burning stove earlier that morning, and the tool-lined building radiated inviting warmth. Two lawn chairs sat beside the stove. Amanda couldn't wait to park herself in one of them.

Nick reached into his sack to retrieve an iron skillet. "Breakfast country-style," he announced.

"You do know how to impress a lady, don't you, Thorn? Gathering around the old campfire for breakfast. Why do I feel as if I have been catapulted back in time? It makes me want to burst into a chorus of 'Yippie Ti Yi Yo.' "

"Just hand me them there eggs an' ham, ma'am," he drawled.

Amanda returned his contagious grin and tossed ham in the skillet. "Thanks, Thorn."

He raised a curious brow. "For what?"

"In case I forget to tell you later, I'm having a good time. I feel as if you have put me in touch with Mother Nature and the traditions of the past. Going back to the earth has a way of cleansing the soul and keeping one's life in perspective."

"Hey, Hazard, don't go getting soft and mushy on me," Nick cautioned. "It's out of character for you, tough, hard-boiled career woman that you are."

"I won't have a career after William's murderer gets tired of these scare tactics and decides to rub me out."

Nick sighed heavily. "Do we have to spoil a good time with *that* subject?"

"I just want you to admit that I might be right. I think the strange occurrences at my house are linked to the fact that I saw the disappearing calf, and the person who kept moving the calf saw *me*."

Nick stirred the eggs. "Okay, Hazard. I think you could be right."

He had finally taken her seriously! Smiling triumphantly, Amanda placed bread slices on the barbecue forks Nick had brought along. Opening the stove, she held the bread over the logs until it was toasted on both sides.

Amanda ate as if she had been on prison rations for months. The food, cooked on the old stove, reminded her of vittles served at family picnics at which everyone ate twice their normal portions.

With a full stomach and thawed appendages, Amanda was ready to tackle another challenging task. "Now what, boss?" she drawled like any self-respecting cowpuncher. "You wanna wrestle a few steers or ride some wild bulls?"

The relaxed, lighthearted side of her personality was appealing—too appealing. Nick reminded himself once again that bringing Amanda home with him had not been a good idea. They had slept side by side, worked side by side and eaten side by side. Memories of Amanda were scattered all over his farm. In days to come, he would look at the gates, the barn and the pasture and see her standing by or in them. He would crawl into bed and feel her there beside him, just a forbidden touch away.

Nick was beginning to like this blue-eyed blond—a lot. But he didn't want to like her. It would have been simpler if he had been in it for the sex, which he wasn't getting. Now he and Amanda were more than casual acquaintances. They were almost friends.

She had stepped into his world, and he was a little too comfortable having her around. She adapted quickly to unfamiliar situations. She invited challenges that tested her abilities and broadened her horizons. A modern woman, Nick thought as he finished munching on his breakfast. Too much woman . . . for her own good and for his.

Nick shook himself loose from his meandering thoughts. "If we can make it to your house, I'll see what I can do about locating your most recent pest and removing it from the premises."

"Thanks, Thorn. I would appreciate that."

For a brief moment, Amanda battled the impulse to lean over and plant a kiss on his all too sensuous lips. But she was afraid she might get carried away. Kissing Nick was like opening a bag of potato chips; she knew she wouldn't be satisfied with just one. They could end up in the sack . . .

Amanda squelched that thought and gathered up the supplies. When they'd returned to the house, she marched off to make the beds. While she was bent over Nick's, she sensed a presence behind her. She turned to see him leaning against the doorjamb, studying her with a smoldering expression on his face. His expression wasn't the only thing smoldering, Amanda noted when her gaze drifted down his muscular physique.

She cleared her throat and cursed herself for doing it. This annoying nervous habit had to stop. "Thanks for putting me up for the night."

"Any time, Hazard. As a cop, it is my duty to serve."

"Is it also your duty to carry a concealed weapon at all times?" She stared at him with mock innocence, but when her eyes bounded off the zipper of his jeans an impish smile gave her away. "Strange place to be packing a pistol, Thorn."

"Damned uncomfortable too," he said dryly. "But I am learning to live with—out it."

When Nick turned and left, Amanda fluffed the pillows and tugged the patchwork quilt into place on the bed. She knew if she changed her mind about what *hadn't* happened last night, Nick would be ready and willing. But just as before, he had given her the option without pressing the issue.

"He's a nice man," she said to herself as she ambled toward the door. "Too bad you've turned into such a chicken."

"What was that?"

Amanda stopped dead in her tracks when she found Nick waiting in the hall. "I said . . . I have this sudden craving for chicken."

Nick smiled an ornery smile and fell into step behind her. "We just had breakfast."

"I'm hungry again."

His eyes dropped to the tantalizing curve of hips clad in trim-fitting jeans. "Me too. But not for chicken, *chicken.*"

Amanda pulled up short, causing Nick to backend her. Before she could scold him for eavesdropping on the conversation she'd had with herself, he nudged her along.

"Move it, Hazard. We have a war to wage against the unidentified monster that has invaded your walls."

"And then we are going to put our heads together and figure out who killed William Farley," Amanda said determinedly.

Fourteen

The roads between Nick's house and Amanda's were snow packed and slick. Amanda kept silent so Nick could devote his full attention to driving. Huge drifts had swirled around her battered pickup in the driveway. It looked as if she would spend the afternoon shoveling just to clear a path. Nothing like extreme physical exertion to wear a body out so a person didn't have to lie in bed at night, wrestling with disturbing thoughts.

Amanda unlocked the door and stepped inside to inhale a whiff of stale smoke. She had been too upset the previous night to determine what had been burned. Hopefully, it was nothing but trash. Yet, she had the uneasy feeling she knew what else lay at the bottom of the can. Amanda opened her briefcase. Sure enough, the Farley financial file was gone.

Clutching Nick's arm, Amanda herded him to the container and reached down to retrieve the large metal clip that once held the file together. "Do you think it the least bit suspicious that my accounting ledger, which held Farley Farm tax reports for the last five years climbed out of my briefcase and jumped into the trash can to be burned?"

Nick stared at the charred remains. "I hope you have an extra copy."

"Of course, I took the precaution of making one. If you recall, I've been suspicious for almost two weeks. I began to take precautions."

"In light of certain incidents, like this fire, it might be wise for you to take up residence elsewhere," he suggested.

"At a motel in the City, for instance?"

"That is one option," Nick agreed, still staring at the trash can. "There is another. We could make it look as if you are still in residence by leaving your vehicle parked in the drive at night, but you could remain under police protection without the knowledge of whoever has been harassing you."

"We'll wait and see what happens next," Amanda decided.

"One morning you might not wake up to see what happens next, Hazard. Desperate people resort to drastic means." His dark eyes locked with hers. "Of course, there are other risks to consider if I offer you protection."

"Like what, Thorn?"

"You know *like what*. The concealed weapon I'm packing in my blue jeans is cocked and loaded. You can't tell when it might accidentally go off."

On the wings of that blunt remark, Nick pivoted to inspect the rest of the house. He found two dead mice in the traps and heard muffled noises in the ceiling. Amanda was still in the kitchen, stuck on the *like what* and wondering how long it would be before she gathered the nerve to take another chance with a man. She was too immersed in thought to respond to the question Nick posed.

"I said . . . where is the entrance to the attic, Hazard?" he prompted in a much louder voice.

Amanda snapped out of her trance, led the way to the utility room and ascended the steps. The attic was colder than the ground level. Icy wind whistled through a broken window pane on the west side of the house, and a fluffy pile of snow stood on the planked floor.

Nick lifted the window to survey the roof. It would have been relatively easy to scale the supporting beam on the back porch and walk up to the attic window. With the glass broken, the window could have been unlocked. Replacing the glass would not deter whoever had sneaked into Amanda's home to badger her. She needed bars on every window and dead bolts on the doors. Or she should vacate the premises until the prowler could be apprehended.

"I know," Amanda murmured dispiritedly. "Staying here is dangerous. I can't keep him or the pests out."

"When we finish up here, gather up just enough clothing to last a couple of days. We want the house to look as if you are living here. Hang a damp towel over the shower rod and leave a few dishes by the sink. Whoever is stalking you is familiar with your habits. Don't deviate from them."

"I'll go gather some clothes," she said dully. "And I'll have to call Mother to tell her I won't be able to show up for Sunday dinner."

When she descended the steps, Nick expelled a muffled curse. He should have listened to Amanda in the beginning. Her protests about the disappearing calf and the soggy wallet had obviously not been the product of an overactive imagination. Chances were, whoever was responsible for William's death had seen her looking for the missing calf. The killer knew Amanda was suspicious and that she was searching for explanations.

Maybe the strange occurrences in her home had been meant to distract her. Or maybe they had been warnings meant to frighten her. But for certain, Amanda's stalker was becoming more insistent and more desperate.

Nick intended to thoroughly question Amanda when he had the chance. He wanted to know what she had found out, who she suspected and why. He also wanted to know about those three canceled checks that had alerted her to the possibility that William might have been killed to ensure his silence.

Nick had access to information which Amanda could spend weeks trying to acquire. His associates at OKC P.D. could open doors and files in the batting of an eyelash. He decided to request a week's vacation so he could devote all his time to this investigation. In the meantime, Amanda would live with him, without the knowledge of anyone in Vamoose.

The problem was, how the hell was he going to pretend that gorgeous blond wasn't under his roof every night? Nick wanted her somewhere else besides under his roof. He was too aware of her. He probably would have functioned far better if they had been as close as two people can get. But Ms. Cold Feet couldn't bring herself to trust him with more than just this investigation. She might have decided he was a "nice guy," but Nick still wasn't getting any satisfaction.

Maybe that was the crux of the problem, he thought to himself. He had been a little too nice to Amanda. She might do some chasing if he gave her the chance. Perhaps he should back off and see how well that strategy worked out.

"Not coming to dinner?" her mother yowled into the phone. "But your brother and his family are coming."

"The roads are hazardous, Mother."

"They aren't that bad over here. And your poor brother needs financial consultation. He'll be broke by summer."

Amanda made an awful face at the receiver, but she said politely, "Brad will be fine. There will be other Sunday dinners." If somebody didn't burn the house down while she slept.

Her mother cleared her throat. "Did you remember to pay your health insurance?"

Amanda strangled the receiver, imagining it to be her mother's neck. The woman was driving her batty.

"Amanda? Are you still there?"

"Yes . . . Unfortunately," she added under her breath.

"Well, if you can't make dinner today, we'll plan another get-together in two weeks. Surely the weather will have cleared up by then. Did you send those birthday cards yet?"

"They are in the mail."

"Good. And don't forget to buckle your seat belt. Goodbye, dear."

Amanda dropped the receiver and drew in a deep, cleansing breath. These phone calls always served to remind her of why she enjoyed her independence so. Her mother could smother her, even over the phone.

Frowning curiously, Amanda watched Nick amble out the door. With little more than a sideways glance, he informed her that he would be back later to pick her up. He had become distant and more businesslike all of a sudden. Amanda wondered at the change in his mood. She supposed she should be relieved. Too bad she wasn't. Damn the man, she didn't know what to do with him, other than the obvious, and she was still too much the coward for that.

Finding other activities to preoccupy her, Amanda packed some clothes in a suitcase and prepared to leave her home. She was about to lock the door behind her when the electrical power was restored. Lights flashed on and the heating system hummed into action. At least she wouldn't have to worry about bursting water pipes.

Amanda stepped outside to see snowflakes drifting on the breeze. Luckily, the precipitation had decreased considerably. The brunt of the storm had swept eastward, leaving the countryside blanketed in white. She had decided to follow Nick's suggestion and drive her truck to the Last Chance Cafe to grab a sandwich. The restaurant's backup generator permitted the proprietors to carry on business as usual.

With the drift cleared from behind her truck, Amanda rumbled off. The citizens of Vamoose who had dug out of snowbanks and ventured to town had one topic of conversation — the possibility Farley was murdered. Or, could it have been suicide? somebody asked. Amanda rejected that theory, insisting someone had reason to want William out of the way. Several customers at the restaurant reinforced her suspicions that Bill might be a prime suspect since he and his father had been in constant conflict.

Amanda was also reminded that Glenn Chambliss, Preston Banks and Frank Hermann had never had a kind word to say about William because they'd had so many clashes with him over the years. The speculation about who might have killed Farley was as varied as the individuals who voiced it. Amanda was becoming more confused by the minute. She had planted food for gossip, hoping to shed light on the issue. What she'd gotten instead was hearsay. Nick had warned her, but stubborn and determined as she was, she hadn't listened. All she had accomplished by her nosing about was to provoke the murderer. And if he or she retaliated, guess who would be the next target? She would!

Stupid move, Hazard, Amanda said to herself. Now the citizens of Vamoose were asking about her theories, wondering what had brought her to such shocking conclusions. Amanda did tell them of the vanishing calf, questioning whether the animal was actually one of William's herd. She also discussed the soggy wallet that had been found at the bottom of the stock tank. She did not mention the canceled checks that she suspected to be forgeries. Only Nick and Bill knew about them. Amanda planned to keep it that way.

For the most part, she had gained nothing but notoriety and the prospect of new clients. Everyone in Vamoose suddenly wanted her as an accountant. The acquisition of clients had not been her objective, nevertheless, she was continually asked to schedule appointments at her earliest convenience. At this rate, she would soon have to rent office space. Her home, which had been overrun by pests and darkened by smoke from the trash fire, would not be suitable for professional conferences. Amanda wouldn't miss trips to the City and battles with rush-hour traffic in the least. But if things didn't go well, she might not be around to counsel anybody. If she didn't watch her step, she could become a casualty of her own impatience.

After thirty minutes of heated discussion, Velma Hertzog, who was taking her customary afternoon coffee break, introduced a new topic of conversation. One of the local celebrities, Billie Jane Baxter, was reported to have been making plans to construct a new home in Vamoose. According to Velma, Billie Jane and her husband were looking for scenic acreage on which to build their house. It would be large enough to also accommodate the members of her country band. Billie Jane, it turned out, was a cousin of Emma Carter who owned the house Amanda rented. And Preston Banks, being a relative by marriage, had offered to sell some of his property to Billie Jane—for the right price, naturally. The acreage, according to Velma, was a very scenic plot of ground that overlooked the fertile farmland near the river.

How very convenient that Preston, who was trying to hold the wolf from the door, had this opportunity to decrease the size of his debt. As Velma had said a few days earlier, Preston had an uncanny knack of resolving his financial problems. The man was obviously as shrewd as William Farley, maybe more so. After all, Preston was still alive and kicking. William was not.

Just as Amanda rose to leave the cafe, Cecil Watts lumbered inside. "Saw your truck. Thought I'd tell you it may be even longer than I expected." Cecil never spoke in sentences with complete subjects and predicates.

"Luckily, I have an alternative mode of transportation."

Cecil nodded his shaggy brown head. "Gotta slip Glenn's farm truck in front of your job. Bankers want it running tip-top for the auction."

Amanda blinked. "They are selling Glenn's truck?"

"Borrowed to the eyeballs to buy it," Cecil confirmed before he turned on his heels and walked away.

Amanda followed Cecil out the door to see the

patrol car cruising past the cafe. Nick veered into the parking lot and rolled down the window.

"Good afternoon, Ms. Hazard."

My, aren't we formal all of a sudden, she thought. "Hello, Thorn."

"I thought I might grab a bite to eat before doing my evening chores."

Amanda waited until two customers filed past her. She assumed Nick was subtly indicating that he would pick her up before he completed his chores. With a casual wave and a smile, Amanda headed for her truck. She expected Nick to be peeved at her for mentioning the missing calf and the wallet while she was at the cafe. He did not agree with the way she had handled her private investigation. But now that he had dedicated himself to the case, perhaps they could proceed in a more professional manner. Amanda never claimed to be an authority on detective work. All she had to her credit were reruns of "Magnum, P.I."

When Amanda returned home, there was a crackling message on the answering machine from Janene Farley. She asked if Amanda could come to the clinic at two on Monday afternoon. There was a matter she wished to discuss. Aha! Perhaps Janene had gotten wind of Amanda's suspicions and was prepared to take her into her confidence. Amanda returned the call, hoping to set up an earlier appointment. No such luck. The phone rang ten times before she abandoned the attempt.

Immersed in thought, Amanda wandered into the kitchen and stopped short. The wooden frame for her college graduation portrait sat on the cabinet. Ashes from the picture filled the sink. Damn it, *he* had been here again!

Amanda darted up the steps to check the attic window. The cardboard Nick had taped over the hole in the pane lay on the floor. Was this actually the route her mysterious visitor had utilized to enter and exit from her house? Or was it a decoy? Perhaps her clever stalker had a key and had broken the upstairs window to throw her off the track.

Spewing curses, Amanda stalked outside to search for tracks in the snow. It was a complete waste of time. Drifting snow had concealed the intruder's footprints. Amanda knew he had been monitoring her activities and had entered the house after she and Nick had left. It was frustrating. She wanted this mystery solved — now.

Maybe she should march herself up to each probable suspect and point an accusing finger. Perhaps that would get immediate results. It would also endanger her life.

Maybe the direct approach wasn't such a hot idea.

Nick had several errands to attend before he picked up Amanda. His first order of business was to place a call to an old friend from OKC P.D. and ask for information. The second call he made was to the county sheriff's office to request time off. That accomplished, Nick drove to Farley Farm to put himself back in touch with the finding of William Farley's body draped over the stock tank.

That Amanda had imparted details concerning Farley's death to the public disturbed Nick. She had been, and still was, obsessed with the notion that the vanishing calf held a key that could unlock the mystery. Nick could not imagine what the calf had to do with anything. He had seen, and dealt with, his share of newborn calves. Amanda had not. But then, it was possible that his close association with livestock and farming put him at a disadvantage in this instance. He may have overlooked an important clue that Amanda had spotted.

Nick pulled into Farley's driveway, but he didn't bother to stop at the house since Bill's truck was nowhere to be seen. He simply plowed his way through the drifts to reach the scene of the accident. No one had bothered to chop ice on the stock tank during the power outage. The floating heater was just beginning to thaw the ice that encircled it. To accelerate the process, Nick unplugged the deicer and set it aside to hack a semi-circle of ice out of the tank. That accomplished, he hooked up the hose to run water into the tank. No one had bothered to replenish the water supply for the cattle, Nick noted. The tank looked as it if had the same amount of water as it had the day he'd found William floating in it.

The lack of attention to the needs of the livestock left Nick wondering who was in charge of overseeing William's cattle operation. Bill Farley obviously hadn't taken time to tend to the chores, and Janene wouldn't think of dirtying her hands with feeding and watering livestock. That left only Luke Princeton who had plenty to do to keep him busy at the clinic, plus the task of examining the cows for complications of calving. This chore, by all rights, should have fallen to Bill Farley. So where was he?

Nick glanced up to see the Farley cattle trotting toward him from the far end of the pasture. Sure as the dickens, they were thirsty and probably hungry. There was no wheat pasture available to appease their large appetites, and it did not look as if the herd had been fed hay or supplemental cubes since William had passed on.

Hurriedly, Nick scooped up the chunks of ice in the tank and tossed them aside. Before the cattle reached him, he replaced the floating heater and continued to fill the tank to capacity.

What the hell did Bill Farley think these animals were, camels? The entire herd stampeded up the hill and abruptly stopped to stare at Nick. Finally, one of its braver members took a few tentative steps forward. Nick backed off, knowing the cows and their calves were suspicious of his scent. They were familiar with William who was out among them daily, but they were leery of a stranger in their midst.

Even after Nick climbed into his pickup, the herd was still hesitant to approach. Although they had been deprived of water and appeared eager for it, they avoided the tank. Odd behavior, Nick thought as he surveyed the herd.

His gaze shifted from one cow to another. A wary frown plowed his brow when he noticed brands that did not match Farley's Flying F. True, the brands could have belonged to the original owners, and Farley had yet to make the change, just as Nick was waiting until spring to mark his herd. But it seemed highly suspicious that Rocking C and Lazy B brands were etched into some of the cows' shaggy coats. He was beginning to think Amanda might have stumbled onto something after all.

Nick shifted gears and headed toward the stack of round hay bales William had fenced off beside the pasture. Within a few minutes, he had stabbed a bale with his hay fork and hauled it back to the herd. The cattle practically knocked him down trying to eat while he cut the strings that held the prairie hay together. The herd had veered away from the stock tank, forgoing a drink to eat to their hearts' content. That further aroused Nick's curiosity. The cattle must have found a water supply elsewhere if they had no need of the tank.

Studying the obstacle course of snowdrifts, Nick navigated across the pasture to the creek. A quick inspection indicated the cattle had indeed broken through the ice to drink. Luckily, the stream wasn't deep enough to drown them. They had an alternative water source.

Since there was no pond in this particular pasture, William had not run the risk of losing cattle on this ice. He had, however, taken a chance on losing newborn calves in the creek. The wobbly calves could easily fall into the stream and drown before William came along to lend assistance . . .

That thought triggered speculation. What if William had found one of his calves stranded in the creek and struggled to retrieve it. The physical exertion of catching the calf and carrying it up the steep incline to safety could have caused the kind of stress and strain that initiated his heart attack. William could have made it as far as the stock tank and set the waterlogged calf down for its mother to tend. Then his heart might have given out on him. Or, the mother cow might have charged him, throwing him off balance. The blows combined with excessive physical strain could have resulted in his death. That could also explain how William's wallet had been jarred loose from his pocket.

The ailing calf could have struggled to its feet after Amanda had erroneously pronounced it dead. That would also explain why the cow and calf in question had sought shelter from the cold in the grove of willows before wandering down to the creek. Perhaps it was there that the calf had actually died. Someone had later removed the carcass and inadvertently drawn Amanda's suspicion.

Nick was convinced William's death was accidental. That approach was more logical than Amanda's conjecture of foul play. The strange occurrences in her home could have been coincidences in the beginning. After she started tossing her speculations all over town, ornery teenagers could have decided to play a few pranks on her. Or maybe someone actually wanted gossip about William's death to spread. Now who would gain from such mischief?

Damned if he knew. But at least he had a countertheory that supported what he had believed to be true all along: William Farley had died of a heart attack. Amanda's overactive imagination was responsible for spreading rumor and complicating the incident.

Although Nick had explained the incidents that led to William's death, he could not account for the cows in the herd that carried Preston Banks's and Glenn Chambliss's brands. The theory he had devised was almost too convenient. It explained all the clues . . . save one. William Farley had been keeping some of his neighbors' cattle with his herd. Why? Was it only because the bad fences between Farley's land and his neighbors had allowed the cows to wander away from their home pastures?

"Good question, Thorn. Too bad you don't have an answer." Nick shifted his truck into low gear to plow through a drift and aimed himself toward town. It was time to pick up Amanda. He would see if his theory made sense to her. If nothing else, debating with her would keep his mind off the personal issues that sizzled between them.

Fifteen

"That is the most ridiculous malarkey I have ever heard," Amanda declared after Nick recited his explanation of William's death.

"It is every bit as logical as your speculation," Nick defended.

"You can talk 'til the cows come home but you cannot convince me that William Farley wasn't murdered," Amanda said stubbornly.

He handed her a cup of coffee that was doctored with enough cream and sugar to pass for café au lait and sank down beside her on the sofa. "William overexerted himself and died of a heart attack. That is my deduction, and I am sticking with it."

"Then how do you explain the missing checks I suspected to be forgeries of William's signature? We are speaking of thousands of dollars, Thorn. We are also talking about fraud. And why would this mischievous prankster—the one you have conveniently concocted—rummage through my briefcase?"

Amanda flung up a hand to forestall Nick before he said what she knew he intended to say. "I will admit I should have kept the briefcase under lock and key. But why would this prankster specifically burn the Farley Farm account?"

"To keep you hot on the trail of a murderer who does not exist," Nick said, as if that explained everything. Of course, it did not, not to Amanda's satisfaction.

"Your theory veers off at the same place mine does, but yours goes in the wrong direction," Amanda contended.

"Oh? And where's that, Hazard?" Nick took a sip of steaming coffee, propped his feet up and prepared for a lively argument with Ms. I'm-always-right-and-everybody-else-is-wrong Hazard.

"Starting with the dead calf."

"It was not dead—yet," he qualified.

"Damn it, Thorn. I know dead when I see it!" Her voice bounced off the living room walls to come at Nick from all directions.

"You many know *dying* when you see it, but you don't always recognize *dead*. I've been around livestock all my life. I have walked up on cattle, horses, sheep and hogs that lay like corpses—sound asleep, oblivious to the world. Until you give them a nudge, they don't respond. Now, if the aforementioned calf did spend several fretful hours trying to climb up the slippery creek bank, it could have been near exhaustion and close to death because of prolonged exposure to frigid water, not to mention overwhelming fright. The animal was not likely to get up until its mother urged it to its feet and led it to the protection of the willow grove and, later, to the creek where it finally breathed its last breath and tumbled back into the icy creek."

"And you mock *my* active imagination?" Amanda expelled a caustic sniff. "You really should write fiction, Thorn."

"Think so, Hazard? Come with me."

Nick set his coffee aside, grasped Amanda's hand and hauled her toward the door. Bundled up for an outdoor excursion, they then walked down to the barn to check on the calf they had delivered early that morning. The mother cow had abandoned it to munch on a block of hay that Nick had tossed to her after completing the rest of his evening chores. The newborn lay so still that not even a muscle twitched as Nick and Amanda approached.

"Without touching him, tell me if he is dead or sleeping," Nick requested. "And don't walk any closer to him than you did to the calf you saw beside William's stock tank."

In the shadows, Amanda could not determine whether the creature was breathing. If it was, it was taking shallow breaths. Neither the sound of Nick's voice nor their approach had disturbed the calf.

"At the moment, you are cool, calm and rational," Nick went on to say. "The day you found William I doubt your emotions were under perfect control. Then, you were frantic and upset, having come upon your first corpse — and hopefully your last."

Even after Nick's colloquy, the calf didn't twitch its ears or stir. He ambled over and squatted on his haunches. "Hey, little fella." He stroked the calf's head until it came to its senses and struggled to its knees. After the calf wobbled over to its mother, Nick sent Amanda a gloating glance. "It would not be unusual for a seemingly dead calf to perform a vanishing act if it were alive but groggy from exhaustion and exposure."

"You think you have it all figured out, don't you, Thorn?" Amanda wheeled around and stomped toward the house.

She was not prepared to accept Nick's explanation, though he had an infuriating way of making his theory sound logical. To her way of thinking, there were still too many unanswered questions to consider.

"I know William was upset when he called me the night before he collapsed," Amanda threw over her shoulder before partially leaping over a snowdrift. "He was practically yelling over the phone in his frustration."

"Another reason for his collapse — emotional stress," Nick surmised. "That, compounded with physical exertion could have done him in."

"What about the forged checks?"

Alleged forgeries," he corrected. "Those might have been William's signatures. You have no proof, only conjecture to support the theory you've concocted."

"Hell and damnation, Thorn, you cannot discredit everything I say. I know damned good and well that William was murdered, and I intend to prove it!"

Nick bit back a grin when Amanda's temper flared, and her favorite curse word exploded from her lips.

"Okay, Hazard, don't get your dander up. You might give yourself a heart attack like William did. I already signed up for a week's vacation to investigate the case. I'll see what I can find out about Chambliss, Banks and Bill and Janene Farley."

"And don't forget Frank Hermann," Amanda insisted. "I almost forgot about him myself. He and William butted heads a few times too. William died owing Frank money for damages to a grain truck and for a load of wheat seed."

Nick nodded agreeably and then stipulated, "But at the end of one week, this investigation will be closed. If I am right, I expect your apology."

"If you're right — and I am not yet prepared to agree that you are — you'll have my apology for having caused you so much trouble. And if I'm right, we'll . . ."

For one outrageous moment Amanda had the urge to attach a rider to their bargain. It was a fleeting but very distressing thought that had nothing to do with detection and everything to do with naked bodies lying on patchwork quilts. Yikes! Her mind was beginning to listen to the demands of her deprived body.

Two black brows jackknifed and a scampish grin tugged at the corners of his mouth. "If you're right, we'll *what*, Hazard?" When she refused to meet his stare, Nick clucked his tongue. "Are you suggesting a bribe? And to a police officer, of all people? Shame on you. What happened to that strong sense of integrity you claim to possess?"

Amanda gathered her composure, lifted her chin and inhaled a breath of cold air. There was no sense in denying what Nick had figured out, but she could paraphrase his conclusion to save face.

"It wasn't a bribe, Thorn," she clarified. "It was to be a celebration of the truth of my theory. And anyway, you would have been out of uniform and off duty at the time the deed was to be done."

Nick was getting aroused just thinking about such things. And he had a fierce urge to pursue Amanda's clues and prove her right, for his own personal benefit. Of course, if he conducted his investigation with a closed mind, he would likely conclude what *he* thought to be true.

That's it, Thorn. Keep rationalizing until you talk yourself into a biased opinion that will get you where you have wanted to be for a week—in her bed, or yours. Let's face it, you don't care which.

Amanda left Nick standing on the porch, lost in thought. She peeled off coat and boots and aimed herself toward a waiting cup of coffee. After taking a few sips to warm her insides, she glanced up at Nick who was shrugging off his coveralls.

"Mind if I use your phone?"

"Be my guest."

Amanda called the vet clinic to contact Janene. She didn't want to wait until Monday to hear what the woman had to say. Hopefully the phone call would obviate the visit.

This time, Janene answered the phone. She sounded out of breath.

"This is Amanda Hazard. Are you all right, Janene?"

Not answering Amanda's question, Janene gushed, "I heard the latest gossip, and I want you to know I am not surprised by it. In fact, I have been suspicious since the incident. I moved out of the house for my own protection and to put an end to my disastrous marriage."

Once Janene opened up, it would take a cork to stop her. Breathless as she sounded, Amanda wondered if the woman was afraid for her life.

"I couldn't contact Bill immediately after William died because he was in Oklahoma City instead of Denver," Janene continued in a rush. "I called a mutual friend who'd been at the convention, and he told me Bill had left town early. Bill has a girlfriend in the City. He's been involved with her for quite some time now, and I was tired of his deceit."

Aha! Bill had had quarters from which he could get to and from the scene of murder. Since Bill had not checked into a motel, he would be difficult to track down. But he had had ample opportunity to drive to the ranch and dispose of his father. He could have come and gone without alerting anyone. How he had disposed of William was still a mystery to Amanda. But there was motive and opportunity.

181

Who better to forge William's checks than his son? And who would suspect anything out of the ordinary when they were written for cash at a bank where the family conducted most of its business?

"Besides that, I have been experiencing odd happenings," Janene confessed. "At first I thought nothing of them, but lately . . ."

"What kind of incidents?" Amanda prodded.

"Stacks of papers I specifically remember placing in one location have turned up in another. I suddenly found myself dealing with faulty brakes, though they'd been functioning quite well. I have received phone calls in which I hear nothing but breathing before the line goes dead."

Amanda gulped hard. The incidents had an unnervingly familiar ring. Whoever had been badgering Amanda was also harassing Janene. Since Amanda had told no one but Nick about the odd occurrences in her home, she knew Janene was voicing legitimate complaints. Did the woman have reason to believe Bill had been tormenting her?

Farley was now a prime suspect. He possessed both motive and opportunity. Amanda had an urge to confront him. After she hung up, she pivoted to find Nick looming over her.

"What was that all about?"

"Nothing much."

His dark eyes narrowed, and his thick brows formed a single line across his forehead. "Level with me, Hazard. We are supposed to be in this together. I represent law and order in Vamoose. If you have new evidence, I expect you to share it with me. This isn't a contest, you know."

Amanda relented. He was right, of course. She was withholding information. She simply wasn't accustomed to open relationships with males, not

182

since her divorce. It was second nature for her to keep her own counsel.

"Janene informed me that Bill was staying with his girlfriend in the City when William died. He was not in Denver as he would have the rest of us believe."

"Girlfriend?" Nick blinked, stunned.

"It happens," Amanda assured him in a bitter tone. "I ought to know. According to Janene, the affair was one of the reasons she demanded a divorce. She didn't say how long she had been aware of Bill's infidelity, but she must have known about it for a while if she'd finally reached him at his lover's home."

"Bill . . . a girlfriend?" Nick shook his head, still attempting to accept the fact.

"And that is why a woman can never trust a man," Amanda said, her cynicism rising to the surface.

"Now hold it, Hazard. You can't judge all males by one or two oversexed men," Nick objected.

"One or two?" Amanda smirked. "Check the divorce rate, Thorn. You can blame half the divorces on 'another man' or 'another woman.' William did not approve of Janene, but I doubt he would have tolerated his son's fooling around while he was married."

"And why would that disturb William? I'm sure you've heard the rumors that he slept with Rose Chambliss and her sister Violet Banks for years. Why would he condemn his son for doing what he did himself?"

"Because William Farley considered himself a demigod," Amanda replied. "He played by his own set of rules. Those rules did not apply to those who were less than divine. William expected his son to make no mistakes, to set a shining example. You know the old cliché: Do as I say, not as I do."

"I thought so."

Amanda frowned, befuddled. "You thought *what* so?"

"You have finally resorted to grasping at straws to support your flimsy theory."

"I most certainly have not! More than likely, William discovered the truth about the affair and decided to force Bill into walking the straight and narrow. Maybe that was why William was upset when I talked to him, demanding that we switch the joint accounts. Perhaps that was why he ended up dead."

"God, here we go again!" Nick released a long-suffering sigh. "My first mistake was listening to you when you linked unrelated incidents together in the hope of supporting the theories you have been spinning like a spider. You'll have me so confused that I won't be able to sort anything out."

Amanda marched toward the door. "Fine, you stay here and be confused. I'm going to see Bill Farley."

Apparently, Nick planned to accompany her, confused or not. He beat her to the other side of the room and did not even show her the courtesy of holding the door for her. Equal rights, Amanda reminded herself. Nick had opened the door, so it was her job to shut it.

Sixteen

"Let me handle the questioning, Hazard," Nick requested as they drove toward Bill Farley's home.

"Whatever you say."

Amanda sounded so pleasantly agreeable that Nick cast her a dubious glance. Since when did what he had to say make a damned bit of difference to Amanda Hazard?

"Quit looking at me like that. I said I would back off, and I will," Amanda promised.

"I'll have to see it to believe it."

To Nick's surprise, Amanda behaved admirably while he questioned Bill Farley about his whereabouts on the day of William's death. She simply sat beside Nick on the couch, absorbing information like a sponge. Bill, on the other hand, was squirming.

"What are you insinuating, Thorn?" he demanded after the fifth question.

Nick stared at him in a calm, deliberate manner. "I have reason to suspect that your father was the victim of foul play."

"Foul play?" Bill hooted. "The man had a bad ticker. He'd had it for years. Everybody knew that."

"That made his demise all the easier to arrange," Nick reasoned.

"And you think I did it?" Bill took a hefty swallow of his drink and burst out with, "I did nothing of the kind!"

Amanda wondered if the guilty ever admitted the truth without a painful twist of the arm or the advantage of plea bargaining. She also wondered what had happened to Bill's charming veneer. He definitely had a dual personality, a part of which he kept carefully concealed behind a smile.

"I would like to have the name of the woman you've been seeing in the City so I can verify your whereabouts on the day William died," Nick requested.

Bill's glass tumbled from his hand. He caught it, but not before the drink splattered on the crotch of his jeans. Wide-eyed, he stared at Nick and then at Amanda, who was making an extraordinary effort to keep her mouth shut. That was no small feat, for she was anxious to pose a half-dozen questions of her own.

"Her name is Beth Liken," Bill reluctantly admitted. "She can attest to the fact that we were together."

I'm sure she can, thought Amanda. But would Beth be stating the truth or supplying an alibi for her lover? That was the real question. And Bill was not under oath, Amanda reminded herself. There was no guarantee that he was telling Nick the truth. He could have been mixing fact with lies to protect himself.

"Beth picked me up at the airport when I flew in from Denver. We had a meal and took in a movie that night, and she accompanied me on my errands the following morning."

"What kind of errands?" Nick quizzed.

"Not the kind you think!" Bill blared defensively.

"What do you think I think?"

186

Nick was good at this interrogation business, Amanda thought. He remained calm and emotionally detached, while Bill became more flustered by the minute. No doubt, harsh accusations might send a criminal off the deep end, but Nick was doing a splendid job. Amanda was glad she had let him conduct this facet of the investigation.

She and Nick would make a superb team. She was persistent in digging up clues, and he interrogated suspects with practiced ease. Maybe she should give up accounting and go into investigative work. Hazard and Thorn, P.I.s.

While Amanda was getting carried away by her prognostications, Nick was concentrating on Bill's behavior and his responses.

"I think you think I found some way to murder my old man," Bill spouted. Then he slumped in his chair like a balloon out of air. "Sure, there were times I wished that son of a bitch was out of my life. He rode me hard from the time I was old enough to climb on a tractor and plow my way to hell and back. For years I listened to how the Farleys would own a spread comparable to the gigantic ranches of days gone by."

Bill ruefully shook his head. "The man lived in the past, eaten up with fantastic dreams. He didn't care about money or his family, only about building his empire. He wanted to own the land that joined his fences—in every direction, as far as the eye could see. When he bought another farm, there was always another piece of ground on the other side of that new fence. He wanted to develop a new crossbreed of cattle that the beef industry would rave about. He never had time for my mother or me, unless we accompanied him to check on his precious herds that were scattered all over the county. Only

Rob came close to meeting his expectations. Never me."

Bill swiveled his head to stare grimly at Nick. "You wonder why I was sick of farming and ranching and of him? Nothing I ever did pleased him. It was never enough, never what *he* wanted for me. And things got progressively worse after Robert died. It was as if he blamed me, felt I should have been the one to go instead of Rob. And from then on, Dad constantly threw Rob in my face, expecting me to measure up to his expectations as the heir to a cattle kingdom."

With shaky hands, Bill took a sip of his drink to lubricate his vocal chords. "My wife never suited Dad, and he let me know it often enough, believe you me. If Dad could have had his way, and he usually did, he would have picked out a wife for me and handed her over with his stamp of approval. I think that's one of the reasons I married Janene, just to piss him off. She couldn't have cared less about cattle and wheat. She has a soft spot in her heart for the horses her father raised, but she wouldn't go near a stall to do anything besides fetch a horse to ride. That was her image—rodeo queen."

Amanda forgot her promise to keep her trap shut. "How odd that Janene detests working around livestock while her brother has chosen a profession in veterinary medicine."

Nick shot her a silencing frown. Amanda smiled apologetically.

"Luke does enjoy working with animals," Bill agreed. "Janene likes following the rodeo circuit. She did a lot of that in her younger days. She attended all the parties with the contestants. That's where I met her the second time. The first was at her father's ranch where I conducted an auction."

It seemed to Amanda that she and Nick were doomed to be dragged through a chronicle of the Farleys' marriage. Bill was determined to get the frustration of his divorce off his chest. Maybe then they could proceed with this investigation.

"Janene and I were having trouble before Dad hired Luke as his private vet and set up the clinic," Bill elaborated. "But when Luke arrived on the scene, Janene started running to him after our spats. She spent her spare time with him. It was like old home week, and I was away on business too often. She started accusing me of fooling around while I was on the road, picking up women every chance I got. Then she stopped having anything to do with me when I was home, and I got lonely. I met Beth at a convention in the City, and we've been seeing each other ever since."

Oh sure, thought Amanda, blame your wife for your infidelity. Isn't that just like a man?

"Did William know about Beth?" Nick questioned, his dark eyes probing deeply to gauge Bill's reaction.

"He knew."

"And did he approve?"

"Dad never approved of anything I did, remember? My affair with Beth was no different. He ordered me to break if off. I refused."

Nick glanced at Amanda who wore a smug little smile. He remembered her fierce claim that William permitted flaws in his own character that he allowed in no one else, especially his last surviving son. Nick gritted his teeth when Amanda silently mouthed the words *I told you so*.

"Did you argue about Beth often?" Nick inquired, refusing to cast Ms. Know-it-all another glance. He hoped she gloated herself sick.

Even though Bill had been drinking, he obviously guessed where this line of questioning was leading. Amanda saw Bill's gaze shift back and forth as if he were a cornered cat searching for an escape route.

"We argued often enough and loud enough for Janene to overhear us. But if you think Dad threatened to disown me over it, you are wrong. He would never have done that, not at the risk of letting his precious cattle empire fall to someone who did not go by the name of Farley. I was to be stuck with my heritage, whether I wanted it or not—which I didn't and still don't. I don't like being tied down to morning and evening chores every day of my life. I lived that way until I graduated from high school, and it was enough."

Bill rose to fill his empty glass again. Amanda watched him like a hawk, wondering if he would shoot through the house, dart out the back door and make a fast getaway. She'd definitely been watching too many "Magnum, P.I." reruns. Bill poured his drink and plunked into his chair.

"If you are looking for a suspect in a murder that didn't happen, why not interrogate Glenn Chambliss or Preston Banks? Glenn pulled a gun on Dad a few years back and accused him of selling off two steers that had joined our herd. Preston also had heated words with him—and exchanged a few blows. None of them trusted each other. If a few head of cattle came up missing, they blamed each other's bad fences and selfish greed. And when somebody's bull broke through a fence to breed young heifers, botching up what was to be careful crossbreeding, tempers really flared.

"You could also question my future ex-wife," Bill suggested with a spiteful sneer. "She wanted to kill

Dad a few times herself. He ridiculed her lack of interest in the ranch and her penchant for fancy clothes. She glared daggers at him from across the dining-room table plenty of times."

Bill sloshed his drink around in the glass and took a swallow. "My father was not well liked in Vamoose. You know that, Nick. He would cheat a man out of a few dollars if he had the chance. The more money he made the more he wanted—so he could buy more land and cattle. The money he received for oil-production leases and royalties always went to expanding the ranch. He was so obsessed with doing that he ignored his family. He died doing what he loved, so let it be. I didn't kill him. No one did."

Nice speech, thought Amanda. Run the dead down while they're unable to defend themselves. So much for love of family and fond memories. There was not much grieving going on here. Bill Farley had years of resentment and bitterness built up against his father.

Here was the classic example of two men who could not see eye to eye, even when they lived in the same environment. One never wanted to leave his empire; the other couldn't wait to escape. Bill had chosen an area of the agricultural industry that would put distance between him and his domineering father. That he remained involved in livestock was his only concession; but his profession took him away from home as often as possible.

Amanda could identify with that. She couldn't wait to get away from her mother's overprotectiveness. The thought reminded her to call home. Her mother would become hysterical if she did not occasionally answer the phone.

Nick unfolded himself from the sofa, hoisting

191

Amanda up beside him. "I won't take up any more time, Bill, but I will be in touch."

Outside, sitting in the idling pickup, Amanda focused on Nick. "So, what do you think? Did he or didn't he do it?"

"This is a fact-finding mission, Hazard, not a court of law."

"Cut the detective jargon and answer me, Thorn," she demanded impatiently.

"Possibly. And then again, possibly not."

Amanda threw up her hands in resignation. "If you keep straddling the fence, you'll rip the seat of your pants."

"I suppose you're ready to slap on the cuffs and cart Bill to jail."

"He's a man. He fooled around on his wife, and he didn't get along well with his father."

"Christ! You're condemning him for all the wrong reasons."

"I am basing my decision on several facts." Amanda tilted her chin to that stubborn angle Nick could now easily recognize at a glance.

"Right. He is a man; therefore he's as guilty as original sin."

The pickup zoomed off, giving Amanda whiplash.

"You think I have a few hang-ups, don't you Thorn? And you think they are influencing my logic?"

"Your hang-ups are too numerous to mention and they do influence your ability to reason," came the decisive reply.

"I suppose you think I would be cured for life if we had sex." The presumption was delivered with a sarcastic sniff.

"First of all, we would not have sex. We would

192

make love, Hazard. And secondly, yes. I think it might cure what ails you."

"Don't start splitting hairs over terminology," Amanda snapped. "Fact is, you don't think I can make a reasonable judgment about Bill because he cheated on his wife, just like my ex cheated on me. You think I believe that if a man commits adultery he wouldn't bat an eyelash at committing murder."

"What if Janene was the one who cheated on Bill? Would you be so quick to accuse *her* of murder? You heard what Bill said. Janene didn't like William either. He ridiculed her constantly. Her brother became her salvation, enabling her to put some distance between herself and the two men she had grown *not* to like."

"No one with a pending divorce case has anything nice to say about his or her spouse," Amanda pointed out. "All we have is Bill's version of the problems between husband and wife. Naturally, he's going to blame their incompatibility on Janene."

"Well, you were quick to side with Janene when she suggested Bill might be involved," Nick parried, flinging her an accusing glance.

"That was different." Up went the stubborn chin.

"Right." Nick sighed audibly. "Janene is of the female persuasion. She is a woman; therefore she is innocent of all wrongdoing. Women have been persecuted and stifled for centuries. Ignored or sexually harassed. Abused, verbally and physically. And because they've suffered untold injuries they are innocent of instigating any and all crimes." Nick rolled his eyes and looked directly at Amanda. "Come on, Hazard. I know you are a staunch feminist, but surely you don't believe all that shit. If that were true, there wouldn't be a single female inmate in a penitentiary."

Amanda sat mulling over what Nick had said and then asked, "Am I that prejudiced?"

"If you've reached the point where you can ask yourself that question, I think you already know the answer."

Amanda's lips twitched. "Then maybe I do need a night of good sex to untangle all my hang-ups."

Now it was Nick's turn to grin. "You might view the world from a different angle if you woke up flat on your back," he agreed.

"I never did like looking up to a man."

The insinuations in this conversation were having a profound effect on Nick's anatomy. The picture conjured up by their remarks reminded him of a night when he had been very close to throwing caution to the wind and determining whether Amanda would yield to friendly persuasion. He had backed off without pressing her, however, and had been left to wonder if there had ever been a report of a man dying from sexual frustration. He didn't really want to be the first such casualty.

"I'm sorry you feel that way about looking up to a man, Hazard." Nick squeaked, silently cursing the fact that arousal had constricted his windpipe, among other things.

"Would you mind if I stopped by my house for a minute?" Amanda asked out of the blue. "I need to call Mother."

"You still have to get permission?" he razzed.

Amanda flung him a withering glance. "In case you didn't notice, I completely changed the subject. We are off the topic of sex. My overprotective mother calls at irregular intervals to check on her little girl who is living all alone. If I miss too many of her calls, Mother will have the Bureau of Missing Persons sending out search parties."

194

"I detect a hint of resentment, Hazard. Is it a motive for murder? You certainly tried and convicted Bill Farley fast enough for having similar feelings."

"All right, damn it, I admitted I have a few hang-ups that influence my judgment where men are concerned. But what about you, Thorn? Do you think I don't know why you're in my company? I'm single and old enough to know what is what. I may be chicken, but I am not stupid. You want S . . . E . . . X."

"I know how to spell it, Hazard. And I know how it's done. I'm just not getting any." Nick couldn't actually say why he was teasing her so unmercifully, other than that he enjoyed watching her simmer like Irish stew.

"You're probably thinking I'll give in, that I'll be unable to resist your overwhelming male magnetism and your charming bedside manner. Well, let me tell you something, Dr. Love, I have gotten very good at saying no!"

No kidding, thought Nick. He kept his mouth shut and let her rave since he was amusing himself at her expense.

"You never even asked if I *liked* you. And you never said anything about *liking* me. Oh no, men just want to hop in the sack and see how it goes from there. They form their conclusions not from the brain but from the breeches. That's why half of all marriages end in divorce. Relationships progress from primitive desire to a hop into bed and then to the splitting of sheets. With very little love, trust and devotion in between. I don't want to know how well I will like a man on his back if I don't appreciate him for all the right reasons while he's on his feet."

Nick expelled an incredulous whistle. "You have got some powerful views, lady."

"Think so?" Amanda countered. "If one out of ten men were castrated at birth, how many marriages would take place?"

Nick didn't reply. He was too busy bursting into laughter.

"Not many," Amanda went on. "The marriages that did take place would be based on friendship and companionship, and they would endure because sex, being the root of all evil, would not be involved."

"Jeezus! I can't believe I'm hearing this!"

"Have you ever been in love, Thorn?"

"Sure."

"In bed or out of it?"

"Both."

"At the same time?"

"Once."

"I rest my case."

"On what, in the name of heaven?" Nick was lost. Had he dozed off in the middle of the third degree Amanda had given him and failed to see some connection in the arguments she presented?

"You fell in love but for some reason it didn't work out to your satisfaction. Either you don't believe in forever, or the love of your life didn't believe in it. If I were guessing, I would say you fell hard. When your ladylove left you, you couldn't find anyone to compare so you never married. Nowadays, you want what you can get to appease your basic need. You aren't too concerned about the personality and problems attached to a feminine body because you don't intend to be around long enough to have to deal with them."

"She died, Hazard. Diana was the innocent victim of a drug dealer who was after me. He cut her down to have his perverted revenge. That was when I quit the City force and came back here."

The explanation took the wind out of Amanda's sails. "I'm sorry." Her voice was soft and sincere. "Maybe it would be best if you dropped me at the hospital to have both feet surgically removed from my mouth."

"First you better call your mother. She'll want to know when you are being scheduled for surgery."

Amanda sat quietly in the cab of the pickup, wishing she didn't have a mouth the size of the Grand Canyon.

Seventeen

Outrage exploded in a curse when Amanda walked onto the porch of her house to find the door standing wide open. Cushions from the sofa were strewn across the living-room floor. Broken glass was scattered in the kitchen. The latest assault on her house displayed a burst of someone's temper, a threatening act of violence. A further search of the ransacked house caused Amanda to shriek in disbelief, bringing Nick rushing into her bedroom.

Dried blood stained the sheets. The bedspread had been ripped to shreds.

"This time he came looking for you," Nick said grimly. "Your truck was parked outside when it happened."

Amanda felt herself shaking like a leaf in a cyclone, even while she willfully fought for control of her emotions. This investigation had been a challenging game of wits . . . until now. The earlier incidents had not been life-threatening. She was more convinced than ever that William's death had been the result of murder—a cleverly arranged murder.

It was as if Nick's mind was running on the same bleak track. "I'm convinced, Hazard. I don't want you out of my sight until this case is solved. Let's get the hell out of here."

"I h-have to call M-Mother," she stammered.

"Then do it from my—"

The scratching noise above their heads brought instant death to the conversation. Nick took off like a discharging bullet. Amanda was hot on his heels. The likelihood of her would-be assailant lurking in the attic sent a snake of fear slithering down her spine. She was frightened and yet determined to solve this frustrating mystery.

The instant they burst into the attic, boxes tumbled and the scraping sounds grew more frantic. The sounds that erupted were amplified in the darkness. When an unidentified shadow scurried through the dim shaft of light that beamed through the window, Amanda half collapsed against Nick's shoulder.

"A damned raccoon," Nick muttered. "That must have been what was making the racket in the walls and ceiling."

They watched the varmint scramble out the open window onto the roof.

Nick tested his footing with each step to prevent falling over unseen objects while venturing toward the far end of the attic. When he reached the window, he stacked two boxes in front of the broken pane.

In the distance the phone jingled, and Amanda scurried down the steps two at a time to answer the call. Nick followed protectively behind her.

"Amanda? Where have you been? I've tried to reach you for three days."

"Hello, Mother. Sorry, I have been busy."

"At twelve o'clock last night?" Her mother sounded skeptical.

"I had . . . a date."

"Oh? Who is he? Now you be careful, Amanda. You don't want to be keeping company with a man who is after your money. What does he do for a living?"

How does she know what I want? Amanda thought. She is simply telling me in that annoying way of hers what she wants.

"You are attractive, and you have a high-paying job. You don't want some deadbeat chasing after you, Amanda."

Amanda's mother had a loud voice. Nick could hear the questions and free advice being pumped out over the phone.

"He's no one special, Mother."

Nick sniffed, offended. "Thanks one helluva lot."

After a five-minute conversation in which "Mother" did the talking and Amanda did the listening, the receiver was dropped back into place with a thunk.

"Don't take it personally, Thorn. If I had mentioned your name and occupation, I would have been answering rapid-fire questions for a half-hour. Mother thinks I have yet to escape from Never-Never Land where children don't grow up to live their own lives."

The phone blared again.

"Mother must have forgotten part of her instructions," Amanda speculated, racing for the phone. "Hello?" Her greeting was met with silence. "Hello?"

Nick jerked the phone away to hear heavy breathing and what sounded like an inhuman growl. He slammed down the phone and switched on the answering machine. "Move it, Hazard. We're out of here."

When they reached Nick's farm, his phone was ringing. Nick snatched up it up, and Amanda could

200

hear a hysterical voice on the other end of the line.

"I'll be right there," Nick confirmed.

"Be right where?"

"That was Janene," Nick said on his way out the door. "Someone broke into the apartment while she was gone and ransacked her furniture."

Amanda slowed her step, several thoughts tumbling over in her mind. A shout from Nick prompted her to quicken her pace. Once in the truck, they skidded out of the driveway in second gear and shot off like a launched rocket.

Janene stood by a door that had been bashed in and left sagging on its hinges. Her mascara had run and now streaked her cheeks as she whirled to bring Nick's attention to the living area. Cushions were scattered on the floor, and broken dishes cluttered the kitchen. In between gulping sobs, Janene said she'd made a trip to the supermarket for supplies and had returned to find the place a shambles.

Amanda wandered down the hall and glanced into the bedroom. The bed was neatly made. No bloodstains, no shredded quilt. The damage had not been as extensive as in her home.

"Is anything missing?" Nick asked Janene.

"I . . . don't . . . know. I was too upset to check." Janene dabbed at her smeared mascara.

Nick followed customary procedure, checking the place. He hadn't expected to find much, and he was not disappointed. After offering Janene a few consoling platitudes, Nick paused to glance at Amanda, who wore a ponderous frown.

"Where is Luke?" he inquired of Janene.

"He went to the City this afternoon to restock his veterinary supplies. He was going to see a friend before coming home."

201

"Male or female?" Amanda asked.

"Female. I think my being here might be cramping my brother's style."

"If you would like me to help you straighten up the mess, I'll be glad to stay," Amanda volunteered.

"No, I can take care of it."

When Janene stared at Amanda, Amanda felt the need to console her. "I'm sure Officer Thorn will do all he can to make certain the culprit is apprehended," she said.

"I certainly hope the person responsible will pay for invading my privacy and wreaking havoc in my brother's home. And I don't like being the target of revenge, either," Janene burst out.

Amanda managed a meager smile and ambled toward the door, pausing automatically to replace a cushion in the nearby chair.

"You're awfully quiet, Hazard," Nick observed as he unfolded the sleeper sofa in his living room.

"I've been thinking."

"I thought I smelled wood burning."

The remark didn't faze Amanda. She was too distracted by disturbing thoughts to be teased into good humor.

"Hey. Are you okay?" Nick slid his arm around her waist, instinctively pulling her against him. He had been wanting to do that all day.

Amanda yielded to the tantalizing scent and protective warmth of muscled arms, though she knew she shouldn't have. Nick was too damned tempting, and although she claimed to have become an expert at saying no to reckless desire, she said yes to the tingling sensations that spilled over her like bubbly champagne.

202

Things could get out of hand now. Amanda had tried to convince herself for quite some time that this attraction was purely physical and some defect in her protective armor allowed forbidden sensations to filter through. But the truth was, it had progressed past the point of simple biological need. She liked Nick Thorn. He had a dry sense of humor and he was a dynamic individual. She especially liked that about him, even though the similarities in their personalities often caused them to clash. She appreciated a man who stood up to her.

Amanda was the first to admit that a soft-spoken, mild-mannered man could never be her match or capture her attention. She would walk all over a lesser man, just to prove she could. Even though she preferred to be in a dominant position, she enjoyed the challenge of a strong-willed man.

And what, Hazard, is the point of all this introspection and analysis? Amanda asked herself. Are you trying to rationalize yourself into Thorn's bed or away from it?

The bed . . . Amanda frowned against the collar of Nick's shirt, savoring the scent of him, the overwhelming temptation . . . The bed . . . Either . . . or . . . Fragments of half-forgotten memories shifted in her mind like the colored fragments in a kaleidoscope. The world kept slipping in and out of focus. It was as if the two halves of her brain were functioning separately, one part confounded by tantalizing sensations and the other hacking its way through a morass of troubled thoughts. Although everything felt right while she was in Nick's arms, something was wrong. Something . . .

"If you are going to retreat, Hazard, you'd better do it now," Nick advised in a husky voice. "I'm trying to give you the choice you always seem to want.

I've already made mine. I'm more than willing to enjoy the decision I've made . . ."

His moist breath caressed her cheek. His arm glided over her jeans-clad hips, settling her familiarly against the hard length of him. She could feel his heart beating in accelerated rhythm with hers.

Amanda felt like a chunk of butter melting in a heated skillet. Then desire pulsated through her, her body already far too aware of the man whose lean torso was pressed intimately against hers.

Her gaze lifted to focus on dark eyes that shone like obsidian and on incredibly long lashes. For a moment, thought faded and her attention drifted to his parted lips. Amanda vividly remembered the taste of them, the overpowering pleasure that had seeped into her the last time she'd surrendered to his gentle but soul-searing kiss. She expelled an enormous sigh, savoring the closeness, enjoying the feel of her fingers combing through his wavy hair.

She was tripping along the jagged edge of self-restraint, wondering how long it would be before she took the fall. The woman in her wanted to hold Nick until the intense pleasure ebbed. The leery cynic in her wanted to let go and back off to a safe distance. She lingered, letting her opposing emotions do battle while a fog of disjointed thoughts converged on her mind, frustrating her all the more.

Nick misinterpreted Amanda's silence for rejection, even though he sensed the vibrations that hummed through her body. His arms dropped away, and he turned his back on her to scoop up the bedding.

Stupid move, Thorn. Nick did not delude himself. He was pressing Amanda again to make a decision she obviously was not yet ready to make. Amanda

Hazard, strong-willed though she was, was very vulnerable at the moment. He knew she had been frightened by the ransacking of her home and the bloodstains on her bed, though she was too proud to allow herself to admit any such thing. He had taken advantage of her subdued mood, her need for compassion. He wasn't being fair to her or to himself—even if he had thumbed his nose at the noble malarkey his conscience had been dishing out. He had vowed that he wanted equal and willing participation by both parties or nothing at all. He really hated himself for making that vow.

"We skipped supper. Are you hungry, Hazard?" Nick pivoted around to find that Amanda had vanished into thin air. "Hazard?"

He heard water running in the bathroom. She was probably running a warm bath. He needed to dive headlong into a snowdrift. Why didn't he just chalk that gorgeous blond up as a lost cause? He obviously wanted her a lot more than she wanted him. He enjoyed spontaneity, and she had to have her life mapped out in alphabetical order. It would take more expertise than he possessed to crumble that woman's iron defenses. She didn't trust him, not enough to spend an entire night in his bed, or even a few hours, doing the kinds of things that . . .

Nick cut off the thought before his male hormones started rioting like French peasants storming the Bastille. Scowling, he snapped out the quilt and let it drift into place on the hideaway bed. Wheeling about, he then propelled his throbbing body into the kitchen to build a Dagwood sandwich. A pitiful way to appease the hunger that gnawed at him. Nevertheless, he ate ravenously.

It was late. He had a lot on his mind and a disturbing pressure building in the lower regions of his body. He would have to sleep on his back — again.

Without a glance at the bathroom door, Nick strode down the hall to his room and shed his clothes in frustrated jerks. Utilizing the shower that was situated beside his room, he stepped into cold water. He would have sworn that his body hissed, that steam rose from his skin as it would from molten steel plunged into ice.

Enjoying minimal relief, Nick grabbed a towel and wrapped it around his waist before padding across the room. He flicked on the television, made his customary search through the channels and then plunked down on the bed. He didn't know how long he lay there, seeing nothing but flashing colors, hearing the drone of voices. It seemed like a year. Half an hour was probably nearer the mark.

"Good night, Hazard."

No answer.

Nick thought he heard a motor running. He muted the sound on his television, only to hear the distant hum of the television in the front room. Curious, he got up and ambled down the hall. The hideaway bed he had unfolded for Amanda was unoccupied. A quick check in the kitchen indicated she hadn't bothered to eat.

He glanced at the counter, where he had laid the keys to his truck. *Gone? Damn!* He was halfway across the living room before he remembered he was wearing only a towel and a scowl. Reversing direction, he sought suitable clothing and cursed his missing house guest. Then he cursed himself for pressuring Amanda until she felt the need to run from him.

* * *

Amanda fully expected to catch hell from Nick for borrowing his truck and plowing off without announcing her destination. But she was driven by a curiosity so fierce it wouldn't leave her alone. The confrontation with Bill, the appearance of Janene's ransacked apartment disturbed her. Something wasn't quite right. She wasn't exactly certain what niggled her, but something damned sure did.

Let's face it, Hazard, her conscience taunted her. Curiosity wasn't the only motive that brought you out of a warm, cozy house on a chilly night like this. You were afraid to fight your own worst enemy — yourself.

"Okay, I'll admit it," she said, to the world at large and to her infuriating conscience in particular. "But damn it, I don't want to make the same mistake again. I thought my ex was everything I would ever want in a man. The last time I trusted my heart to lead the way, I turned out to be blind and senseless."

Discovering that Nick had been very much in love once had also contributed to Amanda's fear of walking where angels wouldn't go. What if the women Nick Thorn now took to bed were no more than substitutes for the woman he had lost? Ten to one, he had been on some kind guilt trip, holding himself personally responsible for his girlfriend's death. He probably closed his eyes and saw Diana when he held somebody else in his arms. Amanda had already been cheated on and lied to. She couldn't tolerate the thought of having Nick touch her and imagine himself with Diana.

"Damn, you can really pick 'em," she muttered as she bounced over the frozen ruts.

Why couldn't she have been attracted to a wealthy, studious-looking accountant like the one who worked at Nelson, Blake and Cosmos? Actually, John Proctor had about as much appeal for her as a moldy dish rag. The man was polite to a fault, soft-spoken and considerate. He was cultured, successful . . . and boring.

Amanda's breath gushed out as she took a bump, and she forced herself to concentrate on the ice-packed road that led to Farley Farm. She did not have the slightest idea what she could accomplish, but she was searching for something. Unfortunately, she wouldn't know what it was until she found it. Call it intuition. Call it instinct . . .

She could call it whatever she wanted, but Nick Thorn would call it crazy. He already thought she was a lunatic. For all she knew, he might be right.

Leaving Nick's truck parked halfway between Bill Farley's house and the vet clinic, Amanda stood in the middle of the road, glancing in one direction and then the other. Peeking in windows had never been her forte, but observing a murder suspect when he was unaware might reveal something sinister about his personality. You can always project an image to disguise your true nature, she reasoned. She had seen Bill Farley drop his personable facade once tonight. Should she try for twice?

She hiked off toward Farley's house. Golden light blazed from the front-room window, assuring her that he was still at home. Slipping around like a fleeting shadow, Amanda peered through the sheer drapes to see Bill propped in his recliner, drinking whiskey as if it were about to become unavailable.

He looked perfectly normal. *Right, Hazard. So did the recently apprehended serial killer at the top of the "Most Wanted" list.*

In meditative silence, Amanda watched Bill flip through every television channel. She sighed, marveling at the characteristics of modern man. Instead of settling on a movie filled with violence, fast-moving adventure and gunfire, Bill was watching reruns of Lawrence Welk. Was that the kind of show a murderer would watch? Amanda thought not. But then again, Bill was heavily intoxicated. Chances were he couldn't even see the TV, much less determine what was on this particular channel.

Amanda decided that whatever she thought she was looking for wasn't here. If Bill Farley was concerned about being taken into custody in connection with the death of his father, he didn't show it. She would have expected him to be cramming clothes into a suitcase and making flight connections to South America. Of course, that might have been phase two of Bill's plan. Phase one could have been getting rip-roaring drunk and stomping off to dispose of his estranged wife.

Careful not to slip on the ice, Amanda inched along the side of the house and jogged to the truck. This was probably a wild-goose chase. So far, the only purpose it had served was removing her from proximity to the man who had gotten under her skin.

"This is all your fault, Thorn," Amanda muttered. "I'm out here freezing my butt off because I can't trust myself if I'm alone with you!"

Eighteen

As the rear end of the patrol car zigzagged on the slick blacktop, Nick colorfully cursed Amanda for swiping his four-wheel-drive pickup. He ought to have her arrested for auto theft. He ought to strangle her, shoot or stab her. Maybe all of the above. Where the hell had she gone? Did she expect him to follow her? Probably not. Amanda Hazard expected nothing from men. And Nick didn't even know why he had gone looking for her. It had been an instinctive reaction. He'd been out the door and gone before he'd had the chance to ask himself why.

What was it with that woman? he asked himself irritably. She would make him as crazy as she was if he let her. But hell, now that he was dressed and out on the road, he might as well find her. Of course he had no idea what he would say if he caught up with her.

Nick thought it over and decided Amanda had probably returned to her home, despite its ransacked condition. When he arrived at her house, his pickup wasn't parked beside hers. But considering what had happened to her place, Nick wasn't leaving until he knew whether someone had intercepted Amanda, stolen his pickup and left her for dead.

After circling the house, pressing his face to every

window pane, he breathed a relieved sigh. Amanda was not lying inside in a pool of blood, a victim of the murderer he still wasn't thoroughly convinced existed.

Nick did suspect there was some sort of swindle going on around Vamoose. He wondered if the vandalism in Amanda's and Janene's homes had been done to divert attention. The brands Nick had seen on some of the cattle in William's pasture disturbed him to no end. Leading Amanda to believe a murder had been committed could have been a clever cover for other illegal activity. But whatever the case, someone was going to extremes to confuse issues and Nick couldn't figure out who or why.

Spinning about, he jumped back into the patrol car and swerved down the icy road, wondering where the devil that female cyclone could have gone. To compound his frustration, he saw Velma Hertzog's car, nose-down, in the ditch. Velma was standing beside the road, flapping her arms like a duck preparing for flight.

Nick pulled over and slid to a stop.

"I'm glad you happened along when you did." Velma plopped onto the passenger seat and massaged her frostbitten hands. "I ran out of coffee so I thought I'd drive down to the market before they closed." She paused to blow warm air on her fingertips. "You can see what happened." Smack, pop. "I hit a patch of ice and lost control. Wham! Next thing I knew I was tilted at a forty-five-degree angle, staring at a snowdrift."

"You weren't speeding were you, Velma?"

Velma stopped chomping on her gum and stared at Nick in pretended innocence. "Me? I should say not." When his dark eyes narrowed on her, Velma sighed. "Well, maybe just a little."

Nick switched on the two-way radio and called the dispatcher, requesting that Cecil Watts be contacted immediately. Along with his repair shop, Cecil operated a towing service. If Nick had been in his own truck, which Amanda had stolen, he could have pulled Velma out himself. Instead he had the squad car, and he hadn't taken the time to put on snow tires. So here he was, skidding all over the place. It was like driving on ice skates.

"Nick, would you mind taking me back to my house to get my heavy coat and gloves," Velma requested. "I don't want to freeze to death while I'm waiting for Cecil and his tow truck. You know what gear Cecil moves in. I might be standing out in the cold for an hour."

Nick made a U-turn and aimed the squad car toward Velma's house. It sat beside the garage that had been remodeled into a beauty shop.

"You come by any time, Nick, and I'll give you a free haircut for doing me this favor." Chomp, crack.

"Thanks." Nick tried to smile appreciatively. He failed.

"I've been collecting all sorts of new customers lately," Velma chattered between the snap, crackle and pop of her gum. "That nice accountant, Amanda Hazard, was in twice last week and scheduled another appointment for Monday. We've had the most interesting gab sessions."

Velma gave Nick one of her matchmaking smiles. It put creases in her double chin. "Amanda is single, you know. Maybe you ought to get to know her better. The two of you might hit it off."

Nick would have liked to *hit* Amanda for running *off*. Instead he said, "Yeah, maybe I should."

He applied the brakes and waited until Velma clambered out of the car before he let out a string

212

of curses. He had the inescapable feeling he knew why Amanda—Vamoose's self-proclaimed detective—had been frequenting the beauty shop. She had been collecting and planting gossip to aid in her investigation. Nick was prepared to bet his farm that Amanda had also made several more appearances than usual at the Last Chance Cafe to glean information. What a shrewd female she was. She must have spent a fortune on coffee, greasy hamburgers and hair spray.

Velma took up where she'd left off the second she plopped back onto the seat, bundled up like a polar bear. "Don't you think Amanda is attractive, Nick?"

"Yeah, real cute."

Nick was going to nail Amanda's cute butt to a tree when he caught up with her.

"And intelligent too." Snap, pop. "Everybody in Vamoose is talking about switching accountants. I guess you heard that Amanda suspects foul play in William's death. She did contact you about it, didn't she?"

"She did."

Velma sat on the edge of her seat, willing Nick to impart information that she could pass along the grapevine. No such luck. He only smiled.

"I guess you heard Glenn Chambliss is close to an emotional breakdown. The bankruptcy sale really has him worried. At least I assume that's what's responsible for his odd behavior. I haven't seen him for a few days, but the girls at the shop say he's been cussing everybody up one side and down the other without the slightest provocation." Crack, pop.

Could Glenn's black moods be attributed to facing financial ruin or to fear of being linked to

William's death? In the assaults on Amanda's and Janene's houses, Nick had detected a hint of desperation. Could Glenn have been responsible? And why were some of his cattle stashed in William's herd?

"Well, what do you know!" Velma crowed. "Cecil is already here! He's set a new record for speed and efficiency."

Nick was thankful to see the tow truck. He wanted Velma off his hands and Amanda Hazard in them.

Velma levered herself out of the patrol car and then poked her head back inside, smiling gratefully. "Thanks for the help. And don't forget what I said about that nice Amanda Hazard. Call her up sometime."

With the would-be matchmaker out of the way, Nick drove off, unsure of which direction to take to locate "that nice Amanda." Impulse urged him down the road on which Glenn Chambliss lived. Though he hoped Amanda had more sense than to approach each possible suspect without him, he decided that might not be the case. And if she wound up dead, he would never forgive himself, especially since he had the overwhelming urge to murder her for taking off in his truck.

Nick ground out several oaths when his headlights beamed on a battered pickup wrapped around a corner post at the side of the road. The vehicle was one of Glenn Chambliss's farm trucks, well used and pretty worn out. Having lost his new Ford pickup to the upcoming bankruptcy sale, Glenn had taken to cruising about in this battered vehicle with a hood that resembled an accordion.

Halting at the scene of the accident, Nick walked over a frozen snowdrift and opened the truck's door. Glenn was slumped over the wheel, snoring up a storm. The cab of the truck reeked of whiskey. Glenn had obviously tried to drown his troubles in a bottle and had passed out at the wheel. Well, that earned him a scholarship to driving school.

Nick grabbed Glenn by the nape of his coat and hauled him onto wobbly legs. Slurred fragments of sentences tumbled from Glenn's lips while Nick shepherded him toward the police car.

"Damned bankers," Glenn mumbled. "Takin' ever'thing I goddamn own. Farm prices gone to hell. Cattle industry slidin' down the tubes."

"I know, Glenn. It's rough all the way around. But you won't solve your problems in a bottle. You'll only complicate them. You know better than to be on the road while you're drinking," Nick lectured.

A lopsided smile twisted Glenn's swollen lip. "I wasn't on the damned road. I was in the damned ditch."

"And met a fence post head-on," Nick finished with a disapproving frown. "Do you want me to call Cecil to tow your truck home?"

"Can't do it myself anymore," Glenn muttered. "Damned bankers are takin' all my damned equipment."

Nick radioed the dispatcher to relay the message for Cecil to drive out after he had delivered Velma to her doorstep. He also requested that Benny Sykes drive out to Chambliss Ranch to write up a report on the accident, thereby freeing himself to track down Amanda. And Benny needed to learn the ropes. He was young and green, occasionally too enthusiastic when it came to doing his job. He would catch on, Nick assured himself. Age and experience cured many a fault.

After speaking with the dispatcher, Nick turned back to Glenn, who had propped himself against the door. "Why are your cattle mixed in with William Farley's herd?" he asked simply and directly.

"Shit . . ." Glenn glanced at Nick with bloodshot eyes.

"Shit's right," Nick grimly agreed. "Either you're trying to screw the bank out of what you owe them, or you made some underhanded deal with Farley. Which is it?"

Glenn squirmed and sobered up more than he would have liked to. "It's all that Hazard woman's fault." He scowled. "She started it with her talk of disappearing calves and murder. Everything was fine until she started nosing around."

Nick frowned warily. "What do you mean, Glenn?"

Glenn exhaled like a spewing geyser. "Preston and I made a deal with William so we could cut our herds in half before the assessor came to estimate our worth."

"In half?" Nick stared incredulously at the rancher who was now only two sheets to the wind. "Don't you think the bank will be more than a little suspicious when they discover the collateral diminished by half?"

"I already told 'em I lost several head of steers in frozen ponds and some of my cows to birthing difficulties. It happens, you know."

"And what did William Farley demand in return for stashing your cattle in his pastures all over the county?" Nick wanted to know.

Glenn rubbed his stubbled jaw and stared at his damaged truck that was spotlighted in the darkness.

"He wanted all the calves that his bull bred while our cows were running with his herds."

"Shrewd," Nick murmured.

"He always was a shrewd son-of-a-bitch." Glenn grunted sourly. "But Preston and I were over a barrel and we had to agree."

"Did William give either of you cash to help you get by?"

Nick wondered if the canceled checks Amanda questioned might have been written to William by Glenn and Preston as part of their arrangement.

"William hand out money?" Glenn snorted sarcastically. "What the hell do you think, Nick? William never so much as bought me a cup of coffee. He did, however, sometimes conveniently show up at my house at lunchtime. My wife would invite him to stay. That's the way William was. He had no qualms about taking what he could, but he never gave me a red cent for anything, not even the damages he owed when his cattle broke down the fence and feasted on my hay and wheat."

Nick had heard the rumors that William had paid a few house calls to Glenn's wife. From the sound of things, William was far more closely associated with Glenn's wife than with Glenn. Knowing that, Nick was hesitant to believe Glenn's testimony in its entirety. William might have died because of a vengeful, jealous husband, not because of his underhanded financial dealings. It happened, more times than Nick wanted to count.

Of course, Amanda would leap on that theory with both feet. Since she was suspicious of men in general, she would conclude that Glenn had as much motive as Bill Farley. According to her, every crime committed was the direct or indirect result of infidelity. She would have the cuffs on Glenn in nothing flat. Nick wondered if Amanda had discovered the relationship between William Farley and Glenn's wife. Probably, he decided. After all, Amanda had been spending plenty of time at Velma's Beauty Boutique, the mecca of gossip and the breeding ground of rumor.

Nick cast his musings aside and fastened a probing stare on Glenn. "Were you at William's ranch the morning he died?"

Glenn pushed away from the door against which he had been leaning and snapped to attention. "Now hold on, Nick. Don't go getting any crazy ideas that I had anything to do with this murder that was supposedly committed."

"It does make one wonder. Word is you're desperate and out of sorts—"

"You'd be out of sorts too if you stood to lose everything you had!" Glenn exploded. "But I didn't kill Farley. I would have liked to a few times, I'll admit, and for a few reasons you may not even know about. But I didn't do it."

Nick did know about those "few reasons." So did a lot of other people. That was the problem.

"Just calm down, Glenn. You aren't on trial here. I'm only trying to gain insight."

"I didn't do it!" Glenn loudly proclaimed.

Nick stared bleakly at him. "What about Preston?"

"Aw, come on, Nick. You've known Preston all your life, same as I have. He's a big blowhard, always bragging about how many head of cattle he runs, how many bushels to the acre he makes during wheat harvest. Hell, to hear him talk he's making money hand over fist. He may be a liar, but he wouldn't dispose of his neighbor just because he hated the son-of-a-bitch."

Nick glanced up when the headlights of an approaching vehicle flared in the darkness. Benny Sykes arrived to take command of the situation and deliver Glenn another lecture on the vices of drinking and driving. Leaving Benny to deal with Glenn in his characteristically overreactive manner, Nick circled back to his own house, hoping Amanda had returned. She hadn't, so he decided to check her house again. She had damned well better be there, or else . . . Or else he suspected she was in a lot of trouble.

Nineteen

Amanda vigorously rubbed her hands together and shivered against the icy bite of the wind. At this rate all she would likely gain for her efforts to crack this mysterious case was pneumonia. Inhaling deep breaths, she walked up the driveway toward the apartment behind the veterinary clinic. The battered door had been wedged shut and a dim light glowed through the curtained windows. The pickup that had once belonged to William Farley was parked beside Janene's dented car.

Inching closer, Amanda peered through the gaps between the curtains. The living room had been restored to order, and the television hummed, drowning out all other sound.

Amanda crept around to the kitchen window. Janene had cleaned up the broken dishes. But where, Amanda wondered, was she now? Had she met with another disaster?

A moment later Amanda discovered the answer to both questions. She stared idiotically through the bedroom window, refusing to trust her eyes. The scene before her contradicted everything she'd believed to be true. She blinked once, twice. Then her jaw sagged.

To her astonishment, Janene and Luke Princeton were in bed together—beneath the sheets, wrapped in

220

each other's arms. Amanda had heard that the brother and sister enjoyed a close relationship, but never had she expected them to be *this* close.

Not being prepared for the unexpected was Amanda's downfall. Stunned, she staggered back from the window, too engrossed in the shock of her sordid discovery to watch where she was going. She backed right into a frozen snowbank, was jolted off balance and landed with a thud and a yelp.

"Damn your big mouth," she muttered as she rolled onto her belly and tried to crawl away on hands and knees.

When Luke yanked back the curtain to investigate the source of the sound, shafts of light speared through the window. Amanda dived toward the shadows, hoping he hadn't seen her. But he had.

She scrabbled to her feet on the slippery snow and took off with more speed than caution. She cut a corner short, slipped and skidded into the side of the building. Then despite the pain in her skull, she put on a burst of speed and headed toward the pickup that waited a quarter of a mile down the road.

The pickup might as well have been five miles away for all the good it was doing Amanda. She heard Luke burst out the front door, cursing a blue streak, and knew she was running for her life.

The roar of an engine and the smell of burning rubber rushed toward her on a gust of wind. She glanced over her shoulder and her heart gave a frantic lurch. William's pickup was coming toward her—backward. Luke had lowered the hay fork. Like a spear, it was meant to run her through!

The instant before she was stabbed like a hay bale, Amanda leaped into the ditch. Her fall was cushioned by snow, but her heart was threatening to beat her to death before Luke could accomplish the deed himself.

She bolted back to her feet, but she was much too

slow. Luke flung open the pickup door and launched himself at her.

A pained groan gushed from her lips when he tackled her around the knees. She pitched forward, her face grinding into the frozen snow. Amanda sorely regretted never having taken instructions in self-defense. Before she could land a blow on Luke, he wrenched her arm up behind her back and jerked her to her feet.

Shoving her forward, he forced her to accompany him to the apartment. She tried to wrest free of his grasp, even at the risk of having her arm ripped from its socket. But Luke countered by grabbing a handful of her hair and yanking her against him so that her every movement produced pain.

Wild-eyed, Janene waited at the door. In her shaking hand was a pistol, which Luke grabbed and rammed against Amanda's ribs.

"Her!" Janene exclaimed. Her gaze bounded back and forth between the intruder and Luke. "*Now* what are we going to do?"

"What we should have done in the first place." Luke shepherded Amanda down the hall that joined the apartment to the clinic.

Amanda had found that "something" for which she had been searching when she'd ventured out on this fateful night. Disjointed thoughts and nagging suspicions had led her into trouble. She had sensed an inconsistency hours earlier when she'd seen the condition of this apartment and had spoken to Janene. Her house and Janene's living room had appeared similar in their disarray. That suggested the same person had broken into both places to scatter cushions and smash glass.

However, suspicions had floated around in Amanda's mind until they'd condensed like water vapor, dripping steadily into her thoughts. She had wondered why the bedroom of Luke's apartment had been left untouched while her bed had been ripped to shreds and coated with blood. Now she knew. No one would demolish a bed in which he intended to sleep.

Amanda had also been befuddled by the remark Janene had made earlier. *I don't like being the target of revenge, either.* It was the *either* that had been rattling around in Amanda's brain, clouding her thoughts with suspicion. Amanda had not mentioned to Janene that her rented home had also been a target. So Janene could not have known about the incident unless she'd been involved in it. Too bad Amanda hadn't figured that out hours ago. She wouldn't have been in such a tight scrape now.

Unless she was way off base, and she had the unshakable feeling she wasn't, the attack on the apartment had been a ploy to cast suspicion on Bill Farley. And Janene had lied once or twice about Luke's whereabouts. Luke had undoubtedly been in the bedroom the evening Amanda had come to speak with Janene. He was the man who had been helping Janene rest and recuperate after her accident, which obviously had nothing to do with faulty brakes but was due to Janene's lack of driving skill.

Although Amanda didn't have a clue as to how this brother and sister team had disposed of William Farley, she thought she knew *why*. Amanda would have dearly liked to know for certain the answer to both questions, and some others, before Luke did what they "should have done in the first place" — dispose of Amanda.

Now it was all beginning to make sense to Amanda. The burned-out light bulbs had been planted in her home while Luke was swiping the forged checks. And he had gathered a few nests of mice and rats from the farm, then relocated them in Amanda's house. Luke had burned the Farley accounts to cover up fraud. Everything he and Janene had done was part of a deliberate and clever attempt to cast suspicion away from themselves and on to Bill.

"William found out about the two of you, didn't he?" Amanda prodded, as Luke propelled her toward the cabinets that lined the west wall of the clinic. "That was why he sounded so upset when I spoke to him the night before he died. He felt angry and betrayed."

Janene knotted her fists in the dangling hem of her blouse and looked in every direction except at Amanda.

Amanda's creative imagination went to work, conjuring up the scenario that adequately explained the not-so-accidental accident. "Of course, I don't think William or Bill had the faintest idea that Janene had forged those three checks the two of you stole from my files. William never kept track of his money—"

Amanda flinched when Luke tied her wrists behind her with electrical wiring, cutting off the circulation. "Were the two of you stashing money in a mutual fund to feather your nest? Oh, and don't tell me, Janene, let me guess. Luke is your stepbrother, right? That's why there's no family resemblance."

Still no response. But Amanda wasn't discouraged. She kept putting two and two together, hoping Janene and Luke would eventually give themselves away.

"I doubt your family was pleased about your affair. That's probably why Janene married Bill. But with Bill away on business so often, it was a simple matter for the two of you to see each other. I'm sure Janene's 'meetings' in the City could be better described as rendezvous." She lifted a questioning brow. "Did the two of you have a favorite roadside motel or did you spread yourselves all over town?"

"We—"

"Hush up, Janene," Luke snapped. "Can't you see what she's trying to do?"

Amanda was disappointed that he had warned Janene, then clamped his lips shut, refusing to incriminate either of them. Janene, meanwhile, stood there in her fuzzy slippers, shivering and staring stupidly at Luke and then at Amanda. Janene, Amanda decided, did not have the sense God gave a goose.

When Luke wrapped another coil of electrical wire around Amanda's ankles, fragments of half-forgotten information floated to the top of her brain like cream on milk. She remembered seeing Luke repairing the electrical box after Janene had blown a circuit using some appliances. Somewhere along the way, he had acquired a basic knowledge of electricity.

"Did you work as an electrician in the summer when you were in high school or college, Luke?" Amanda questioned.

He smiled craftily. "Wouldn't you like to know?"

Amanda already thought she did. Men who knew nothing about electricity didn't usually have wiring tools for electrical work at their disposal.

Her speculations were confirmed when she glanced up and saw the object sitting on the top shelf of the cabinet. All the facts she had gathered on her never-ending quest for information gelled, providing the explanation for what had really happened the day William died. Of course, this recently acquired knowledge wouldn't do her a bit of good. She would go to her grave, having solved the mystery. Her hell would be that she'd had no opportunity to convey the information to anyone.

"You were with William the morning he died, weren't you, Luke? And you were still in the pasture when I arrived on the scene. That's why the dead calf kept vanishing and why you sabotaged my house with pests and light bulbs that refused to work. You knew I was suspicious, so you wanted to distract me, to discredit me."

Amanda pivoted to face Luke, who refused to admit to anything. "William picked you up that morning. He'd caught you with Janene the night before. What did he do? Threaten to have you blacklisted so you couldn't practice in any clinic in the country after he fired you?"

"Shut up." Luke scowled at her.

Shut up? Hardly! Amanda knew her minutes were numbered. She was going to ramble on as long as she could. It kept the fear of death at bay.

"You set the stage for William's 'accident' after he saw you and Janene in a compromising situation while Bill was gone on business. William probably reacted the same way I did. First he was shocked, and then he became spiteful and angry. While he was contemplating how he'd retaliate you were setting up your scheme. You knew William and his habits as well as anyone, because you worked with him on a daily basis. You devised the perfect murder for a rancher who methodically went about his chores, and who also had a history of heart trouble. If it weren't for that missing calf, I would never have figured out how you accomplished your dastardly deed—"

Amanda was shaken when Luke wrapped tape around the lower portion of her face. That put an end to her speculating—and to her keeping terror at bay. Luke Princeton was nobody's fool. He wasn't going to admit to anything, and he wasn't going to let Amanda say another word.

He tossed Amanda over his shoulder like a feed sack and carried her back to the apartment, to dress himself in warmer clothes that were more appropriate for the outing he had in mind.

Janene wrung her hands and scurried along in Luke's wake. "What are you going to do with her?"

"I'm taking her for a drive," he explained, shrugging on a flannel shirt. "On these hazardous roads, accidents can happen when you least expect them. You had a wreck just a few days ago yourself. No one will be suspicious when she meets with trouble."

Amanda wondered if Luke would pay close attention to details and remember to fasten her seat belt around her. Her mother would be highly suspicious if he didn't. She constantly reminded Amanda to buckle up. If Amanda hadn't "used" her seatbelt her mother would know something was rotten in Vamoose.

"What do you want me to do, Luke?" Janene questioned anxiously.

"I want you to follow me in William's truck. After I set the scene, we'll come back here together and act as if nothing has happened."

Janene vigorously nodded her head and shucked her fuzzy slippers.

Amanda smiled spitefully into the tape that sealed her lips shut. Luke would confront a stumbling block when he discovered that she was driving Nick Thorn's pickup rather than her own. Maybe that would throw Cool-Head Luke off balance and provide an opportunity for escape. Amanda reminded herself not to get her hopes up too high. Luke was clever—too clever and methodical to be rattled by small inconveniences.

She glanced up at the attractive, blond-haired vet who was built like a rodeo star. What a waste of good looks and intellect! His lust for his stepsister had led him into disaster. Here was yet another shining example that falling in love—or in lust, as was the case here—was the curse of one's life. Luke and Janene had doomed themselves by employing drastic measures to preserve their secret. They had also doomed Amanda. She, like William Farley, knew far more than the pair felt she should. And those who know too much rarely live to tell about it . . .

Twenty

Curses flew like snowflakes. Luke stopped the pickup in the middle of the road and glared at Amanda. "What are you doing with Nick's truck? Where is he?"

Amanda, of course, didn't reply. She couldn't. Her mouth was taped shut. Even if she had been physically able to respond, she would have remained silent. Luke hadn't answered her questions, and if he was wondering where Nick was, that might be useful.

Janene stared apprehensively at Luke. "Now what?"

"Dig in Amanda's pocket and find the keys. We'll take this truck back to her house and get her vehicle."

On back roads, Luke drove Nick's truck to Amanda's place and then deposited her in her own vehicle.

Janene was growing more concerned with each delay. "What if Nick gets suspicious?"

"We'll worry about that if it happens. Just follow me to the bridge. After Amanda winds up in the river, we'll figure out a way to make it look as if Bill's responsible."

Amanda silently decided it was too cold for a swim.

Nick pulled to a stop and stared, disbelieving, at

his truck which now sat in Amanda's driveway. Her jalopy was nowhere to be seen. What the sweet loving hell was that woman up to? Nick scowled irritably. He wished he had his keys so he could climb into his truck and roar off in pursuit. But he was stuck with the patrol car. Damn it, he had half a mind to throw up his hands in resignation and go home. But he couldn't shake the uneasy feeling that Amanda needed his assistance, whether she thought she did or not.

Luke eased the pickup off the gravel road onto the highway. Diligently he searched for a slick patch of ice that could be blamed for the accident Amanda was about to have. A devilish smile curved his lips when he found what he wanted. Fifty yards from the bridge was a stretch of glazed road. Shifting into low gear, Luke veered the truck off the pavement and down the sandy path weekend fishermen often took to try their luck at catching channel cat. Before reaching the steepest incline that plunged to the river, Luke halted. He reached over to rip the tape off Amanda's mouth, only to hear her opinion of his scheme.

"You won't get away with this." Though trite it seemed the appropriate thing to say.

Luke shrugged, unconcerned. His gaze was focused on the steering wheel. Before Amanda guessed his intention, he grabbed her by the hair and slammed her head against the wheel. The combination of superior strength and forceful impact caused excruciating pain to explode within her skull.

The world went black a split second later, and Amanda slumped into oblivion.

* * *

After Luke untied Amanda's hands and feet he shifted to the passenger side to guide the truck in the direction he wanted it to go. He then positioned Amanda behind the wheel. With the vehicle in gear, he stepped on the accelerator, and the truck bumped along down the hill, gathering momentum.

With the stage properly set, Luke flung open his door and leaped to safety. As he'd anticipated, the truck plowed through the underbrush and plunged into the icy river.

Wearing a triumphant smile, Luke jogged up the river bank toward the side road where Janene waited. By this time, she was so edgy she was about to chew her well-manicured fingernails.

"We have seen the last of Amanda Hazard," Luke said with absolute certainty.

Below, in the river, the old truck gurgled and hissed in the frigid water. Amanda lay with her nose mashed into the steering wheel, sinking . . .

Nick tensed when he saw an eerie light skim the river, casting incongruous shadows on the far bank. Either a UFO had landed on the ice or some unfortunate traveler had missed the bridge and plunged into the water.

He pulled onto the shoulder of the highway the instant he saw the thick patch of glazed road. He knew the patrol car could never make a return jaunt up the steep incline. He would have to walk down to check on the condition of the accident victim.

Quickly, Nick put in a call for Cecil, who had been having one helluva busy night, to report to the bridge. His second request was for his deputy's assistance.

With flashlight in hand, he started down the slope.

230

When he recognized the half-submerged truck and heard the rumbling muffler, Nick burst into speed. Bellowing Amanda's name at the top of his lungs, he slipped on the slick ruts left by the truck and skidded halfway down the hill. Regaining his feet, he raced ahead. Without breaking stride, he leaped into the bed of the truck that sat at a precarious angle in the river. Shielding his eyes and snatching up the tire iron, Nick smashed the rear window. Glass shattered and danced across the ice that rimmed the river.

Cursing a blue streak, Nick thrust his head inside the waterlogged cab to grab hold of Amanda. He knocked jagged bits of glass from the base of the window and dragged her backward, careful not to let her limp body scrape against the remaining chunks of glass that lined the frame.

"Damnfool female," Nick muttered as he lifted her into his arms.

The pickup sank another two feet. Nick slung Amanda's limp body over his shoulder and eased down from the truck. Adrenaline pumped through Nick's veins, leaving him oblivious to the stress of the extra weight on his shoulder and the chill of the night air. He headed for higher ground as fast as he could.

A whining siren and flashing lights drowned out his muffled curses as he dumped Amanda on the ground and leaned down to check her condition. She was frozen stiff but still breathing, he noted. The flashlight beamed down on her blue-tinged face.

A purple knot was swelling on Amanda's forehead, and Nick assumed what Luke Princeton wanted him to assume. She had been driving too fast, considering the hazardous road conditions. The truck had slid across the patch of ice and swerved toward the river. Amanda had struck her head when it plunged into

231

the river.

Footsteps pattered behind Nick, and he swiveled on his haunches to shout a command. "Call an ambulance, Benny."

"An ambulance. Right."

"Hurry it up! We've got an emergency here!" Nick grumbled at Benny's unconscious habit of repeating the last few fragments of conversation.

"Emergency. Right!" The patrolman-in-training turned around and dashed back in the direction he had come.

Cecil skidded down the incline to offer assistance. "Don't look good." Cecil spit an arc of tobacco and shook his shaggy head. "I'm feeling responsible. Tires needed replacing. Should have done the job on her car before I overhauled Glenn's truck. She should've been driving her own car."

Nick was shouldering part of the blame himself. If he had been a little less persistent Amanda would have been at his house, cuddled up under the quilts on his hideaway bed. He would still be doing without, but at least she wouldn't be lying here unconscious and frozen like an iceberg.

After what seemed like hours, the ambulance arrived on the scene. Amanda was loaded onto a stretcher and carted off. A sickening feeling gnawed at the pit of Nick's stomach while he watched the ambulance drive away in a flash of lights, the siren screaming. He was reminded of the night he had found Diana. The details were too gruesome to bear remembering. Damn Amanda Hazard for dredging up those tormenting memories.

Nick gave his deputy a brief account of what he assumed had happened and left the scene. He wanted to be at the hospital when Amanda regained consciousness. He was going to strangle her for scaring ten years off his life. He was also going to kick himself for getting mixed up with her. She was shattering his emotional tranquillity. And when she recovered—she had damn well better recover—he was going to steer clear of her forever.

Amanda Hazard was a woman who attracted trouble. She had the kind of curiosity that was responsible for the deaths of cats, and she was as independent as the American flag. Nick wished he had never met her.

"Right, Thorn," he said to himself. "And we grow younger."

Spotlights blared and then evaporated into darkness. The world shifted sideways. Voices echoed at the end of a winding tunnel. Amanda drew a shallow breath and shivered uncontrollably. Where the devil was she? In hell? Wasn't it supposed to be hot?

She licked her lips and fought her way through the cobwebs that cluttered her mind. When she finally remembered where she was, or rather where she thought she was, she lashed out, trying to claw her way out of the cab of the pickup. She gasped and shrieked when an unidentified object pinned her down, making it impossible to free herself.

"Easy, Hazard. You're just fine. Lie still."

Amanda relaxed and then pried open her eyes to find herself surrounded by darkness. A shadow moved closer, and the firm grasp on her shoulders lessened. A groan tumbled from her lips. She suddenly felt as if an axe was protruding from her skull.

"You scared the hell out of me, you know."

Vaguely, Amanda recognized Nick's voice, though

it seemed amplified due to the fierce pounding in her brain. His hand folded around her icy fingers, giving them a comforting squeeze. Or so she thought. Her appendages were too numb for her to be certain.

"I . . ." Amanda swallowed. Her vocal chords had frozen shut and her teeth were chattering to beat the band.

"Dr. Simms said you needed to rest. I just wanted you to know I was here. I'll be right here all night if you need anything. Do you want me to call your family?"

Family? What family? Did she have one? Fuzzy images swam through her mind. Oh yes, now she remembered. She did have a family, an overprotective one.

Amanda mustered the energy to give her throbbing head a negative shake. Her mother would have a fit of hysterics and would appear within hours, smothering Amanda with the kind of sympathy and concern she didn't need.

"L . . . uke . . ." Amanda gasped for breath. God, remaining conscious took more energy than she could generate. Valiantly, she struggled to name her assailant before she drifted back to that black abyss from whence she had come. "L . . . uke . . ."

"What?" Nick frowned, puzzled.

Lord have mercy, Dr. Simms must have been correct in his diagnosis. Apparently Amanda had suffered a concussion. She didn't seem to know where she was or to whom she was talking.

When Amanda's lashes fluttered against her pale cheeks and she succumbed to the prescribed medication, Nick sank into his chair. He stared pensively at her sleeping form. For the life of him he couldn't figure out what harebrained crusade Amanda had been pursuing in her effort to avoid him. She had sped off in his truck without one word of explanation. Where she had gone was anybody's guess. Only Hazard and the Lord knew for sure.

Why Amanda had switched trucks still had Nick baffled. She had taken his four-wheel-drive and then had climbed into that run-down rattletrap with four bald tires. Why would anyone of sound mind give up a three hundred and fifty horsepower engine and snow tires? It made no sense to Nick.

Exasperated, he slumped in his seat. This was not the way he had envisioned spending the evening. But then he should have anticipated something like this. It was his penance for hanging around with this wacky blond.

Nick wondered if he could persuade Dr. Simms to prescribe at least one week's bed rest for this particular patient. That should give him time to conduct a thorough investigation — without Amanda's assistance. It would also keep her off the road and out of rivers, and would save wear and tear on Nick's nerves. Amanda Hazard, with her wild escapades, had already put him through quite enough.

Twenty-one

Amanda woke with a start, but for her it was as if the past few hours had never existed. The medication she had been given left her oblivious to her conversation with Nick, still trapped in a nightmare, reliving that frantic split second when Luke had grabbed her head and shoved it toward the steering wheel. Overwhelmed by a sense of panic, Amanda thrashed beneath the blanket, imagining herself in a liquid hell.

"What the—?" Nick croaked when flailing appendages caught him on the side of the head. Before he could fully rouse from his catnap and get his bearings, a barely clad body surged off the bed and landed in his lap.

It was only then that he developed an appreciation for hospital gowns that open down the back. He had clamped hands on the quaking body sprawled on top of him, his fingertips making contact with smooth flesh—Amanda's well-shaped derriere to be specific.

Amanda's second shriek was muffled in the collar of Nick's shirt. Like an overturned beetle trying to upright itself, she struggled to determine which way was up. Where the blazes was she anyway? Where was the icy water and the looming death she had anticipated? And whose hands were molded to her skin as if they were part of her anatomy?

When Amanda's elbow accidentally connected with Nick's crotch, he let out a yelp. Other patients were now awake. And Nick's bark of pain was followed by the patter of footsteps.

Amanda turned her head toward the light in the hall, watching silhouettes gather in the doorway. She raked tangled strands of hair from her face to survey her surroundings. This wasn't heaven. It wasn't hell, either. It was a hospital, she finally realized.

"What happened?" one of the nurses questioned.

"I think she fell out of bed," Nick replied, arranging Amanda more comfortably on his lap.

Amanda glanced down at him before swiveling her head around to see his hands resting familiarly on her exposed fanny. Before she could slap them away and pull her gaping gown back into decency, a host of nurses descended on her. She was hoisted off Nick and planted on the bed, where she lay like a model patient until the nurses departed. Then she threw her bare legs over the edge of the bed and stood up.

"Where do you think you're going, Hazard?"

"I don't think; I know, Thorn."

"Get back in bed. Doctor's orders."

If Nick expected silent obedience, he was disappointed. Amanda felt her way around the cot toward the closet. She had just grabbed hold of her clothes when Nick latched onto her arm.

"Damn it, Hazard, give your guardian angels a break, will you? They're already working overtime."

"They'll have to clock in again, Thorn. We have a murderer to arrest."

Nick decided that she was not in proper command of her mental faculties. "Why don't you lie down and we'll talk about it?"

"Don't patronize me. I know where I am and what I'm doing."

"You've had a rough night. In case you've already forgotten, your truck slid off the road and nose-dived into the river. I saved your life."

"Thank you kindly for the assistance."

"You're welcome."

Amanda grumbled at the soggy condition of her clothes. She had wanted to wear something more stylish than a hospital gown when she apprehended William Farley's killer. But if she had to walk out of here in a blanket, she would!

When she wormed loose to propel herself toward the bed, Nick breathed a relieved sigh. It was short-lived. Amanda scooped up the blanket without breaking stride and headed toward the door. Scowling, Nick darted after her, clamped a hand on her arm and halted her in her tracks.

"Either you get back in bed and stay there or I'll have you restrained," he threatened.

"I am perfectly fine, Thorn."

"Oh really? Dr. Simms suspected a mild concussion. How many fingers am I holding up?"

"None. That's your thumb, and if you don't let me go, I'll tell you where you can stick that thumb of yours. For your information, I did *not* lose control of my truck and plunge into the river."

"Funny thing, that's where I found you. You're sick. Go lie down."

Amanda expelled a frustrated breath, unclamped Nick's fingers from her forearm and explained,

"The so-called accident was Luke Princeton's doing. He staged a second murder, but luckily I didn't stay dead."

"What?"

Even in the shadowed room Amanda could see the enlarged whites of Nick's eyes.

"Something Janene said kept bothering me. That's why I left your house."

When Nick's dark eyes narrowed, silently accusing her of lying about the real reason she had abandoned him, she shrugged evasively.

"Well, that was part of the reason I left," she amended. "I was instinctively drawn to Farley Farm and the vet clinic. You will never guess what I found when I got there."

Now that she had distracted Nick with the telling of the story, Amanda wrapped the blanket around her like a toga and stuffed her feet into her boots. "Guess who I found in bed together?"

"Certainly not us," Nick grunted sarcastically.

The comment did not go unnoticed, but she didn't respond to it. "Janene and Luke."

"What!" he yelled.

"That's what I said when I peered into the bedroom window and saw them snuggled up like two bugs in a rug. Unfortunately, I made too much racket trying to make my getaway. Luke tried to run me through with the hay fork on William's pickup, and then he tackled me in a ditch."

Nick sank down on the edge of the bed, thinking he might fall down. "Janene and Luke?"

"Ever heard of brotherly love, Thorn?" Amanda asked dryly. "Luke is carrying that phrase to the extreme. Fact is, Luke and Janene are stepbrother and sister. William must have caught them together, just as I did. He didn't live long enough to

239

expose them, and I wasn't supposed to survive my swim. Luke tied me up and purposely drove my truck off the road. He knocked my head against the steering wheel, and that's the last thing I remember."

Amanda didn't wait for Nick to recover from his shock. She was out the door and gone, knowing he would catch up with her when he had absorbed the hasty explanation she'd tossed at him.

"I'll handle this," Nick declared, having caught up to her with long, hurried strides. "You go back to bed."

"Oh no you don't, Thorn," Amanda protested. "I'm going along." Up went the stubborn chin.

Nick glared at her. Not to be outdone, she glared right back—even harder.

"Apprehending criminals is not your field of specialization, Hazard. If it were, you wouldn't have ended up taking a midnight swim in January."

"Be that as it may, I intend to go with you, so you might as well get used to the idea. I know exactly how Luke pulled off the murder, and I intend to be at the clinic to collect the evidence. It might be too late now. He could have destroyed it already. Every minute you delay by standing here and arguing with me could be an expensive waste of time. Our only hope is that Luke believes I didn't survive."

Amanda hustled off, but she pulled up short when a brigade of nurses blocked her exit.

"It is against the policy of this hospital to release a patient without a formal dismissal," said the nurse who had appointed herself spokesperson.

Despite her bedraggled appearance, Amanda drew herself up to a dignified posture. "You are hereby notified that I am leaving this hospital," she said. "You can inform my physician if you feel obliged to get a second opinion on the state of my health, but I am definitely signing myself out."

Nick bit back a grin. He appreciated Hazard's relentless determination when she wasn't directing it at him. The nurses looked to him for support and reinforcement. When he only shrugged, the congregation dispersed to fetch the physician, save for one stout angel of mercy who volunteered to blockade the exit.

"Were you born with this stiff-necked stubbornness, Hazard? Or is it a learned behavior?" Nick inquired, propping a sturdy shoulder against the doorjamb.

"If I had not developed backbone in my youth, I would have been meek and incompetent to this day. Mother wanted to, and would have, lived my life for me. I declared my independence years ago, although Mother refused to acknowledge it."

Amanda frowned thoughtfully. "Mother approved of my husband. That in itself should have tipped me off that the marriage was doomed to disaster. She and I have always held opposing views and had contrasting tastes. The only time I agreed with her, I lived to regret it."

"And your father?" Nick questioned, curious to understand what influences had molded this sassy female into the headstrong woman she had become.

"Daddy believes in allowing his children to live up to their potential without interference." Amanda eyed Nick warily. "Why are you trying to distract me from the matter at hand, Thorn?"

"I have always been a student of psychology, and you are a most fascinating case. Besides, what else do we have to do while the nurses track down Doc Simms?"

"We could be discussing our plan of action," Amanda suggested.

"*My* plan," Nick clarified. "You are only along for the ride. I am taking you with me so I can keep an eye on you. If I leave you here you might try to escape."

"You're a smart man, Thorn."

He flashed her one of those dazzling smiles that display pearly teeth, the kind of smile her mother would ooh and ahh over. "I like to think so, Hazard."

"And what in your vast and varied background has given you such an abundance of self-confidence?" she quizzed him.

"I was born with it. It came with the name."

"Oh sure, you let me expose my background—and my backside—to your scrutiny, but you reveal nothing about yourself," Amanda complained.

Nick reached out to bring her famously stubborn chin down a notch. "Hang the past, Hazard. I'm just thankful you're still alive. I've developed a certain attachment to you over the past few weeks." The forefinger that had curled beneath her chin began to caress her, and his voice rustled huskily. "I like you."

"I like you too, Thorn," she admitted in the same raspy tone.

The spell was broken by the echo of approaching footsteps as Dr. Simms marched down the hall, bookended by two nurses.

"I hear we have a belligerent patient."

Nick smiled at the gray-haired doctor who had been practicing at the county hospital for thirty years. "Indeed we do. But I am investigating a case and I'm in need of Ms. Hazard's assistance. She has information which could help solve a crime. If you can release her, I would appreciate it." His lips quirked in wry amusement, and he added, "I also think you would be doing yourself and the hospital staff a great favor. If I leave Ms. Hazard here, it's not likely she will be an agreeable patient."

Dr. Simms made a quick examination of the dilation of Amanda's pupils and the knot on her forehead. When he reached out his hand, one of the nurses produced a clipboard with the necessary forms. Amanda hastily scrawled her name on the dotted line and managed an appreciative smile.

"I will return your blanket tomorrow."

Nick was quick to note that she hadn't *asked* to borrow it. She had assumed she could use it. Amanda Hazard did not request when she could demand. That was another example of her dominant personality.

Despite Amanda's protests, Nick scooped her up, blanket and all, and carried her to the squad car. "This is not necessary, Thorn. I have my boots on, and I can walk."

Nick levered her into one arm to open the door and dumped her on the seat. "You're welcome, Hazard." Swiftly, he rounded the car and took his position behind the wheel. "Now, I want a complete recap of your activities since the moment you stole my truck—"

"I did not steal your truck. I borrowed it," Amanda corrected and then sneezed her head off.

"It was auto theft," he said, his voice like a pounding gavel. "And do not even think about putting up a fuss when I detour by your house so you can change into something warmer and more con-

243

cealing than a hospital gown and blanket. As much as I enjoy the view granted by your gown, we are definitely taking time for you to dress."

Amanda curled up under her blanket and shivered. "I was going to suggest that myself." Another sneeze. "I may be determined to get to the *bottom* of this case, but not with mine exposed."

Nick smiled to himself. He didn't want that shapely behind exposed to the rest of the world, either. The tantalizing view had distracted him enough already.

With intense concentration, he listened to Amanda offer her concise account of the incidents leading up to her late-night swim in the river. It was a story full of startling revelations. Nick absorbed the information and linked the facts to those he'd acquired the day he had returned to the scene of William's death. He too had been puzzled by the behavior of the cattle herd that gathered around the stock tank.

As Amanda spoke, the pieces of the confusing puzzle began to settle into place. If Nick's and Amanda's assumptions were correct, the scheme was ingenious. It soothed Nick's pride to realize anyone would have had difficulty believing the "accident" was actually a well-plotted murder.

While Amanda was in her bedroom, wrapping herself in several layers of clothing, Nick fastened himself into his bullet-proof vest and put in a call to the county sheriff, requesting backup. His main concern was keeping a woman like Amanda safely in the background, just in case the unpredictable occurred. If he'd thought he could sneak out and leave her where she was, he would have. But knowing Hazard as he did, he was certain that would only slow her down. Nothing would stop her, short of tying her up and securing her to a tree. Though she would try to uproot the tree and drag it with her. Amanda Hazard was a female hurricane.

Twenty-two

"Okay, Hazard, this is how it's going to be," Nick announced in a no-nonsense tone. He brought the patrol car to a halt at the clinic and rounded on Amanda. "No life-threatening heroics. If Luke or Janene resort to desperate measures to escape, you are not going to risk life and limb to apprehend them. Understood? The sheriff is sending a squad in case we need assistance."

Amanda gave him a snappy salute. "Yes, sir."

"For once, I want you to remain a step behind me. I know it's hell on your feminine pride to be upstaged by a lowly officer of the law, but try to remember your place just this once."

Amanda fell into step behind Nick. When she unconsciously quickened her pace to walk beside him, he curled his arm around her waist and placed her behind him, as if he were her shield of defense.

"And stay there, Hazard," he commanded.

"Very chivalrous, Thorn," she commended. "But unnecessary."

"Just humor me," Nick demanded before he turned his attention to the matter at hand.

After he'd pounded on the door twice, Luke appeared. Nick followed customary procedure, notifying him that he was being taken into custody for questioning. He had only begun his spiel when Luke wheeled around and made a mad dash across the living room. Characteristically, Amanda took matters into her own hands. The instinct to give chase was as natural to her as breathing. She slipped past Nick with eel-like agility and burst through the door to bring Luke down.

Earlier that evening, Luke had tackled her, leaving her to mutter curses into the snow. Turnabout was fair play, she thought. And besides, she was not going to give Luke time to collect a weapon, hole up in the apartment, and stage a shoot-out like the ones in the Old West.

"Damn it!" Nick roared when Amanda blazed past him like a speeding bullet. She had charged off as if she were wearing invisible armor, as if she were invulnerable. Curse the woman!

Nick plunged into the room, watching in frustration as Amanda made a spectacular leap over the sofa. She locked her arms around Luke's legs, causing him to stumble and crash to the floor, cracking his head on the edge of the coffee table.

Like a starved dog pouncing on a bone, Nick attacked. He shoved Amanda out of the way and jabbed his knee into Luke's back, efficiently pinning him down. Swiftly, he grabbed Luke's arms and cuffed them together. Before the stars completed a revolution around Luke's head, his hands were bound behind him and two hundred pounds of taut muscle was weighing him down.

Nick stabbed a hand into the pocket of Luke's jeans and retrieved the keys to his own truck. "I can't wait to hear you explain how you came to have these in your possession. You just added auto theft to your list of crimes, Princeton."

"You have the right to remain si—"

"That's my job, Hazard," Nick growled. Then he focused his stormy gaze on Luke. "You have the right to remain silent . . ."

While Nick was reading Luke his rights, Amanda hauled herself off the floor and darted toward the bedroom. She found Janene propped up in bed, clutching a quilt to her chin. The shock of learning that Amanda had survived her "dip" in the river held Janene paralyzed.

Headlights glared through the window, heralding the arrival of the backup squad. While Janene lay abed, her mouth opening and closing like the damper on a chimney, uniformed officers swarmed inside. Within minutes, Janene and Luke were propelled toward the county sheriff's squad car and deposited on the back seat. Nick was all business until the apartment had been abandoned. Then he turned on Amanda, breathing fire.

"Hazard, did I not tell you to let me handle this arrest? Can't you follow simple directions?"

"I can when I feel like it," she informed him proudly.

"Well, I sure as hell wish you would feel like it more often. Luke could have taken you hostage. You almost got yourself killed once tonight. Wasn't that enough?"

"He was about to get away," she insisted.

"How far could he go?" Nick called her attention to the compact apartment with an all-encompassing sweep of his arms. Then he jerked open his shirt to gesture toward the bulletproof vest he had taken the precaution of wearing. "I had protection. All you had was that rock of a skull for a helmet."

"I was being careful."

"Like hell, Hazard!"

"I just responded instinctively," she said in self-defense.

Nick snapped his shirt back together, glaring at Amanda all the while. "You responded stupidly," he corrected in a harsh tone. "Just because I've had the hots for you for a couple of weeks, don't think I'll overlook your idiocy. I ought to arrest you for interfering in the apprehension and arrest of a suspect."

"Interfering?" Amanda parroted, highly affronted. "I was trying to prevent a shoot-out."

Nick drew in an enormous breath. The snaps on his shirt strained against the expansion of his chest. He exhaled slowly, giving his emotions time to regroup. "Hazard, you've been watching too many detective shows. Actors and stunt men get paid to make theatrical leaps to apprehend fleeing criminals. You placed yourself in a dangerous situation, and I'm fed up with watching you flitter from one calamity to another."

"Well, it seemed to me that it would have been wiser to take Luke by surprise the moment he opened the door," Amanda countered.

"According to the law, everyone is presumed innocent until proven guilty," Nick contended.

"Oh sure, Thorn. Protect the alleged murderers. Give the bad guys all the breaks. Lord, what is our judicial system coming to?"

"I'm beginning to wonder the same thing. It has gotten to the point where a law-enforcement officer cannot perform his duties without some busybody butting in and instigating more trouble than a policeman already has to face."

"Well, if you ask me—"

"Nobody did."

Amanda was not to be put off by the snide remark. "I think we should just hang the criminals and be done with it."

"My, my, the milk of your human kindness has curdled, hasn't it?"

"I think society has bent over so far backward to be 'fair' that we have forgotten what 'fair' is!" she declared. "Criminals are lucky they aren't shot or stabbed on the very spot where they committed their crime. Our prisons are overflowing with convicted killers who whine that their rights have been infringed upon. *Their* rights?" Amanda expelled a disgusted snort. "It seems to me a criminal waives his rights when he breaks the law and deprives fellow human beings of *their* rights, *their* property or *their* lives. If you take something away from your neighbor, then you should not expect to be protected by the same set of laws you broke."

It was glaringly apparent where Amanda Hazard stood on the issue of crime and prison reform. Not that Nick didn't agree with her, because he did. Doing time in the pen wasn't supposed to be a vacation. It was supposed to be punishment for offenses against John Q. Public.

"People cannot have it both ways," Amanda went on to say. "Either they respect and observe the laws or they don't. And if they don't, *they* made the choice and *they* have to live with the consequences."

She inhaled deeply and then plowed on, much to Nick's chagrin. "We have prisoners sitting in penitentiary lounges and watching cable television, who demand better conditions and plenty of entertainment. I don't even have cable TV! I work for the money I make, and I'm not provided with three square meals a day, a place to bed down, medical care, workout rooms and a college education.

250

"And another thing, I'm sick and tired of middle-class America shouldering all the expenses of ineffective government agencies."

"Like the Department of Corrections?"

"To name only one."

Nick had been afraid of that.

"My tax dollars are being squandered. Government officials have ten aides and secretaries to do the job of two. I don't even have a secretary. We're bogged down in the quicksand of bureaucracy, and no one has the gumption to swim out."

Nick's lips twitched with barely suppressed amusement. "I suppose if the world came into alignment with your theories and beliefs then it would be a better place for all of us."

Hazard's approach to cutting waste in government and society, Nick decided, would be to see heads roll. She was not what Nick would call conservative, not by any stretch of the imagination.

"I do have a few suggestions about getting this country back on its feet, yes."

Nick grabbed the arm she was flinging about expansively. "Don't be modest, Hazard. You have a thousand suggestions. I'm sure the Department of Corrections, as well as all the other government agencies, will be eager to hear your ideas after we wrap up this case." He glanced around the apartment. "Now where is the storage cabinet you said contained important evidence?"

"On the west wall of the clinic." Amanda set her complaints aside and zoomed down the hall.

Nick groped for the light switch and then crossed the room to search the cabinet. He spotted the object that had drawn Amanda's attention several hours earlier. An electrical de-icer identical to the one that floated in William Farley's stock tank, as

251

well as to those in other tanks in the area, sat on the shelf. Nick picked up the appliance and inspected it. The insulation that housed the wiring on the power cord had been cut away and painted black. At a glance, it would have been difficult to tell that the heater had been tampered with.

At the spot where the power cord threaded through the protective metal coil that fastened onto the heating element, the insulation had also been stripped and the wires painted black. Live wires protruded downward, concealed by the circular red float.

"I think this is the heater Luke plugged into the electrical source the morning I found William Farley draped over the stock tank," Amanda said with reasonable certainty. "Luke has enough knowledge of electricity to plot such a scheme, even if he refused to admit it to me. I saw him repairing electrical circuits the day I came to question Janene.

"If my theory is correct, William insisted on having a private conference with Luke after he caught Janene fooling around at the apartment. While William was reading Luke the first and second paragraphs of the riot act, he was also doing what he did every morning, checking his cattle and the water level of the stock tank. Luke was there beside the idling pickup, ready to watch William fry. When William noticed the ring of ice on the water tank, he naturally suspected the faulty heating element."

"And Luke was very clever in rigging this de-icer so that no matter how careful William was, he would receive a fatal shock," Nick added, pointing an index finger at the dangling wire and the exposed connection. "Even if William employed every precaution he would have made contact with live voltage."

Amanda nodded pensively. "William was given just enough shock to daze him before he pitched forward in the tank and drowned. Luke quickly switched off the circuit and removed the de-icer. Then he drove back to the clinic to retrieve the properly functioning heater and placed it in the tank. He also removed the work gloves that William always wore when doing his chores. The wallet probably fell in the tank while Luke was jostling the body around to retrieve the gloves. No one found burns on William's hands because the burns from the electrocution were on the gloves."

Now Nick understood the cattle herd's peculiar behavior when he returned to the scene to study the surroundings. The cattle had refused to drink and had opted to obtain water from the creek. Just as cattle learned to respect an electrical fence which gave them a jolt when they ventured too close, the herd backed away from the tank to avoid shock. The electrical current in the water was strong enough to electrocute a man or a small calf, but could only scare off a thousand-pound cow.

"There were two unanticipated hitches in Luke's plan," Nick said. "One of the small calves came to drink from the tank while voltage was running through the water. The calf met with the same end as William. And Luke didn't know about your early morning appointment with Farley. You showed up before he could remove the calf and hike off across the pasture to return to the clinic."

"Luke probably sought refuge in the grove of willows when he heard me coming," Amanda said thoughtfully. "He hadn't counted on the body being

253

discovered so quickly or on a dead calf that was seen."

"When you drove off to flag me down, Luke dragged the calf to the willows and the mother cow followed," Nick speculated.

"Luke probably hightailed it back to the clinic on foot to have Janene help him. With Bill out of town, Janene could come and go without detection. She probably drove around the section and dropped Luke off on the road beside the willow grove to watch what would happen next. After you and I returned, Luke had Janene drive up to the house to serve as a distraction."

"Since you refused to accept accidental death as the explanation, Luke must have decided to plant pests in your home and set up the other difficulties with which you'd have to contend. He wanted to divert your attention, distract you from your suspicions and discredit you in my eyes," Nick added. "When the story spread that you suspected William had been murdered, he decided to stage the same kind of incidents in his own apartment, hoping to frame Bill. The estranged husband who was known to be cheating on his wife became the prime suspect. Luke was doing all he could to get both of us to suspect Bill."

Nick located a paper sack and dropped the faulty de-icer into it. "Luke's attempt to stage your accidental death was an admission of his guilt. We have enough evidence to put him away and to convict Janene as an accomplice. William will have his way after all. Farley Farm will remain in the family. That should please him."

When Nick strode toward the door, Amanda glanced around the vacated clinic. "Luke and Janene embezzled money from William's account so

254

they could live in the manner to which they had grown accustomed. Unfortunately, William discovered their relationship. For Janene to divorce Bill would no longer be enough to ensure that the lovers could stay together. William was a threat. What a shame that Luke was willing to go to extremes, in the name of love. And money. It only proves that ill-fated affairs can ruin a man or woman's life."

"Right, Hazard. Love and lust are the curses of everybody's life," Nick muttered. "Let's go. It's been a long night, and it isn't over yet. I have reports to file with the sheriff and evidence to present to the D.A. I'll drop you at my place. One of us ought to get some sleep."

"I'll come with you," she volunteered.

"Don't do me any more favors."

"I happen to be an injured victim who lived to tell about it," Amanda reminded him before switching off the light.

" 'Injured' is the key word, Hazard. That's why you are going to bed to rest and recuperate. You can give your statement to the sheriff tomorrow."

Despite Amanda's objections, and she had plenty of them, Nick dropped her off in his driveway. She was still protesting when he shut the car door in her face and skidded onto the icy road.

She let herself into the house, thankful for its cozy warmth. She was chilled to the bone, and a dull headache tapped at her skull. She gulped in shock when she walked into the bathroom to brush her teeth and spied her reflection in the mirror. A goose egg bulged on her forehead, and tangles of blond hair protruded at odd angles from her face. She looked like a witch in a cyclone. No wonder

Nick had ordered her out of the car. In her condition, she didn't appear to be a dependable witness. She resembled a circus freak.

Although Amanda plopped down on the sleeper sofa, looking the worse for wear, she was brimming over with satisfaction. She had solved a cleverly plotted crime. William Farley might not have been the most likable individual on the planet, but he deserved to see justice served for the crime committed against him. His son also deserved to be cleared of suspicion.

Bill Farley had been as much a victim as his father. His wife had driven him away and had tried to frame him for murder. There was no question about it, Janene had been more of a curse than a blessing to him. Amanda could identify with that. Her ex-husband had been an unpleasant part of her past. The lessons she had learned had been difficult ones. Now, trust and devotion did not come easily for her.

She rolled onto her side and heaved an exhausted sigh. Although she had planned to congratulate herself more for her efforts in William Farley's behalf, she fell asleep the instant her head hit the pillow.

Since Amanda was sleeping as if she were in a coma, she didn't hear Nick enter the house in the wee hours of the morning, and he didn't bother to rouse her. He was still peeved at her for throwing herself in harm's way twice in the same night.

That "nice Amanda Hazard," as Velma was so fond of calling her, was a lot of trouble for one man to handle. She looked a sight, lying there with a purple knot between her eyes and a mat of blond hair tangled around her face. Sometimes Nick wanted her so, he was afire. At other times she made him mad enough to spit nails.

Amanda had opted to go out and darned near get herself killed rather than spend the night with him. Obviously she did not consider him a man to die for but one she'd die to avoid. Now was that the ultimate insult, or what!

Only a few hours earlier, Nick had admitted to Amanda that he cared about her. To repay him for that heartfelt confession, she'd darted over furniture in her reckless attempt to apprehend a fleeing criminal. She had no consideration whatsoever for the fear and concern Nick had experienced while he'd watched her go from calamity to calamity. Did she ever stop to think how he felt when she thrust herself into life-threatening situations? Did she even care?

Years ago, Nick had watched Diana being carried away after she had been caught in the middle of a fight between him and a vengeful criminal. Wasn't once enough?

True, Amanda had solved a difficult case that he might have overlooked. And his male pride was smarting. He wasn't accustomed to having a woman steal the limelight. Neither was he accustomed to battling for dominance or, at the very least, equality with a woman.

After Nick had reported the incident and explained Amanda's involvement, the sheriff had sung her praises until it turned Nick's stomach. He could see the headlines in the *Vamoose Gazette* now. ACE ACCOUNTANT CRACKS CASE. The publicity would probably go straight to Amanda's head. She wouldn't have time to handle the new clients that would be flocking around her because of all the criminal investigations she would take it upon herself to conduct. She wouldn't have time for Nick, either. He would be a forgotten file in her cabinet.

Anyway, if Nick knew what was good for him, he would steer clear of this crime-solving accountant who was quickly becoming a household word in Vamoose—in the whole damned county!

"Atta boy, Thorn," Nick grumbled on his way to bed. "Keep it up and you'll talk yourself out of this crazy fascination. As well you should!"

He peeled off his clothes and fell into bed. He liked sleeping alone. He enjoyed lying spread-eagled on the sheets without anyone crowding him. He didn't need frustrating emotional involvements to complicate things. He liked his life just the way it was.

Amanda Hazard lived her life in alphabetical order. *T* for Thorn would always be at the bottom of her list. If Nick couldn't be on the top—in more ways than one—then to hell with it!

Come morning, Nick promised himself he was going to take Amanda Hazard home and get on with his life. Oh certainly, he would see her now and again. They couldn't help but cross paths occasionally. But he would keep a respectable distance, just as he had vowed to do in the first place.

On that determined thought, Nick fell asleep.

He awoke twice in a cold sweat. He cursed a blue streak and tossed in the bed. He wasn't going to torment himself over that wacky woman. He'd heard more than enough of her weird theories and cynical opinions. This was one hazard he could do without!

Twenty-three

Amanda stared at the financial ledger in front of her, seeing nothing. The past two weeks had passed in a flurry of hectic activity. She had battled a cold after her chilling swim in the river. Dr. Simms had prescribed medication to prevent complications and now Amanda was on the mend. She had been interviewed by the reporter from the *Vamoose Gazette* and had received accolades for her part in seeing justice done. She had given her statement to the sheriff and had had the pleasure of seeing Luke Princeton and Janene Farley arraigned. The work gloves William had been wearing the day of the "accident" had been recovered from behind the seat of his pickup, providing more evidence for the trial.

And Glenn Chambliss's bankruptcy sale had been postponed because Emma Carter, his mother-in-law, had intervened to pay off the interest and part of the principal owed on his loans. All had not been lost — yet.

Phone calls had been coming in as fast as Amanda could answer them. Suddenly, she was in great demand as an accountant. With all the new clients she had collected in Vamoose, she had decided to rent office space in the vacant building across the street from the Last Chance Cafe, and had set up shop there at the beginning of the week. Now she was up to her ears in paperwork.

Interviews with prospective clients had taken up a tremendous amount of her time, as had frequent trips to the City. Amanda didn't want to sever her professional connection with Nelson, Blake and Cosmos, but being her own boss held great appeal. She had finally agreed to keep several of her ongoing accounts in the City and to go there once or twice a week, depending on her work load in Vamoose.

The publicity she had received had launched her career into orbit. Business was booming, and her landlady's insurance company had paid for the vandalism and smoke damage to the house, so Amanda's life and her home were back in order. Everything was coming up roses—except for one Thorn.

Since the night of her life-threatening ordeal with Luke Princeton, Amanda had seen very little of Nick. She had volunteered to help him do his farm chores the following morning, but he had responded with a clipped no thank you. He had helped her gather her belongings and had transported her home. Then he had detoured to Cecil's shop to have a long talk with the mechanic, insisting that her Toyota be returned in good working condition—immediately. The old truck, however, would be under repair for a month, considering how slowly Cecil worked.

Nick had not taken a vacation since the Farley case had been resolved. He had busied himself patrolling avenues and country roads and tending his cattle and sheep.

On impulse, Amanda had driven past his home one evening to see him repairing a sagging stretch of fence between pasture and wheat field. He

260

hadn't even bothered to wave when she'd passed him.

From all indications, he had plenty of other interests to occupy him. Not that Amanda cared . . .

"Well, I don't!" she burst out when the mocking voice inside her scoffed at the stubborn declaration.

She heaved a sigh and stared out the window of her new office. She watched the traffic buzz by and monitored the comings and goings of the patrons of the Last Chance Cafe. When the patrol car pulled into the restaurant parking lot, Amanda felt her pulse accelerate. Nick Thorn unfolded his six-foot-two-inch frame from the car and ambled into the cafe.

Amanda checked her watch. Eleven A.M. A little too early for lunch, unless one had skipped one's breakfast — which she usually did. Hunger pains knotted her stomach. It was a hunger pain, Amanda assured the infuriating little voice. Maybe it wasn't in her stomach, but it was a pain just the same.

I could use a break, she told herself.

Billie Jane Baxter's mother had called to say that her famous daughter would be flying in to consult with Amanda at one P.M. Since Billie Jane had decided to build herself a country estate near her home town, she wanted an accountant in the area to handle her personal finances. Billie Jane was taking time from her singing tour to finalize the purchase of land from Preston Banks. She intended to interview the publicly acclaimed accountant during the same trip. But the upcoming consultation with Nashville's country sweetheart was two hours away. Now was the time for a lunch break.

Amanda scooped up her coat and purse, locked the office and darted across the street. Self-consciously, she straightened her business suit and ran a hand through her hair. She was only grabbing a bite to eat before her appointment, that was all. She hadn't had a greasy hamburger and fries for a week. If her cholesterol count shot up she'd have something to talk about.

Projecting a casual air, she made her entrance into the Last Chance Cafe. She was greeted by every patron—save one. Nick Thorn sat in the corner booth. His fist was propped under his chin, and his elbow was stuck to a table which had yet to be cleaned from the previous customer. Nick was staring at the wall on which Amanda's interview with the *Vamoose Gazette* had been posted. Her picture smiled back at him, but Nick was as sober as a judge.

"Mind if I join you, Thorn?"

"It's a free country." His voice registered as much indifference as was humanly possible.

Amanda eased onto the seat, but not before she flicked the crumbs to the floor. "So how is the police beat in Vamoose?"

"All's quiet," Nick replied, still staring at the article on the wall. "No murders reported. Sorry, Hazard. I know you live for the excitement of investigation and the thrill of the chase."

Her pleasant smile slid off the corner of her mouth. "My, aren't we snide and sarcastic this morning? Get up on the wrong side of the bed, Thorn?"

When the waitress ambled over to clean off the table, Nick graced her with an appreciative smile. It seemed everyone in Vamoose was accorded a slice of Nick Thorn's charm—except Amanda. She was being treated with chilling tolerance.

After Faye Bernard assured Nick that his order

262

would be ready in a few minutes, she took Amanda's request.

Easing back in her seat, Amanda stared meditatively at Nick. "You've been giving me the cold shoulder for two weeks, Thorn. Would you mind telling me why?"

That was Hazard through and through. No beating around bushes. Just dive right into the heart of the matter.

"My shoulder is neither hot nor cold," he said. "I am simply performing the duties of a law officer and a farmer."

Amanda swallowed the comment she had intended to make and waited for Faye to place Nick's order in front of him. When Faye ambled off, she said, "The newspaper article and the publicity I received stole your thunder, and you resent it. Is that it?"

"No." Nick plucked up a french fry and stuffed it into his mouth.

"Then why are you sulking?"

"I am not sulking," he snapped and grabbed another french fry.

"Right."

The conversation had hit a dead end and showed no potential signs of life. So had her relationship with Officer Thorn of the Vamoose P.D., Amanda decided. She knew when she wasn't wanted. She had learned that during her divorce. If Nick perferred to eat his lunch alone rather than in her company, then he could have his wish.

With quiet dignity, Amanda rose to leave. Nick grabbed her wrist and pulled her back into the booth.

"I am not sulking, Hazard. I am simply staying out of your life and keeping you out of mine. That's

263

what you wanted in the first place—no strings attached, no complications. You didn't want us to become serious, except that you wanted me to take your suspicions seriously. I let you play by your rules, but I reserved the right to decide how long I planned to play by them. I wanted more; you wanted less. We were playing different games on the same court. It just didn't work out."

Amanda felt her lower lip trembling, and she bit into it. She should have been relieved that he hadn't pressed her for more than she was prepared to give. He had simply given up, gone away and left her alone. So why did she feel this strange coil of emptiness in the pit of her stomach? That nagging little voice did not hesitate in telling her it wasn't because she was ravenously hungry.

Nick grabbed his hamburger with both hands and took a bite. The slice of tomato slid out of the bun and splattered on his french fries. He stared at the basket and then at Amanda.

"I knew you didn't want to be pressured so I backed off. Now I'm seeing one of the secretaries at the County Court House. Our friendship has promising possibilities."

That old familiar feeling of rejection hit Amanda right where she lived. Nick's colloquy reminded her of the one her ex had delivered years back. *Sorry, Mandy. There is somebody else. I waited too long to tell you because I didn't want to hurt you.*

Had Jason thought telling her sooner rather than later could lessen the degree of pain and humiliation she suffered? Well, it hadn't. Jason had broken her trust. Now Nick Thorn was stabbing holes in her mending heart.

Amanda had been here before, so why was she

getting teary-eyed about it now? She could cope with this rejection. It was no big deal. Right? Wrong!

The silence between Amanda and Nick was as thick as tar. They sat in the booth for what seemed eons, staring in every direction except at each other. When Faye returned with the hamburger and fries, Amanda requested the order to go. Without another word to Nick who was swallowing his food like a python to prevent conversation, she followed Faye to the counter.

You should have stayed at the office, Hazard, Amanda told herself as she breezed out of the Last Chance Cafe. Last chance was right! She wasn't taking any more chances with romance. It was highly overrated as far as she was concerned. Who needed the torment? She didn't know what she'd thought she was doing, chasing after a man. That had never been her style. Yet, she had reached out to Nick. To get her hand slapped and her feelings trampled. Well, she would never make that mistake again.

"Get over it, Hazard. What did you expect from the male of the species?" she asked herself on her way across the street.

Resolved never to give Nick Thorn another thought, Amanda entered her office and switched on the radio. Billie Jane Baxter's twangy voice blared at her, the song about a broken heart and a woman done wrong.

"Ain't it the truth, Billie Jane," Amanda muttered before poking a french fry in her mouth.

Amanda honestly could not imagine what brought Billie Jane such fame and fortune in Nashville. The woman might have a porcelain face and a voluptuous figure that she poured into form-fitting blouses and skin-tight jeans, but she had a voice like a gong.

"Don't be so critical," Amanda said to herself.

She was in a sour mood, compliments of Nick Thorn. Well, she hoped he and his secretary girlfriend were immensely happy. Ms. Secretary probably fawned all over the Tom Selleck look-alike, morning, noon and night. Men sucked up that sort of devout attention like sponges. It fed their egos. Was it Amanda's fault that she was difficult to please and that she didn't go around flinging compliments at those of the male persuasion unless they richly deserved them? If Nick Thorn didn't like her style, then that was that.

Meanwhile, back at the Last Chance Cafe, Nick was downing his third cup of coffee. He was just preparing to leave when Velma Hertzog plopped down in the booth.

"When are you coming in for the free haircut I promised you, Nick?" Smack, crack. "You could use one." She reached across the table to tug at the dark hair that drooped over his left ear. "I have an opening at two o'clock."

"Thanks, but—"

"It will only take a few minutes." Chomp, chomp. "I won't be satisfied until I've paid you back for picking me up the night I slid off into that snowdrift."

"That's—"

Velma cut him off to pose a question. "Did you ever give that nice Amanda Hazard a call? You should, Nick, and you better do it quick." Snap, crackle, pop. "Randel Thompson was in the shop yesterday, pumping me for information about her."

266

"Randel?" Nick frowned, bemused.

"You know, that tall, sexy-looking cowboy Buddy Hampton hired to help him on his horse ranch." Crack, crack. "Randel is breaking Buddy's yearling colts to the harness and getting them groomed for the horse shows. I hear Randel is really good with animals. He used to follow the rodeo circuit until he got tired of all the traveling." Velma leaned closer to convey her confidential remark. "Horses aren't his only specialty, or so I have heard. He has an appreciative eye for the ladies. He wants me to fix him up with Amanda."

"I really have to get back to work," Nick insisted, trying to escape from the booth.

Velma clamped a hand on his forearm. "Give Amanda a call before that hot-dog rodeo rider tries to rope her."

"Velma, you really should stick to styling hair and leave everybody's love life alone," Nick said.

Having offered that advice, to which he doubted Velma had bothered to listen, Nick stood up and left. He didn't want a haircut or a matchmaker. He wanted to be left alone. It was his life and he could screw it up all by himself!

The greasy hamburger and fries Amanda had consumed at lunch sat on her stomach like a pint of acid. A pack of Rolaids later, Billie Jane Baxter swanned into the office as if she were taking to the stage to perform for a packed house. Her long, curly black hair fanned out around her shoulders and hung there—pasted into position with hair spray. Her neck was encircled by a silver necklace inlaid with gawdy chunks of turquoise. Amanda thought the jewelry looked like a fancy hangman's noose.

Billie Jane thrust out a lily-white hand spiked with fake fingernails. "Nice to meet ya, Mandy," she drawled.

Only Amanda's ex-husband called her Mandy. She had always hated it. "It is nice to make your acquaintance, Billie Jane. Won't you sit down."

Billie Jane fluttered into the chair and crossed her legs at the knees, causing her tight jeans to tug at their seams. "I just flew in from Nashville to sign the deed for the land I'm buying from Cousin Preston. The contractor is supposed to meet me later this afternoon to go over the blueprints for my house."

Amanda wondered if Billie Jane's husband took offense to their collective possessions being referred to as "my" and "mine." Probably. One would have thought Billie Jane was the sole supporter of her family. Maybe she was. Amanda would know for certain if she agreed to take Billie Jane on as a client.

"Since my singing career took off like a rocket, I have so many engagements and obligations that I barely have time to keep up with my finances. I want someone who will be as conscientious with my money as I am. You come highly recommended by everyone in Vamoose, Mandy."

"Thank you." If Billie Jane called her Mandy one more time Amanda was going to choke the country music star with her own turquoise necklace.

Billie Jane ranted on for an hour about her blossoming career and the fabulous home she was building on Preston Banks's land. It was her dream house, equipped with a gigantic music studio and enough guest rooms to accommodate her band and all her celebrity friends.

After demanding to know Amanda's professional

qualifications, Billie Jane decreed—in her fake Southern drawl—that she would become a client. Her financial records, Billie Jane announced with a toss of her curly head, would be delivered to Amanda's office by her mother the following day.

Amanda expected the bills and canceled checks to arrive in boot boxes. There would be dozens of them for Amanda to sort through. What a fun way to spend an evening.

"I'll send you an autographed photo and my latest album," Billie Jane promised before she sailed out the door like a flying carpet.

"Goodie, goodie," Amanda mumbled when the door swung shut.

Just what she needed. An eight-by-ten glossy of the human gong and an album of songs to remind her of a woman done wrong.

Twenty-four

Amanda returned home that cold, dreary evening, depressed by the meterologist's report that another winter storm was approaching. Great. Snowbound for the weekend. Her social life had fallen into decay while her professional life blossomed. If that was to be considered some compensation, Amanda did not feel satisfactorily rewarded.

Supper would be an uneventful affair—canned tuna and crackers. Well, thought Amanda, if she was going to mope around and feel sorry for herself she ought to do it right. Nothing could be duller than tuna in a can. She would be sure to eat the variety packed in oil to boost her cholesterol count.

One glance out the kitchen window proved the weather forecast correct. Huge snowflakes fluttered past the window and danced in the wind like a parade of winged fairies. Amanda was all set to drop down to a lower level of depression when an insistent rap rattled the hinges of the front door. Setting her can of tuna aside, she went to answer the knock.

"Hello, Hazard."

Amanda frowned bemusedly at the handsome policeman she had officially written out of her life five hours earlier. "What's the problem, Thorn? Has the safety sticker on my Toyota expired? Or is it the license plate?" Amanda extended her arms and lifted her chin. "Okay, go ahead and cuff me. Haul me off to the slammer. I don't have anything special planned for the weekend anyway."

Nick's lips twitched. "May I come in?"

"Not unless you have a search warrant."

"This is a social call, not a professional one," Nick informed her.

In a mocking parody of courtesy, Amanda stepped aside and made a sweeping gesture with her arm. "By all means."

Nick ignored her snide theatrics and ambled inside. "I have a confession to make."

"Then go see a priest," she suggested flippantly.

He drew himself up in front of her, eclipsing the lamplight that came from behind him. Then he reached around Amanda to close the front door, wondering if he was still going to feel a cold draft. Sure enough, he did, but he sought to raise the temperature in the room a few degrees to thaw out Amanda's icy facade by brushing against her in the pretense of shutting the door.

When Nick leaned close, the musky scent of his cologne infiltrated Amanda's flared nostrils. She was reminded of other times and other places when she had breathed in his scent and battled overwhelming temptation. The man still affected her on an elemental level. She was still too aware of him . . .

Don't frustrate yourself, Hazard. You know how men are. They will tear your heart out if you let them.

Nick advanced even closer, and Amanda plastered herself against the wall, in retreat. "What do you want, Thorn. My supper is getting cold."

Nick glanced over his shoulder to see the open can of tuna, soda, crackers and milk. He smiled wryly at her flimsy excuse.

"That was just a figure of speech," she muttered without daring to breathe for fear she would get another whiff of his tantalizing scent. "If you want me to be blunt, then I will. Go away. You are bothering me."

"Am I? Good. That makes us even." Nick effectively erased the narrow distance between them. He stood there, blocking every avenue of escape, keeping Amanda sandwiched between the wall and the scintillating temptation of his masculine body. "You have been bothering me for one helluva of a long time, Hazard."

"Then take your complaints to the police department," she croaked, mentally kicking herself for allowing his disturbing nearness to alter her breathing and her voice.

He moved even closer so that there was barely enough space between them for a gnat. "I *am* the police department, if you recall."

"Then I would like to register a complaint. Quit crowding my space, Thorn."

He didn't back off. He cushioned his muscular body against hers and braced his arms against the wall on either side of her shoulders. "I came here to confess that I don't really have a girlfriend working at the court house."

"No? Did she get fired? I'm sorry to hear that. Now why don't you go console her and leave me in peace!"

His right arm curled around her waist, guiding Amanda into the hard contours of his body. "There is no new girlfriend," he murmured against the pulsating column of her throat. "I invented her to protect myself. But I'm tired of pretending I don't know you're alive. I want you in the worst way, and I like you, Hazard."

272

Amanda shoved her hands against his chest, holding him at bay before he lowered his head and kissed her senseless . . . and she let him. "Oh fine, Thorn. Make me spend a miserable afternoon, feeling sorry for myself," she pouted. "What is it it with you men? Do you get your kicks out of trampling all over a woman's feelings?"

"No," Nick explained as his hand wandered off on a journey of discovery on the curvaceous terrain of Amanda's body. "What I was doing was protecting my own feelings from someone I was afraid would never feel anything back." His dark head dipped lower, teasing her with the nearness of full, sensuous lips. "Feel anything, Hazard?"

This dynamic man took up so much space that Amanda couldn't breathe without inhaling him. "I feel cramped and cornered." She strove for a light, playful tone, but the rattle of unfulfilled need gave her game away.

"Feel anything else?"

His lips grazed her throat, finding that ultrasensitive spot. Her Achilles' heel was beneath the ear. The touch of his lips on her skin went through her like a bolt of lightning, leaving her to sizzle and burn. If Nick realized her weakness, she would be a goner for sure. His masculine body molded itself familiarly close, and Amanda became vividly aware of the changes in his anatomy, aware of her own burning needs.

Okay, Hazard. Admit it. There is a definite attraction here, and it has been here for over a month. Ignoring this elemental magnetism hasn't proved one hundred percent effective. Avoiding it didn't make the feelings go away, either. So what are you going to do about it?

"I feel like a dieter craving a slice of chocolate

273

cake, even when I'm accustomed to self-denial," she admitted on a strangled wheeze.

When moist lips feathered over the column of her neck to again settle on that vulnerable patch of skin beneath her ear, Amanda felt like a quivering jellyfish. Now Thorn had really done it. The craving had evolved into starvation. Canned tuna and crackers simply weren't going to cut it. Her appetite had swelled out of proportion.

"So, what are you planning to do about the craving, Hazard?"

Amanda had already asked herself the same question. The answer was becoming more evident by the second. She was going to do something she hadn't done in a very long time — throw caution to the wind and take a chance.

Her hands climbed the ladder of his ribs, scaled the broad expanse of his chest and linked behind his neck. "Are you off duty, Thorn?" she questioned in a sultry voice she hadn't employed in years.

"I'm all yours until eight o'clock Monday morning," he informed her.

"If you're off duty, then shouldn't you also be out of uniform?" Amanda pressed her hips suggestively into his. She smiled mischievously at the vivid evidence of his reaction. "Loaded pistols and handcuffs make me nervous."

"Oh really? And all this time I thought you were the kind of woman who liked living dangerously."

His hands drifted over the rounded curves of her buttocks. The pleasure he experienced reminded him of the night he had enjoyed touring her shapely backside while she was wearing that gaping hospital gown. She had a fabulous fanny, if he was any judge of the back end of a woman's anatomy. And he liked to think he was.

274

"I'll drop my holster"—a wry smile pursed his lips, making his dark eyes sparkle like obsidian—"but I will still be well armed, if you get my drift . . ."

Oh yes, she definitely got his drift, the arousing scent of him, the sensual feel of his eager body reacting to hers.

When his mouth slanted over hers, Amanda gave herself up to the tingling feelings that tap-danced on her every nerve ending. The demanding pressure of his kiss caused the knot of longing to coil tightly inside her, and in less than a heartbeat fire begin to burn from inside out.

It had definitely been too long, Amanda decided. One touch and she was blazing like a forest fire. One kiss and she wanted to gobble Nick alive. Suddenly, she was kissing him back without one smidgen of self-reserve. It was shameful, but oh, so enjoyable.

And how, Amanda wondered, was it going to look when she threw this gorgeous, delightfully amusing and sexually stimulating cop on the floor and attacked him, especially after she had kept him at arm's length for a month? Uncharacteristic? You betcha! But what the hell, she said to herself. Nick Thorn might as well know, here and now, that she could be very passionate when she felt like it. And he definitely made her feel like it!

Just when things were really getting good, the shrill demand of the phone blared through the tantalizing silence of two bodies sending sensual messages to each other.

"Damn," Amanda muttered when she came up for air.

Nick groaned. "Don't answer it."

The phone rang . . . again . . . and again. Nick

was tempted to yank the damned thing right out of the wall!

Amanda inhaled a fortifying breath, then wormed free from temptation and crossed the room on legs as stable as cooked spaghetti.

"Hello?"

"Hi, doll. It's Mother."

"Not to worry, Mother. I had my teeth cleaned last week." Amanda cursed her mother's sense of timing and her own smart-ass remark.

"I should hope so. You don't want to end up with a mouthful of dentures like your Uncle Dean, not if you can help it. Uncle Dean can't get used to the change. His false teeth spend more time soaking in Polident than they do sticking to his gums. Regular brushing and checkups are a must for healthy teeth and gums, you know."

"God, your mother isn't going to burst into a long-winded dissertation on the benefits of dental floss and regular brushing now, is she?" Nick muttered.

Amanda strangled a laugh when he beat his head against the wall in frustration.

Her mother cleared her throat. "So, what's new in Vamoose? Are you seeing that same man on a regular basis?" She cleared her throat again. "Oh, did I tell you what your brother did last week? You know how he squanders his hard-earned money . . ."

Amanda was not allowed to comment or to respond to questions. Her mother was yammering ninety miles a minute. She held the receiver away from her ear and put an occasional uh-huh in to the lopsided conversation.

After five minutes of nonstop chatter, Nick crossed the room to strip the receiver from Amanda's fingertips. "Nick Thorn here . . . Yes, I'm the new boyfriend." He didn't allow her mother to squeeze in another word. "I'm afraid you'll have to call back later. Supper is boiling over on the stove. Nice visiting with you."

When Nick dropped the receiver onto its cradle, Amanda clucked her tongue. "Now you've done it, Thorn. She'll demand a full review of our evening together and she'll insist on a complete account of your life history, beginning with your date of birth and ending with the immediate present. You let her think we had something going."

Nick scooped Amanda up in his arms and directed himself toward her bedroom. "We do have something going, Hazard," he assured her in a voice that was reminiscent of a purring lion's.

"I told you I wasn't good at casual affairs and one-night stands."

"Then we'll do it lying down." He waggled his thick black brows before he tossed her onto the middle of her bed.

Amanda propped herself on an elbow, fighting like the devil to remain calm and rational, even when the deprived woman inside her wanted to rip off Nick's uniform and satisfy the wanting she had long refused to acknowledge.

"We need to establish a set of ground rules here, Thorn."

"Fine," Nick said agreeably. "Rule number one: there are no rules. I like you and you like me. Sometimes you drive me crazy, organizing your life in alphabetical order and spewing your theories like a geyser. And sometimes I frustrate you because I like spontaneity and inconsistency. We are never going to see eye to eye on everything because you are stubborn and I'm a little bullheaded—"

"A little?" Amanda begged to differ. "Give your-self full credit, Thorn. You are *a lot* bullheaded."

"Then we are equal, Hazard. That should please you." A rakish smile spread across his lips, and his eyes sparkled with deviltry. "And I am going to make a conscious effort to please you as often as I can in the next few days, the next few months . . ."

She looked him over once or twice and smiled an impish smile. "Oh, I think you'll please me very well—if you ever get past your lengthy recitations." She crooked a finger at him. "Come here, Thorn . . . if you please . . . and let me see what I can do about pleasing you back . . ."

The invitation was eagerly given and quickly accepted. Off came the holster and the handcuffs. The uniform followed shortly thereafter. Amanda's business suit fell to the floor beside the other discarded garments, and she didn't even give a thought to putting them in their proper places.

For a moment, Nick was content just to lie with her, comparing his fantasies with reality. His imagination had not done the lady justice, and he was a man who believed in seeing justice served.

Amanda Hazard had it all, and in just the right places, Nick observed with masculine appreciation. He was more than willing to take this gorgeous blond to all those intriguing places they had never been together.

He reached for Amanda, but she flung up a hand to forestall him.

"Now look, Thorn, we still haven't—"

"I am looking," he murmured, all eyes. "The view is spectacular."

"The scenery isn't bad over here, either, but . . ."

He hooked his arm around her waist, bringing her body into suggestive contact with his. The kiss was intense and penetrating, imitating the intimate promise of what was to come. After a long, breathless moment, Nick dragged his lips away. His hands, however, refused to be still for a moment. They moved quickly, memorizing every bit of flesh that sensitized his fingertips.

"Was there something you wanted to say, Hazard? If so, better make it fast. You know how we cops can be at times—trigger happy." Nick sucked in his breath when Amanda confiscated his weapon.

He had no idea she had been so well schooled in police training.

"Just one more thing, Thorn," she insisted.

"What is it, Hazard?" Nick struggled to breathe while she was doing the kinds of things that took over a man's mind, as well as his other vital body parts.

"Before the fireworks start, could you, just this once, call me by my name."

He grinned and made a vow to himself that this was going to be the first of many times that Amanda Hazard enjoyed looking up to a man. "Whatever you say, Amanda. I make it a policy never to argue with a woman holding a gun."

Amanda smiled back. She had the instinctive feeling this was going to be the beginning of something very, very good . . .

And once again, a good while later, Amanda's instincts proved her right.

She'd rather thought they would . . .

If you enjoyed Amanda Hazard's first foray into murder, you'll enjoy a sneak preview at her next adventure.

Spring has come to Vamoose, but there's a chill in the air when Amanda stumbles upon another dead body. Will her life again be placed in jeopardy or will the irresistibly attractive Nick Thorn come to her aid? The Last Chance Cafe and Velma's Beauty Boutique are the places to gather clues as Amanda tackles her second mystery and tries to figure out why Elmer Jolly was found . . .

DEAD IN THE CELLAR

Dead in the Cellar
An Amanda Hazard Mystery

The jingling phone shattered the silence. Amanda Hazard stuck a well-manicured forefinger on the piece of paper in front of her to keep her place and reached for the receiver.

"Hazard Accounting Agency."

"Missy? Elmer Jolly here."

"Hi, Elmer. What can I do for you?"

"I need to see you PDQ."

That was Elmer Jolly through and through. The old man never had the time or inclination for social amenities. He said what he wanted to say and then he got off the phone. Some of Amanda's elderly clients had a tendency to ramble incessantly about their families or most recent ailments, but not Elmer. He was a plainspoken recluse who lived several miles northeast of Vamoose. Elmer ventured into town twice a month to purchase supplies and then returned home having made as little contact with the outside world as possible. But for some reason he had taken an instant liking to Amanda. Perhaps it was because she was also a no-nonsense kind of individual who did not mince words. Whatever the case, Elmer had handed his accounts and tax forms over to Amanda with a decisive nod of approval, declaring she was "the best damned accountant" he had ever met.

"Do you want me to come see you tomorrow morning, Elmer?"

"Not good enough, missy." Elmer's gravely voice boomed back at her. "Those sons-a-bitches are trying to have me committed, damn their sorry hides! I won't stand for it, I tell you! When I depart from this earth, I'm leaving my money and property to whomever I want to leave it to, and *nobody* is going to try to change my mind!"

"*Who* is trying to have you committed?"

Apparently Elmer didn't hear the question. Either that or he was too frustrated to listen. It was also obvious to Amanda that Elmer wasn't wearing his false teeth. He was gumming the words and smacking his lips each time he paused for breath.

"They're trying to have me declared incompetent so they can steal me blind. But I fixed 'em good! I wrote up my will and had the banker witness it. I named you the executor of my estate, and no matter what, don't you believe a word of the lies!"

Elmer had worked himself into a lather, and he wheezed as he tried to catch his breath. After a moment of sputtering and coughing, he plowed on. "I'm leaving you my critters, missy. I know you'll take care of them the same way I would. And all the cash that I have stashed in the house in canning jars is yours to pay the critters' expenses."

When Elmer sputtered again, Amanda leaped at the chance to interject a comment. "I'm flattered that you'd trust me to oversee your estate, Elmer, but I think a lawyer would—"

"Lawyer? Lawyer!" Elmer crowed like a rooster. "I ain't messing with no damn lawyer, and that's final! The first and last lawyer I dealt with tried to swipe the mineral rights to my land in exchange for conducting a legal transaction. I refuse to deal with them. They ain't getting a penny from me, either!"

At seventy-three, Elmer Jolly was a hot-tempered eccentric, and his mind was encased in cement. Amanda knew it was a waste of breath to argue the virtues and benefits of attorneys or anything else. Elmer also harbored trepidations about computers, newfangled electronic devices, and the tortures of retirement homes. Amanda knew better than to get Elmer started on those sensitive subjects. What he did not completely understand, he didn't trust. He believed what he believed, and no one could change his mind.

"All right, Elmer, if you want me to handle your estate when the time comes—"

"You're damn tootin' that's the way I want it! You hightail it out here after lunch so I can get things squared away. I'm putting my will in your hands."

"But—"

"I won't be able to rest until you've seen the will. I don't want anybody stealing my notes and my money. By God, I'll find a way to take them with me first!"

Elmer had worked himself into such a tizzy that Amanda was willing to say anything to reassure him. "Don't worry about a thing, Elmer. I promise you that I'll see your wishes carried out to the letter."

"I knew I could count on you, missy. I'll simmer down, eat my lunch, catch the farmers' market report on TV, and then we'll talk."

The line went dead and Amanda frowned at the receiver. My, but Elmer was in a fine temper this morning. She was beginning to wonder if he hadn't developed symptoms of paranoia as well as senility. But then, who was she to criticize? If she lived to be seventy-three, she might have a few eccentric tendencies herself.

Up to this point, Elmer had possessed a sharp, alert mind, but he had definitely been raving like a madman this morning. Something had upset him. Hopefully, he would calm down after he had lunch and listened to the farmers' market reports, as he did faithfully each day. Then perhaps Amanda could get the details on exactly who "they" were.

Tucking the conversation in the back of her mind, she returned to the papers on her desk and completed her calculations. When thunder rumbled, she glanced out the window of her new office on the main street of Vamoose to see cumulo-nimbus clouds piling up.

It was springtime in Oklahoma, and this region of the country wasn't called Tornado Alley for nothing. Amanda had developed a wary respect for thunderstorms over the years; so had the citizens of this farming community. When lightning streaked across the sky, tractors and implements ground to a halt; cattlemen gathered their fencing tools and headed for shelter. Too many folks had been struck down trying to repair barbed-wire fences or zapped while their plows were half-buried in farm ground.

No one took tornadoes and severe storms lightly in Vamoose. Weather was a serious determining factor in farming and ranching. Mother Nature had a way of dipping her hand in the pocket of profit, just when everything was coming up roses, or rather, coming up cotton, wheat and alfalfa, as the case happened to be in Vamoose. Amanda had become as conscious of weather conditions as her rural clientele in small-town America. When storms approached, all eyes turned skyward. Televisions and radios were tuned into the meteorologists' forecasts. Storm alert teams from Oklahoma City swarmed the countryside to dramatize disaster . . .

And therein lay a most baffling question. Why would anyone in his right mind chase dangerous storms and stand out in lightning, wind and rain to present a "live" report? What was the matter with those people?

Amanda had never understood why news teams scampered off to areas that were about to be struck by an oncoming hurricane or bombed by third world countries. While all the sane people were packing up and leaving, an influx of reporters and camera crews rushed *into* impending disaster. And these people were thrust upon the viewing audience to give an intelligent summary of the news? Folks who didn't even have enough sense to come in out of lightning and rain! And Amanda had questioned Elmer Jolly's mental facilities. Elmer had nothing on the media.

Another crack of thunder rattled the windowpane and brought Amanda straight out of her chair. A quick glance at her watch indicated that she had just enough time to grab a greasy hamburger and fries at the Last Chance Cafe before she drove out to Elmer Jolly's farm. Amanda intended to be within running distance of a storm shelter if severe weather threatened. From the look of the blackening sky, hell was going to break loose somewhere in Tornado Alley before the day was out.

Amanda dashed across the street to Vamoose's one and only restaurant just as the church bell chimed high noon. As usual, the Last Chance Cafe was packed with farmers and cattlemen. Speculations on how the weather would affect crops and livestock were buzzing around it. One stubble-faced farmer in OshKosh overalls was comparing this year's weather patterns to the 40's, while his companion was contradicting his every word. Faye Bernard, the harried waitress, was scurrying from one table to another, delivering hamburgers and refilling coffee cups.

Amanda caught a glimpse of Officer Nick Thorn, Vamoose's chief of police, in the corner booth, surrounded by three cattlemen. When Thorn noticed Amanda's arrival, his dark eyes flicked over her business suit. He nodded a greeting before turning his attention back to his companions. Without a second glance in Thorn's direction, Amanda headed for the counter to order a hamburger to go.

Since she had cracked her first murder case a few months earlier, she and Thorn had become acquainted—intimately, in fact. Their . . . relationship . . . was one of the best-kept secrets in a town where everybody liked to keep abreast of everybody else's business.

Velma's Beauty Boutique and the Last Chance Cafe were hotbeds of, and breeding grounds for, gossip. Amanda had used that fact to her advantage in solving her first murder case. Of course, Nick Thorn had scoffed at her techniques for gleaning information about a murder he'd refused to believe had even been committed. But he had come around to Amanda's way of thinking eventually. In the end, they had made a fine detective team. Their . . . relationship . . . might have progressed at an accelerated rate if Amanda had not been so swamped during tax season and Thorn had not been busy making his appointed rounds and keeping abreast of his part-time farming and cattle operation. In short, their promising romance had been put on the back burner because their professions took precedence.

After solving her first murder case, Amanda had

gained so much notoriety that new clients had flocked to her in droves, forcing her to rent office space in town and spend only one day a week with her previous Oklahoma City employers: Nelson, Blake, and Cosmos Accounting. Seeing Thorn reminded her that these days, the *only* thing she got her hands on was her calculator.

Suddenly Amanda felt a presence beside her, and she knew instantly who had approached the cash register to pay for his meal. She would have recognized that tantalizing masculine scent anywhere, even if it *had* been a long time since she'd been even closer to it. There were some things a woman did not forget. Nick Thorn was one of them.

"Hello, Hazard. It looks as if we're in for a stretch of rough weather, doesn't it?"

Nick leaned leisurely against the counter, his uniform straining against the expanse of his broad chest. Amanda had a most outrageous urge to reach out and touch him. Damn, it really *had* been too long since she and Thorn blew off a little steam . . .

She cleared her throat and silently cursed herself for emulating her mother's annoying habit. "Um . . . yes . . . rough weather, Thorn," she agreed while her hormones rioted.

"How's the accounting business coming along? Any relief in your workload?"

Nick wanted to grab this sexy blond and disappear with her for a couple of hours. One look at Hazard and his temperature rose ten degrees. If he'd had his way, their affair would have been common knowledge long before now. Unfortunately, Miss Propriety had been leery about making a public commitment after her unpleasant divorce seven years earlier.

Since Hazard had only resided in the small town of Vamoose for a year, and now handled almost everyone's accounts except his, she had a fanatic desire to ensure that her high-profile image remained unblemished. She cringed at the idea of being the subject of juicy gossip. Nick, however, had no qualms about letting folks know she was his woman. He liked Hazard, and she claimed to like him — in private. In public, Hazard expected him to play the role of casual acquaintance.

Nick reminded himself that they'd both been so busy there hadn't been time lately for anything except work. But that didn't alter the fact that he was about to blow a fuse for want of this woman.

"Hazard, I need a little relief," Nick murmured just as Faye Bernard scuttled over to bring Amanda her hamburger to go.

Amanda nearly dropped the paper sack she'd received in a handoff. "Keep your voice down, Thorn," she hissed.

"I can keep my voice down, but that's about all I can keep down." He leaned over to hand Faye a five-dollar bill to pay for his lunch. Straight-faced, he whispered, "A man can stand only so many cold showers. I've reached my limit. Your place or mine?"

Amanda darted a discreet glance in every direction. "Yours. But if you grin and strut on your way out of the cafe, I'll hold it over your head for the rest of your life."

No cold shower tonight! thought Nick. But with the nonchalance and reserve befitting an officer of the law, he stuffed his change in his pocket and ambled toward the door. He paused to make small talk with Chester Korn who was lounging in a booth with his son. The tactical maneuver provided time

289

for Hazard to catch up with him without the crowd at the Last Chance Cafe knowing they were planning a long-awaited tête-à-tête.

When Amanda stepped outside, she cast Thorn an aggravated glance. "Confound it, Thorn, she could have overheard you."

"Who? Faye? She was too busy counting change and serving meals to give a thought to anything else. Besides, I think it's time Vamoose knows we're an item," he said, flashing Amanda a heart-melting smile. "I gave up clandestine work when I resigned from the narcotics squad of the Oklahoma City police force."

"Well, I don't want to wind up as news on the bulletin board at the Last Chance Cafe, or the hottest gossip at Velma's Beauty Boutique," Amanda huffed as she moved toward her compact Toyota.

"If you had any pride in the fact that we are more than casual acquaintances, you wouldn't mind letting Vamoosians know we're having an affair."

Amanda winced at the *A* word and clutched her paper bag in a tight fist. "I believe in being discreet," she muttered. "One does not publicize one's private life."

"Then I suppose you want me to pick you up at your place and drive you to my place so nobody will suspect anything is going on." Nick tossed her a goading grin. He had always derived excessive pleasure from ruffling Hazard's feathers. "Are you going to duck down in the seat of my truck like you did the time Velma Hertzog met us on the road?"

Amanda blushed beet red and flounced into her car. She supposed Nick had a legitimate point. Maybe she was carrying this secrecy thing a bit too far. But she had never been worth a damn at casual

. . . relationships. Her old-fashioned midwestern ideals nagged her to death. What she and Thorn had was good, especially in the bedroom. Okay, better than good, Amanda amended. *Aw, come on, Hazard, tell it like it is*. Oh, all right, she and Thorn were dynamite together, Amanda admitted. Thorn was the first man who had gotten past her bedroom door since her divorce. However, that did not signify that she had lost all sense of logic. She had made one mistake. She was *not* going to blunder blindly into another.

Stabbing her hand into the greasy sack, she grabbed her hamburger and ate as she drove. She and Thorn would hash out the terms of their . . . relationship . . . tonight. The thought sent a tingle of anticipation down her spine. Thorn was right. Cold showers were for the birds. It had been too long since they had enjoyed any privacy.

A naughty little grin curved her mouth upward as she bit into her hamburger. Nick Thorn in uniform had always been a sight to see. His good looks were impossible to ignore. But out of uniform, Thorn was something else again . . .

Amanda switched the air conditioner onto MAX to cool off. The last thing she needed was to get hot and bothered before consulting with Elmer Jolly.

Discarding the lingering vision of Nick Thorn naked, Amanda switched on the radio and concentrated on the problem at hand. The fact that she was living in Tornado Alley struck her when the meteorologist interrupted regular programming to issue a special bulletin. Vamoose and the nearby town of Pronto were under a tornado warning. A strong low-pressure air mass had plunged across the Great Plains to collide with the warm, moist air that had been sucked up from the gulf. A dry line had formed over Oklahoma, and conditions were ripe for tornadic activity.

Great. Just great.

To emphasize the grim report, lightning flashed and thunder exploded overhead. Amanda instinctively ducked and lost her grip on her hamburger. Her high cholesterol lunch kerplopped onto her lap, leaving a noticeable stain on her linen skirt.

Before she could pick up the half-eaten sandwich, her Toyota sideswiped the gargantuan clump of weeds and gravel that lined the country road.

"I swear Commissioner Brown and his road-grading crews screw up these roads on purpose!"

The insufferable condition of the country roads had always been one of Amanda's pet peeves. In winter, the rural byways were frozen into deep ruts that could, and did, wreak havoc on her compact car. In spring, the ditches boasted such an array of weeds that the roads were reminiscent of the paths carved out by covered wagons in the pioneer days. Grass grew in the middle of the road, and huge mounds of downed weeds, gravel and dirt lined both sides like guards rails. Meeting another vehicle on a one-lane path was treacherous business. A driver could get high center in no time at all on the piles of graded weeds.

Still muttering about the road conditions, Amanda opted for the middle and prayed she didn't meet oncoming traffic when she topped the hill. She cringed to think what would happen to these roads when the torrential rains came. On her return trip from Elmer Jolly's farm, she might wind up in a ditch, up to her axles in goo.

She forgot her irritation with County Commissioner Brown and his road brigade when another weather alert blared over the radio. A wall cloud had been sighted. The projected path of the storm put the communities of Vamoose and Pronto in jeopardy. Worse, Amanda was heading directly into the path of the approaching storm in her crackerbox car. What else could go wrong?

She craned her neck to get a better view of the swirling clouds that hung from the sky like vaporous stalactites. "Holy hell!" Amanda floored the accelerator and created her own cloud of dust, hoping to reach Elmer Jolly's farm before disaster descended. From the look of things, she and Thorn might not have a choice of her place or his. One or both homes might be blown to smithereens before the sun went down.

Huge raindrops pelted the Toyota, and Amanda switched on the windshield wipers. As lightning illuminated the darkening sky, the meteorologist urged everyone in the path of the storm to seek shelter—immediately.

"I'm trying, for God's sake!" Amanda yelled at the radio. She still had a mile to go before she reached Jolly's farm. If she didn't kill herself first driving at seventy miles an hour on impassable roads, the storm would probably swallow her alive.

She gritted her teeth and zoomed toward the farm, serenaded by thumps as gravel put dents in her Toyota. Up ahead, Amanda spotted another cloud of dust left by a speeding vehicle . . . or was it the makings of a tornado?

Amanda stamped on the brake to make the turn on two wheels. The Toyota skidded sideways in the loose gravel and scraped the corner fence post that marked Elmer's driveway. She cursed and plowed on ahead. In the distance she could see the cloud of dust swirling off in the raging wind, assuring her that it was definitely another speeding vehicle, not a tornado, that caused the billowing brown fog.

Just as Amanda stuck a pantyhose-clad leg out the door, the clouds opened. Rain hammered against the tin granary and barn, amplifying the feeling of oncoming disaster. The fierce wind that had been blowing from the southeast switched directions, practically ripping the door off the car and succeeding in tossing Amanda off balance. The Toyota wobbled on its wheels when another blast of wind pummeled it.

Amanda inhaled a fortifying breath and dashed toward the porch. It was then that she saw what she hadn't wanted to see. Black clouds churned counterclockwise, sucking up debris from the ground below. She and Elmer Jolly were in serious trouble! If the tornado touched down within the next few minutes, she and Elmer would be goners. She had seen homes and buildings wiped off their foundations by F5 tornados. Hiding in a hole was the only sure way to ride out a destructive twister. She had to get Elmer into the outdated storm cellar that sat behind the house, and she had to do it *now!*

"Elmer!" Without awaiting an invitation, Amanda barreled through the front door. The small black and white television in Elmer's front room was blaring to accommodate the elderly farmer who was hard of hearing and refused to wear auditory devices. The meteorologist was indicating the dark patches on radar, pinpointing the strongest cells in the storm. And of course Amanda was in one of the dreaded dark patches!

She glanced anxiously around the house. Elmer's half-empty plate sat on the table. One corner of the square tablecloth which was draped over the round table nearly touched the floor. And Elmer's chair had been left sitting at an angle instead of being pushed into its normal position. The pudgy tom-cat — Hank was his name — was prowling the confines of the room, looking every bit as uneasy as Amanda felt.

"Elmer? Where are you?" Amanda scurried down the hall, scooping up Hank to cuddle him protectively against her.

Elmer's bedroom stood empty, but several drawers in his antique walnut dresser were gaping open. The unmade bed looked as if a tornado had already struck. The sheets had been pulled away from the mattress and lay in a pile. Wherever Elmer was, he was not in bed.

When hail pounded against the roof, Amanda whirled around and dashed to the kitchen. In her mind's eye, she could see her shiny Toyota being beaten by golfball-sized chunks of ice. She also pictured herself buried beneath falling debris.

"Elmer!" she howled while Hank squirmed and caterwauled in her crushing grasp.

The electrical power shut down. Lights and television flickered off as the snapping of tree branches mingled with the steady thump of hailstones. Amanda was running out of time. If Elmer had already taken the precaution of huddling in his storm shelter, she was likely to be the one blown away while trying to rescue the elderly farmer from disaster.

Yielding to a sense of panic, Amanda plunged out the back door with Hank clutched to her bosom. Hank sank his claws in and squirmed when rain and hail descended on him, but Amanda held onto him and darted toward the cellar.

The warped cellar door lay open, the hatchway lined with rotting wooden steps slick with rain. Amanda tossed Hank inside and made a grab for the door, but the howling gale prevented her from shutting them in. Muttering unladylike curses, she stumbled down the steps, steadying herself against the damp walls of the underground shelter that looked as if it should have been bulldozed in long ago. A musty smell saturated her as she descended into the darkness.

"Elmer?" Amanda squinted into the shadows to see remains of wooden shelving which had tumbled to the floor. Broken glass jars littered a floor three inches under water. Green beans, beets, peaches and pickles were strewn about like casualties of war, but there was no sign of Elmer.

When Amanda realized a deadly calm had settled over the cellar, she pivoted on the slimy step and scrambled up the stairs. She made a frantic grab for the rope that served as a handle on the inside of the door, and the wooden portal clanked into place a split second before a roar, like that of a locomotive, rumbled overhead.

Amanda clamped both hands on the rope to secure the door and prayed for all she was worth. Visions of the dilapidated cellar caving in around her danced in her head. The cement walls and arched ceiling were already cracked and bulging. Streams of mud and water seeped inside the cellar and dribbled down the walls. The violent force of a tornado could leave this flimsy structure a pile of rubble.

A yelp burst from Amanda's lips when the door was sucked upward, drawing her up too. She clung to the rope as if it were her salvation, and the door dropped back. Minutes passed, and the storm raged on. Hail pounded like fists on the wood above her, and unseen objects banged into it. She wondered if Thorn had had time to seek cover before the storm struck. She hoped his streak of machismo hadn't gotten the best of him. She liked him—too much for her own good, if the truth be known. Even if she had been discreet and wary of gossip, their . . . relationship . . . had promise. Indeed, if it were not for Amanda's excessive workload and Thorn's career and farming obligations, this might be a romance in full blossom. It would definitely bloom tonight, Amanda promised herself. If they both survived this calamity . . .

A deafening crash shook the wooden door and Amanda squealed. With her luck a tree had been uprooted above her, trapping her inside this outdated cellar. No one knew where she was. She would die of starvation before somebody thought to look for her.

No, Amanda assured herself shakily. She wouldn't starve. She could munch on the fruits and vegetables that floated in the rising ground water. Yummy. She could pry the air vent off the ceiling and stuff Hank through it with a note tied around his neck. She might be rescued . . . in a couple of years.

Depression closed in on her as the howling storm had. "Ah, Thorn. I guess I shouldn't have made such a big deal of keeping our . . . relationship . . . a secret. Maybe we could have seen more of each other, if only from two to six in the morning."

Thorn really was something special. He was far superior to her frivolous ex-husband who had gone bankrupt without her to manage his finances, which was what he deserved for having an affair. The unfaithful jerk.

The wind wailed and hail pounded on the wooden door. Amanda wondered if she would emerge from the inky darkness to find herself surrounded by Munchkins, viewing the Land of Oz in living color. Elmer Jolly would be the great and wonderful wizard who . . .

Where the hell was Elmer anyway? If he had made it to the cellar, why hadn't she heard a peep out of him?

"Elmer? Are you down there? It's me . . . Amanda," she yelled over the storm.

Hank meowed.

Another few minutes elapsed before the second eerie calm settled over the black hole Amanda had shut herself into. Deeming it safe to emerge, she shoved her shoulder against the door and pushed. It wouldn't budge.

Climbing a step higher, Amanda crouched under the door to use the strength in her legs. The door creaked, but only opened a few inches. Cursing loudly, she fumbled down the steps to locate a piece of wood to prop the door open wide enough to wriggle out.

Once she had lifted the weight of the door, she shoved the board into place, snagging her pantyhose and jacket sleeve in the process. Another expensive ensemble torn to hell. For sure, she was overdressed for coping with the destruction left by a tornado.

Worming through the narrow opening, Amanda emerged like a turtle poking its head from its shell. The scene before her did nothing to improve her bleak mood. Fallen tree branches testified to the intensity of the storm which had cut a swath across the countryside. Wood from the barn and tin from the sheds were scattered hither and yon. The screen door on the back of Elmer's house sagged on its hinges, and shingles littered a lawn covered with a white glaze of egg-sized hailstones.

A whine from the barn demanded Amanda's attention. Still lying prone in the mud, she swiveled around to see Pete, the three-legged dog, hobbling toward her. With a wag of his soggy tail, Pete licked the cobwebs and goo from Amanda's face.

"Hello, Toto. Did the storm blow us all the way to Kansas?"

Pete limped off to join Elmer's other critters. Lucky, the duck, was having a field day digging roots from water holes. The chickens were on a worm hunt, and Amanda could hear Elmer's pigs squealing in their pen beside the barn, carrying on as if they were trying to tell her something. Now, if only she could locate Elmer, all would be present and accounted for.

Amanda scraped her muddy self off the ground and surveyed the tree limb that had crashed onto the cellar door. Bracing her legs, she tugged on the branch. One shoe was sucked off her foot as she struggled with it. The other red pump fell by the wayside on her second step backward. Shoeless, Amanda nonetheless managed to dislodge the branch that blocked the cellar door.

Glancing around, she tried to locate a rag to wipe the mud and sap from her hands. Then, with a hopeless shrug, she grabbed the hem of her silk blouse. The costly ensemble had suffered irreparable damage already. What did a little mud and sap matter?

A groan came from Amanda when she caught a glimpse of her Toyota. The car looked as if it had sprouted leaves. She didn't even want to imagine the size of the dents in the top and hood, not to mention the damage the hail had done.

"Elmer, come out. Come out wherever you are," Amanda yelled at the top of her lungs.

No answer. Where was that old man?

After pulling the branches from her car to determine whether the damage was as extensive as she suspected — it was — she propelled herself toward the house. A thorough search of it turned up nothing. Elmer was simply nowhere to be found. Maybe he had been in the speeding car she had seen topping the hill when she'd arrived at the farm.

Amanda ventured back outside to free the tomcat from the cellar. Two kitty, kittys later, Hank still refused to slink out. Muttering, Amanda descended the stairs. Her foot slipped on the broken bottom step, and she plummeted over the fallen shelves that had once held Elmer's supply of canned goods. Hank meowed from somewhere in the shadows.

"Come here, you stupid cat," she snapped.

Hank caterwauled, but he didn't come.

Crawling on hands and knees, Amanda inched over the shelves until her foot connected with what felt suspiciously like a body. Amanda glanced sideways and automatically recoiled as if she had been snakebit. Now she knew what had become of Elmer Jolly. She had touched his bony body with her foot, and the thin shaft of light that fell into the cellar spotlighted the outstretched arm that protruded from the overturned shelving. A hand, resembling a bird's scaly claw, was barely visible in the water. Amanda looked down into a pair of glassy eyes and swallowed hard.

Obviously Hank had found Elmer a half-hour earlier, but Amanda had not been able to understand his feline call for assistance.

Elmer Jolly, Amanda was sad to realize, had weathered his last storm. The "they" who'd threatened to have him locked away were no longer of any consequence. Elmer was headed to that Great Barnyard in the Sky, and now Amanda was responsible for the critters he had bequeathed to her. The recluse of Vamoose would never again have to worry about humanity crowding in on him. Elmer would have all the space he wanted in the netherworld far, far way . . .

*MAYBE YOU SHOULD CHECK
UNDER YOUR BED . . . JUST ONE MORE TIME!
THE HORROR NOVELS OF*

STEPHEN R. GEORGE

WILL SCARE YOU SENSELESS!

BEASTS   (2682-X, $3.95/$4.95)

BRAIN CHILD   (2578-5, $3.95/$4.95)

DARK MIRACLE   (2788-5, $3.95/$4.95)

THE FORGOTTEN   (3415-6, $4.50/$5.50)

GRANDMA'S LITTLE DARLING   (3210-2, $3.95/$4.95)

*Available wherever paperbacks are sold, or order direct from the
Publisher. Send cover price plus 50¢ per copy for mailing and
handling to Zebra Books, Dept. 4267, 475 Park Avenue South,
New York, N.Y. 10016. Residents of New York and Tennessee
must include sales tax. DO NOT SEND CASH. For a free Zebra/
Pinnacle catalog please write to the above address.*